THE
STROKE
OF DEATH

D0921219

THE
STROKE
OF DEATH

Jessica Mann

ROBERT HALE

ST. JOHN THE BAPTIST PARISH LIBRARY
2920 NEW HIGHWAY 51
LAPLACE, LOUISIANA 70068

First published in 2016 by
Robert Hale, an imprint of
The Crowood Press Ltd,
Ramsbury, Marlborough
Wiltshire SN8 2HR

www. crowood.com

www.halebooks.com

© Jessica Mann 2016

All rights reserved. No part of this publication may be
reproduced or transmitted in any form or by any means,
electronic or mechanical, including photocopy, recording
or any information storage and retrieval system, without
permission in writing from the publishers.

British Library Cataloguing-in-Publication Data
A catalogue record for this book is available from the
British Library.

ISBN 978 0 7198 1996 4

The right of Jessica Mann to be identified as author of
this work has been asserted by her in accordance with the
Copyright, Designs and Patents Act 1988.

Typeset by Catherine Williams, Knebworth

Printed and bound in Great Britain by
CPI Group (UK) Ltd, Croydon CR0 4YY

The stroke of death is as a lover's pinch
Which hurts, and is desired.

Shakespeare, *Antony and Cleopatra*.

I AM INTERESTED IN DEATH. I admit it freely. In fact I'm proud of it. This is a boast. Everyone ought to be interested.

Birth and death, the two universal experiences. And how little we know about either.

Oh, physically it's done and dusted. We know how a foetus grows, how it's born, after how many months it will kick or wriggle. It's alive as a snail or a toad is alive. But when does actual life get into it, humanity, the uniqueness of the individual – when? At conception, on birth, at some point in those nine months in-between?

And where does the life go when it leaves the body? Is that the end or another beginning? Sometimes you see the body become still and feel the room fill with a death that is finality. Finito. Over. But sometimes it's as if the closing of one chapter of existence is the beginning of another. You shut the staring eyes but don't feel that's it, done and dusted. Something, someone, is still there.

I've heard of places where they open the window to let the soul fly out and away. We close the eyes, pulling the lids down with thumb and middle finger, we pull a covering up to hide the face, and drape the corpse in cloth, perhaps to keep whatever is or was there, there.

I am certain that we will know one day. Eventually humans will understand death. Perhaps that's the day we become superhuman. I always have the feeling that the answer is nearby, waiting for me, and if I watch the moment of transition often enough and carefully enough I will come to understand.

Yes, as I said, I take a great interest in death.

IN THE SMALL hours of the night, just for a short while, the pavement was deserted. Looking out from a top floor window, Dr Hope could see the wide yellow line painted on the paving, a rectangle marking the point beyond which protesters should not go.

Ever since President Clinton had signed his Access Act they had been supposed to restrain themselves, up to a point. But since the police were on the protesters' side, no attempt was made to make them do so. The marked-off area looked like a bag-lady's den, scattered with paper cups and sheets of paper blown around in the wind.

They had all gone home. Time for bed, Doctor. The words came into his head with an accent, the voice of his latest, about to be ex-wife. Time for bed, without her, and because she was still occupying the apartment they had rented in both their names, he had taken temporary refuge upstairs on the attic floor of the clinic, officially out of use and out of bounds to the clinic staff. He'd stayed there before, when Kylie got into one of her states. It was uncomfortable sleeping on a bed designed for hospitals, too high, very hard and, being made of fabrics that could withstand boiling water, sweaty and scratchy. Private, though. And in case anyone did wander up, conveniently riddled with nooks and crannies for hiding things in. As the only medic working in this clinic, Euan Hope had unrepeatable opportunities, and it would be idiotic not to take them, so he had managed to accumulate enough supplies to last for some years if he left this job. No, *when* he left.

Doesn't look like Kylie will come round this time, he thought. In which case I'll be off.

How quiet it was.

It was very rare that any peace or quiet could be found here. The perpetual shouts or chanting, the intrusive cameras and above all the fear of violence – justified by experience – were beginning to get him down.

After a while one grew used to the noise and even able to interpret it. Triumph when they had dissuaded some poor woman from going into the clinic; fury, threats and warnings to any woman brave enough to make her way past the 'Life Chain', a shoulder-to-shoulder line of placard carriers, waving their messages in her face: 'Abortion Kills Children', 'Abortion Stops a Beating Heart', others with hugely magnified photos of aborted foetuses. The worst were the self-styled Army of God, who committed arson and acid attacks. The women who came here had to run that gauntlet of shouted threats, pleas and character assassination.

There! Euan caught sight of the first protester of the day. It was the flat-faced, pale man who behaved like a clergyman, might even be one, but a nutter none the less. Die, damn you, just drop dead, why don't you? he thought. God, what wouldn't he give to be able to shoot them, the whole lot of them. He imagined himself with a machine gun, sweeping sudden death across the grimacing faces, silencing them for ever.

He heard the scrape of metal being pulled across the paving stones. There were five of them now, four men and a woman. They were moving the fence away. One of them was holding a large poster ready to attach to a poster board. It read, 'WE WON!!' A stout woman bustling up the sidewalk was carrying a large poster reading 'VICTORY'.

Another of the protestors was crouched down with a newspaper spread out on the ground. She was meticulously cutting out an article from the front page. Makes no difference which paper it is, he thought morosely, they'd all have the same lead story. The antis had won their case. The Supreme Court had decided that '... *a ban on protesters at abortion clinics infringed upon the First Amendment rights of anti-abortion activists.*'

'What about the patients' rights?' Euan said aloud. It was not long before he could see the answer to his rhetorical question. A perfect example. One of the clinic's more pathetic patients: a 13-year-old with the mental age of a toddler and the body of a beauty queen. Her mother didn't even know which of her lodgers it had been, but somebody had forced the child, held her down. She'd still had bruises three weeks later, when her period was a fortnight late. He'd seen them on her arms, legs and body. The mother thought there had been several men. One of them had hit her, had got off on hitting her. And one of them had made her pregnant. Euan had not hesitated for a second. Get rid of it quickly, the sooner the better.

The anti-abortion campaigners weren't interested in true stories. Freed by the judge to move in close, three of them had homed in on the girl, tugging at her arms, her long hair, waving pictures of blood-covered foetuses before her face. The mother couldn't shield her daughter. She was yelling something. 'Backward! Can't you see she's backward?' I haven't heard that word since I was a child, Euan thought. It was certainly easier to say than 'mentally challenged'. Today's noise was an unfamiliar sort of howl. It was easy enough to understand: triumph; victory.

Euan was standing to one side of the window with the bullet-proof glass just a sliver open, so he was safe enough, but all same did not want to be seen. He hoped that the rest of the clinic staff would have the sense to do as they had been told in instructions circulated the previous evening.

Do not come in and out of the building's main door, sneak in through the side entrance. Do not stand at a window in full view. If you are questioned, say you don't know anything. And don't on any account comment on the Supreme Court judgement.

One of the night staff must have heard the commotion, and had gone to open the door. The mother and daughter, both crying hysterically, came into the lobby. It was a struggle to shut the front door. 'The enemy', as Euan had come to think of them, were banging on it rhythmically, shouting and then chanting.

Murderer. Killer. Assassin. Actually, he'd been called much worse in his working life. His first job stateside had been in Oregon where doctors were permitted to speed up a dying patient's death. Euthanasia, or mercy killing, had been legalized; and there too, self-righteous citizens had gathered to shout their disapproval. 'Murderer' was one of the milder accusations; he'd heard worse.

He looked for trouble. Two of his wives had made the same comment. When there were so many specialties that brought doctors respect and admiration, why choose to be despised? Couldn't he do better for himself – and her?

He wasn't about to explain that he was lucky to be working at all; that back home he wouldn't be in a job, he wouldn't be on the list of qualified medics. They hadn't struck his name from the register – yet. Struck off – words with a scary finality about them. But they'd told him, if he went abroad and never tried to work in his own country again, then he could continue as a doctor. Which, after all, was the only thing he knew how to do.

'Murderer.' 'Child killer.'

For some reason it hurt this time. The words hit home. He'd never given all that much thought to the ethics of his work. Abortion had been legal back home since the 1970s and didn't worry him any more than performing a tonsillectomy. It wasn't human life he was taking, it was potential life. If one worried about it, why stop there? Baptize the menstrual flow every month?

And if these idiots cared so much about every potential baby why didn't they care about them a bit more after they were born?

Did they help the useless mothers, did they feed the hungry children, did they ensure the rescued kids got the same chances as their own pampered brats? Did they hell. As he turned away an unfamiliar thought leapt into his mind and clung on. I don't have to take this shit. Maybe it's time to move on. Without consciously wondering where his passport might be, he found himself at his desk searching for it. Got to be somewhere in here. Is it still valid? How many years since it was last – ah, here it is.

'Dr Hope?'

He was startled by the nurse's voice, but turned to face her. She looked curiously at the tiny dark red booklet and said, 'Planning your vacation?'

'I wish!'

'Me too. I always have to go home to Mom.'

'Somewhere nice?'

'Baltimore. But I can dream.'

'And do you?'

'Somewhere there's a sunbed beside a blue pool with my name on it. I'll get there in the end. What about you?'

'I haven't ever thought about it.'

'You don't go to England?'

'Haven't for a long time.'

'No folks back home?'

'Family? They bring out the worst in me, we're better apart. Anyway, when would I go?'

'Too busy? Me too. And your first patient's ready for you. But I think she's been upset by the demo, poor kid.'

'I daresay,' Euan replied in a sombre tone. 'Haven't we all?'

PRESUMABLY GORDON HOPE had informed their elder son when his mother – mercifully, at last, after a protracted living death in a care home – died, but Euan hadn't turned up for her funeral. Not quite three years later, when Gordon himself became seriously ill, it was Tamara who had managed to track down Euan's email address on an obscure website, and had written him a message.

Dear Euan, I'm sending you this message to let you know that your father is dying. There is no immediate urgency, but if you wish to see him again you had better come within the next few weeks. He is in The Radcliffe Infirmary in Oxford.
With all good wishes, Tamara Hoyland Hope.

There had been no answer, but ten days later Tamara sent him another email telling him that Gordon was weakening fast.

Early the next morning Tamara answered the phone to someone with a professionally sympathetic voice. Gordon Hope had passed away in the night. Would Tamara be coming to collect his things or should they be given to his son if he came back again?

His son?

Tamara drove back to Oxford on an exotically perfect morning, February pretending to be June. She opened the roof and went slowly, looking at the countryside, wishing she was in it. She didn't get to the hospital until mid-morning. She was told that Euan had arrived the previous afternoon. The greeter wore the blue and red uniform of the non-professional staff, but she had evidently not yet been trained in the art of uttering a lot of words and saying nothing. Eventually she would learn never to comment on any patient or visitor but today spontaneous burble poured from her lips. She'd met Euan. 'Isn't he a lovely man, so friendly!' the woman enthused. Later, carrying an awkward bundle of her father-in-law's possessions, Tamara was told by another member of staff that she needn't trouble herself with the usual formalities, Dr Hope had dealt with all the documentation. The younger Dr Hope, that is. And would Tamara care to view the body? Never mind if she didn't, but many people found it comforting, and there was nothing to be afraid of.

Some dead bodies I have seen, Tamara thought. Counting in her head as she followed signs to the mortuary, walking down a seemingly interminable green corridor, Tamara had reached number eight, of which two had died naturally, and two others had died as a result of Tamara's actions. She hadn't thought about Mike and Rory for years, but now she did, realized that she still felt as guiltless as she had when her secret machinations worked exactly as she had planned and they were killed by the bomb they had made themselves. They, or their co-conspirators, had murdered the man she was going to marry. It was a just execution.

But she had never seen a body after the cosmetic technicians had done their best. Her father-in-law's face seemed smaller than in life. He had been carefully shaved and there was lipstick on his mouth. He looked not at all like himself.

She exclaimed, 'What have you done? Why is he all tarted up?' She waved her hands in a baffled gesture. 'It's not going to be an open-casket funeral.'

'Dr Hope asked us to tidy his father up.'

Tamara extricated herself from the mortuary. She was sorry the old man was dead and intrigued that the elusive Euan had turned up and taken a hand. Maybe he'd deal with some of the admin, Tamara thought. She really dreaded having to embark on the process of organizing the funeral, of reading the will, of receiving polite sympathy for the loss of a father-in-law she had known for nearly twenty years without ever having found a topic of conversation that interested both of them.

UNTIL THEY WERE fifty-two, the Cannings had led charmed lives. They met at uni where for two years they were just friends, running around with a biggish crowd of other students, all from middle-class families. When one of them claimed to be skint, everyone knew that in the last resort they'd be rescued. When one was ill, Mummy would come in a big estate car to take the invalid home. They played ping pong and tennis, cricket and croquet, they rode and rowed and the chaps played soccer or rugger. Some of them didn't care about getting a good degree; some were hell-bent on scoring a first.

Robert Canning got his first-class degree in law, was taken on as a pupil at a glamorous set of chambers, and twenty years later had become one of the most successful barristers of his day.

Polly always knew she wanted to have lots of children, and that she would look after them herself. So she had decided to train as an 'early years teacher', a profession that allowed career breaks, and would fit in well with having a family.

They got married as soon as Robert qualified, had two daughters and one son, and by the time he was eighteen and went to Exeter University to study law, the family was living in a small but quite stately home, a red-brick Georgian former dower house in Hampshire. They also had a small flat just round the corner from Gray's Inn, so that Robert could spend the night when he had a heavy case. For family holidays they had a Provençal farmhouse which they had rescued from dereliction.

'We're so lucky to have all this,' Polly would say.

Robert always replied, 'It's not luck, it's judgment and damned hard work. We've earned it.'

As a family they were sporty. In the garden they all played every game, but in the outside world they had specialized so as not to have to compete with each other. One of the girls was a tennis player, her younger sister a swimmer. Their son rowed in the summer and in winter played rugby – in fact, was in the university team.

His last rugby match for the season was an away game somewhere in the Midlands. It would also be his last match with this team. By the next season, he'd be living in London, studying for his Bar exams. He'd signed on to travel with the other chaps and warned his parents they'd be late back.

'Good luck, darling, I hope you go out with a bang,' Polly said.

'Thanks, Mum.'

Amanda was going to give her brother a lift to the bus, and had already brought her car round to the front door. She hooted impatiently.

'See you later,' Dave said.

'Have fun,' Polly called.

'Go out and win,' Robert added.

'I bet he will, too,' Polly said. 'Time for another cup?' She held the coffee pot up and poured the last of it into Robert's mug.

Robert would spend the morning at the golf course, Polly was going to join him at lunchtime. As she often said, quoting her late father who was himself quoting Voltaire, 'Everything is for the best in the best of all possible worlds.'

'I'M NOT A fool,' Thea told herself. To boost her morale she took a business card from her bag. Professor Dame Thea Crawford, DBE DL DLitt FBA FSA wasn't foolish, whatever else she might be. 'I don't have a death wish. I know what post-menopausal women are supposed to do if they notice certain symptoms. And I did try to see the doctor. Is it my fault they couldn't fit me in that week? And then I was committed to be away on an excavation, and then I'd promised my son to come to Cape Cod for a fortnight and then I had that lecture tour in Eastern Europe....'

The upshot of all this, whatever the excuse or reason, had been delay and procrastination. It was a good eight or nine months between noticing the occasional spot of blood and actually mentioning it to her GP, who looked very grave when Thea admitted how long it was since she had needed to use sanitary pads, and that she found herself needing more and larger ones.

So that was a week wiped off the calendar. Various hi-tech diagnostic procedures took the time when she would normally have been at her desk. She saw specialists and technicians, had scans and tests and gave samples and was increasingly bored and restless. 'I really don't have time for all this,' she said.

And then came the consultation with the surgeon himself. Young enough to be Thea's son, busy enough to see symptoms and signs but not the personality they were attached to. He did not actually look at Thea as she came in and sat on the chair facing him. He was silent while he refreshed his memory about the various test results. Then he slotted a photograph into a viewer, saying, 'It's very clear. Look, you can see, here and here? That's the villain of the piece. It's something of a pity that you didn't seek medical advice when you first noticed there was a problem.'

'I had too much on, simply didn't have time.'

'Mmm. Well, if we operate this week and then—'

'I can't possibly this week. I'm terribly busy. What about, perhaps, at Easter? That would give me the holiday to convalesce.'

'That's months away!'

'Far more convenient though.'

'I'm not sure you have taken in what I was saying, that's quite usual,' he said. 'In any case, I'll need to see you again as soon as possible. Perhaps you could bring somebody with you? It's often easier to discuss alternatives with another family member present. Your husband perhaps, or a friend.'

Thea looked at him – no doubt he was a perfectly nice man, probably much liked in private life and he had a horrible job, giving bad news to women like Thea. All the same, he shouldn't treat her like an idiot.

'I'm so sorry,' she said. 'I hadn't quite realized the implications. I don't need anyone to help me understand, I'm concentrating now.' She listened carefully as he spoke about post-menopausal bleeding, what it might signify, what treatment was necessary,

15

what was the long-term prognosis.

'Very good of you to explain so clearly,' she said. 'And I'm afraid I've taken up more than my share of your time.'

'I'll be writing to your GP. But I strongly advise you not to put this off any longer. The consequences might be … shall I say, regrettable. You would regret them.'

As I SAID before, I'm interested in death. I find it fascinating in all its guises; slow or quick, painful or peaceful, sudden or forewarned. I'm not the only one either. Today I came upon someone else watching, as I've watched, standing silently and unnoticed.

Until I noticed.

He's obviously a medic or a nurse, because I first saw him through the spy window in the door of a high-dependency single room. He was adjusting the patient's drip. I'd been sent to see if the patient needed more sleepers, but as he was fast asleep (drooling and snoring) I didn't go in.

Then I saw the man again this morning, in the basement corridor. I often go down there when I'm doing a stint in this hospital. At the far end is the morgue. He stood aside, and so did I, to let a trolley pass, its passenger completely invisible under a green cover and the expression on his face probably matched mine, curiosity and a kind of – maybe *yearning* is the word I need. A kind of lust.

We looked at each other as it was wheeled out of sight into the morgue. Then he followed it, and I went back to the ward. But I saw him later in the canteen and we got talking, cautiously at first, both of us putting forward practical reasons for being such careful observers. We looked at one another with, I'd guess, the identical expressions on our faces. The words we said were true as far as they went. But we both left out the important part, the fascination, the addictive thrill of hearing that last inhalation, and waiting, waiting to know if there will be another. The silence when there isn't. The beauty of the finality.

I don't know who he is. He could be on the staff, though he was in civvies, or he could have been visiting.

But I could feel what he was thinking.

You don't believe me.

Never mind. I know what I saw. He'll be back.

So will I.

TAMARA HOYLAND HAD been visiting a site that turned out to be of much less archaeological interest than its metal-detecting finder had hoped, mainly because nearly the whole of whatever it had been was irretrievably buried under the cellars of a hospital built in the 1930s. In the circumstances – the pouring rain that seemed to have become the permanent climate – she was lucky not to be grovelling round in a sea of mud. She got away well before she'd expected.

In better weather she would have stayed and had a look around, not knowing this part of the border country between England and Wales, but the combination of rain and a raw wind made the idea unattractive. This time last week it was like summer, she remembered. The thought crossed her mind that she might have dismissed the site too quickly. Did I skimp the job because of the weather? No, surely not. There wasn't any space for investigation, one couldn't dig beneath the hospital itself. Thea wouldn't have given it any more time, Tamara thought.

Thea Crawford was Tamara's model for the role of archaeologist, and had been ever since Tamara, a still gauche and countrified student, had first encountered her. At the time Thea was still married to a journalist, a well-known voice from the world's trouble spots, but they had parted shortly after that. Thea was clever, decisive, original and elegant. She'd been a professor in Edinburgh University's Fine Art and Archaeology Department when Tamara went there as a student. Later she had acted as Tamara's referee for her first job as an archaeologist in a government department.

Those had been good years, her twenties. Free, solvent, and with too much to do, Tamara had somehow fitted everything in to a standard-length day – her publically official and publicized work on ancient monuments for the Environment Agency, and her secretly-official commissions for Department E. She had been recruited almost by accident, after her boyfriend, an operative in that secret department, was killed. His boss, the enigmatic and obscure Mr Black, had met Tamara with Ian and apparently been impressed by her common sense, resourcefulness and energy. His first task for her was to travel to the remote island where Ian's mother lived and under the cover of doing archaeological field work, find out what conspiracy was brewing.[1] Tamara had learnt very much later that Thea, having been on the island briefly, and then having learnt through her husband of Tamara's double role, had written a confidential letter praising Tamara's performance working undercover there.

Later there had been other adventures. Tamara discovered things she had never known about her family and things she could never let anyone else know about more famous families. Tamara's father, a tweedy and benevolent solicitor, turned out to be acquainted with Mr Black, and to have been involved in the secret world himself decades before. Alastair, however, knew little about such things and intensely disliked the idea of his wife having anything to do with them. When she was pregnant, Tamara resigned.

Mr Black became uncharacteristically lachrymose but told her that if she hadn't resigned, he would have sacked her. Apparently he believed that a foetus took in its mother's thoughts and moods. He advised her to listen to good music, and gave her a stack of

1 *No Man's Island* by Jessica Mann

suitable CDs as a leaving present. And as she handed over the tools of the trade a nameless functionary warned, 'You're still bound by the Official Secrets Act.'

Twenty years on, Tamara was an archaeologist, a wife, a mother but nothing else; and Thea Crawford's views still counted for a lot. Worrying away at the thought of the site she'd seen that day, Tamara was pretty sure that Thea would have said, 'Let it go. Some sites are just impossible and that's all there is to it. Forget it.'

It was still early in the afternoon when Tamara reached Oxford's outskirts. She felt overcome by reluctance to reach her destination. I don't want to spend this afternoon shut up in that house, she thought, considering her mental list: arrangements with the undertakers: done. Tomorrow's funeral service: arranged. Service sheets: printed and paid for. Vera's seeing to the house and all the food and drinks are organized. And I did say I wouldn't get there till quite late.

Feeling like a naughty girl skiving off from school, she turned from the dual carriageway onto the slip road and followed signs for the city centre. It felt good to be aimless. And there (a miracle, surely, or at least a very good sign) was a legal parking place. Tamara had got to know Oxford quite well during the years of taking her boys to visit Alastair's parents. More recently her work had been based in a modern building in a business park on the city outskirts, though with children at day school in London she wasn't often in the office, and didn't deviate into the town when she was. She had long since done all the requisite sight-seeing. But now it seemed amusing to stroll along watching the solid phalanx of umbrellas under which were the crowds of visitors who still had the sights to see. She stopped by a dress shop and admired some original designs. Could I wear that? No; it's for teenagers, it would look ridiculous. She stood for a while listening to a busker who was making a lovely job of some Schubert Lieder from *The Winter Journey*. 'As a stranger I arrived/As a stranger I shall leave ...'

19

Next stop: food, drink, weight off feet. One café was too crowded, in the next the music was so loud that the whole building seemed to be quivering. The next one had a poster in the window announcing that there would be a 'Drop-In Death Café' here, £5 per head, 4 p.m. on Thursday the – but that's today, Tamara realized. The time was twenty to four. She pushed the door open, and a bell rang loudly. Inside was very pink. The walls, the cloths on the half-dozen tables, all laid with cups and saucers, the lino floor. On the counter stood a cake stand loaded with pink-iced fairy cakes. Three other customers were there, at one table two women wearing black. One of them looked as if she had recently been crying and might start again any minute. On the far side of the room, a stout grizzled elderly man in scratchy-looking tweed, seated in a belligerent posture, knees wide apart, both hands on the handle of his walking stick. Tamara smiled slightly at each of them, took off her raincoat and hung it dripping on a hanger on a coat stand and sat at an empty table. She caught the eye of the waitress (Manager? Proprietor?) and ordered Earl Grey tea. The woman went through a doorway obscured by dangling rows of multicoloured beads and returned quite quickly with a tray. Tamara was given a cup and saucer, a teapot and a plate of biscuits, and as she set them on the table the woman said, 'Here for the meeting, are you?'

'I wasn't, actually, but may I stay for it?'

'I don't see why not, the ad says it's first come first served.' She went back with the empty tray and Tamara heard her lowered voice talking to someone in the kitchen.

Ginger biscuits. Tamara was about to give in to temptation when the door opened and a small horde of people came in. Far more women than men, far more old than young, and all a little uncertain as to whether this was where they were sure they wanted to be. Eventually they had taken off their sodden coats, found chairs, ordered and received their refreshments, and started to look round the room to see what would happen next. Then a young woman with a cushiony mound of black curls tapped a pencil on her table and stood up to speak – or rather, to shout, making herself heard over the noise of the heavy rain battering at the café's windows.

'Hi everyone, wonderful to see so many of you here, at Oxford's first death café.' Lots of foot-shuffling and not-meeting of eyes. Undeterred, she went on, 'I'm Lucy and I'm here to facilitate your discussions. The idea of the death café is very simple. It was thought up by a Brit, who set up the first one in his own house in London. The Americans picked up the idea and ran with it. Over there it's even more difficult to speak candidly about this universal experience than it is here. The idea is to break the taboo by providing a casual, comfortable space to talk about death and dying. In this environment of openness, respect and confidentiality you can say what you like, express your deepest feelings. You could be practical and discuss wills or funerals or hospices. Or if you want to, spiritual – heaven or hell? – or even ethereal. If you've had a near death experience, for example, or if you just want to speculate about what will follow this life. It's for you to decide.'

A silence followed this speech. Feet were shuffled, eyes not met. Tamara noticed that someone was standing just the other side of the bead curtain, presumably watching and listening. In the unresponsive quiet, the beads were making an irregular clicking sound. Lucy paused briefly, and then went on.

'I think we should start in small groups. Please begin to get to know each other. You, madam, what's your name?' The reply was an inaudible mumble, but Lucy said, 'And your neighbour?'

A seedy-looking middle-aged man said, 'My name's Simon. Simon Brighouse. I'm an accountant.'

'Oh, we'll just go by first names here,' Lucy said. Going round the room, people whispered or declaimed. Tom, so obviously an ex-soldier that he hardly needed to say so, Eileen (very old and shaky), Alan, a sales rep, who could have been called Everyman, since he was without a single identifying feature, Mary (newly widowed), Gloria, who announced that she was a nurse, another much younger Mary. When it came to her turn, Tamara said clearly, 'Anna. I'm a teacher.' She had surprised herself. What made me say that? Anna was the cover name she had used during one of her more dangerous assignments. Was instinct warning her now to be careful, to observe, not to give anything away?

Lucy's timetable required conversations in small groups first, then opened up to everyone. Tamara found herself explaining 'Do Not Resuscitate' orders to a grey-skinned ancient who looked as if she could well have been brought back from the dead herself.

'Now it's time for our group discussion,' Lucy said brightly. That proved to be an unsatisfactory experience dominated by long-winded accounts of prolonged last illnesses.

'Those doctors! You know the saying "Thou shalt not kill but need not strive officiously to keep alive". Officious! It's a good word. Their endless treatments and procedures—'

'You were lucky! My Edgar might be alive today if the NHS had funded the right medicine, but some high-up know-all decreed it was too expensive for ordinary health service patients …'

'Well, all my poor husband wanted was to be allowed to die in peace, and they wouldn't stop the treatment, he was in such misery—'

'That's why we need a new law. Join Exit. Exit believes that if you're of sound mind, and over twenty-one, you should have the right to choose how to die, and where.'

'There was some bloke who said he'd charter a so-called death ship, so as to be able to euthanize people out at sea, in international waters.'

'Or you could join Dignity in Dying. That's full of people who want more choice and more autonomy at the end of their lives.'

Still doggedly smiling, Lucy eventually interrupted. 'We've made a very good start,' she exclaimed brightly. 'Now we've got to know each other a little, next time we'll get down to the nitty-gritty. Do come next week, same time same place. And come prepared to explain your wishes.'

Tamara was almost out of the door when she heard something that pricked her curiosity. 'Oh, my gloves,' she said, and started searching through her bag, careful not to show that she could hear a conversation being carried on in the neighbouring room. One voice was Lucy's. The other – who was it? Not the waitress who was clearing crockery onto her tray at the same time as she listened to one of the customers, a military-looking man who, having introduced himself as Major Simpson, had wept as he described his father's deathbed ordeal, undergoing ever more desperate procedures by medics who seemed determined to keep him alive. Whoever it was that Lucy was talking to spoke in whisper, perfectly audible but impossible to identify whether male or female.

'You promised me.'

'I know, and I'm sorry. How was I to know the courier would be arrested? She's in prison in Mexico City, it must be ...'

'I should give a damn what it must be? So one mule's out of the game – find another one.'

'As yet we haven't ...'

'Listen, Luce, I like you. I really do. But if we don't get those barbies, you know what happens. It's not my decision.'

'I'm doing my best. I did my best. And you're not the only one. There's a queue.'

'I know what they fetch. And how much you've had already.'

'Can I help, Anna, have you lost something?' It was the lachrymose Major Simpson, now restored – but for his red eyes – to dapper self-confidence.

'Oh thanks so much, no, I'm fine, it was my gloves, and I found them.'

'Can I give you a lift anywhere?'

'Sweet of you, but my car's parked nearby.'

And so it was, with the addition of a penalty charge notice because she had overstayed by ten minutes.

Next stop, the supermarket. Gordon's housekeeper Vera had taken on the responsibility for the funeral baked meats, but there'd still have to be supper for tonight; some fruit, some cheese and bread.

It was the rush hour now. As she inched from hold-up to hold-up Tamara dismissed the question of the drug smugglers for the time being – one would need to be sure that barbies, presumably short for barbiturates, were forbidden drugs before taking action. And then, the question, What action? She no longer had any contact with officialdom. A quandary to consider later on. 'It's none of my business,' she said aloud. She wasn't a civil servant any more, either openly in the Department of the Environment, or secretly in Department E. What's it got to do with me? Answer, nothing. Nothing at all. But she found her thoughts returning to that eavesdropped conversation. Barbies. Barbiturates – they were heavy-duty sleeping drugs, which surely had been legally prescribed not so long ago. Seconal. Soneryl. There used to be a bottle of them in the bathroom cabinet. Mum took them, and doled them out, if one couldn't get to sleep. Tamara didn't think you got high on them. So why were they banned?

Stop it, she admonished herself. Not your business. Just now, think about the house, and about Alastair's father. His death was having the usual effect, softening her memories of the old man, reviving the lost affection she'd felt for him before he became so sorry for himself that other people felt they needn't bother.

In earlier years she had admired Gordon and after a while, even loved him. When Alastair first took her to meet his family, Gordon was not yet sixty and his wife was still well. He was at the peak of his powers as a doctor, an expert in the theory and actuality of general practice, and on the way to the heights of worldly success. He was an Elder of the Church of Scotland. The civic honours, the honorary degrees, the newspaper profiles came in the following decade. If he had died at the biblical three score years and ten, he'd have died happy. But the inevitable decline, both in his powers and his reputation, soured him.

He wasn't a good grandfather, being hypercritical and impatient with young children. His own had been brought up to sit strictly silent at mealtimes – the exact opposite of what Tamara had been taught, that it was the duty of everyone at the table to keep interesting conversation going, to contribute if they could and seem interested if they couldn't.

In the Hope household, if there was anything to discuss, it was deemed unsuitable for mealtimes. If the grown-ups spoke at all, it was in ritual platitudes. Euan and Alastair were supposed to put their hands on the table, empty, between courses.

'It sounds incredibly old-fashioned,' Tamara had remarked, when Alastair first described the meals of his childhood.

'We're not going to have our family seen-and-not-heard.'

'Of course not.'

'Promise me you won't ever revert to type!'

Suddenly serious, he pulled her in to his arms and said, 'Don't you realize, I love the life you've had almost as much as I love you. I want our kids to be free and self-reliant and unafraid. I was always nervous that I was doing something – anything – God knows what – wrong. My parents were never satisfied.'

In which case, how anxious they must have been about their elder son. Having qualified as a doctor, Euan couldn't settle for a specialty. Inexplicably he always seemed to choose the dodgy jobs. Or perhaps, he was only offered the dodgy ones. He had qualified, he was on the medical register, but he'd only just scraped through every exam. How he must have resented his brilliant younger brother, Tamara thought.

Euan moved from one dead-end post to the next. His real life was elsewhere, in nightclubs, at parties, in fast cars and drinking dens he couldn't afford. He was suspected of illicitly supplying prescription drugs. It was embarrassing for the old man but he could still influence his sons, and eventually he decided that Euan had better go abroad. Tamara had been married to Alastair for nearly three years at the time, and was pregnant with her first child. She described the scene to her father.

'It was as if we were living in a Victorian novel, all "more in sorrow than anger", and "this hurts me more than it hurts you". If it had been snowing he'd have turned Euan out into it. As it was, Gordon was taken by surprise, he'd no idea that Euan would just up sticks and go. And now he's kicking himself because Euan's disappeared without a trace.'

'Nobody leaves no trace.' Tamara's father was a solicitor. She was herself skilled in secret and sometimes hardly legal investigations. He added, 'Do you want me to...?'

'No, Pa, thanks. I think he's well lost. We're better off without him.'

There wasn't much that could surprise or shock Rob Hoyland. 'Well, my dear, he'll be back when your father-in-law is ill or seems to be dying. He's trouble, that one. You might want to consider having your security system checked.'

He knew, and she knew he knew, that officialdom ensured her security was state-of-the-art – or, at least, had been. In any case, she wasn't going to be taking risks. Going into danger was a game for the unattached. Tamara had realized that her sons needed her more as they grew, not less, and they came first. Always. No matter what. Had to. The fantasy that she might go back to her secret work when the youngest went to school was just that – a fantasy. Which was not to say she didn't miss the excitement, and the feeling of being an insider, the knowledge of having unusual, illicit, hard-acquired skills and insights and the chance to use them.

Back in the skin of herself when much younger, she suddenly put her foot sharp down, skidded and swerved past the stationary sheep-like cars – and braked, and slowed. Stop it, Tamara, you're a middle-aged housewife now. A mother. An archaeologist. An administrator. Your speeding – or did she mean spying? – days are over.

That conversation with her father had been several years ago and by now Rob Hoyland himself was dead. And if the nurse was right and Euan had been to see his father in hospital, there had been no other sign of him. But she thought he might well turn up now, and hoped he would, because the idea of a funeral without family was too depressing.

Tamara herself was the youngest of four children. They had eight first cousins on their father's side and eleven on their mother's. There were also about two dozen slightly more distant relations or connections with whom they kept in frequent touch. It could well be that one of Alastair's charms, for Tamara, had been his lack of extended family. Gordon had no relations. Or, if he had, he'd allowed himself to lose touch so thoroughly that his direct descendants didn't even know of their existence. When they were first together, Alastair had seemed to revel in the large Hoyland 'cousinage'. More recently he'd been less enthusiastic, as Tamara had not been able to help noticing. She hoped he wasn't reverting to type.

It had taken three-quarters of an hour to get from the city centre to her father-in-law's house in south east Oxford. The road was quiet and peaceful, the only traffic a few commuters' cars as they returned home. The street had been developed in the 1930s, and by now it was an expensive area, the houses all detached and sheltered from view by flowering cherry trees or hedges of conifers. During the day when most of them were empty, unwary walkers were sometimes greeted by a pack of dogs, pets that had escaped from the gardens they were supposedly locked into. The houses didn't seem to have numbers but each had a gatepost or hedge with a name plaque: The Hive, Coromandel, Honeysuckle Cottage. The Hopes' house was called Swallows. Painted off-white, with green woodwork, it looked like a picture in one of the mid-twentieth century Ladybird books for children. Its front garden was bounded by a tall privet hedge, much in need of trimming, and some sparse mauve tulips were scattered in the otherwise empty flower beds.

When Tamara went in she found that Vera Fleming was still there. She had been for many years Gordon's nurse, secretary and housekeeper; if anything else as well, as Tamara always supposed, nothing was ever said. She was finishing off the dining room. She'd looked out white, stiffly starched damask table cloths, never previously used that Tamara knew of, and numerous small silver salt and peppers. Vera had a curator's enthusiasm for the contents of the house.

'Tamara. Oh, it's you!'

'Who else?'

Vera whispered, pointing her finger up to the ceiling. 'Someone's here.'

'Oh, has Euan turned up?'

'It's his ... his partner.' She seemed to be gathering her thoughts before explaining, when Tamara heard someone coming down the stairs, heavily but fast.

'Hi, you must be Tara! I'm Leslie – spelt ell-ee-zee-ell-eye.'

'Lezli? That's unusual.'

'Yeah, that's what I thought.'

A man, surely, Tamara thought. A man in a caftan. There was an Adam's apple; and the hands and feet, though manicured and with crimson-painted nails, were outsize even for a man.

Lezli had arrived not long before Tamara. It took a while for Vera to be convinced that this bizarre apparition had a right to come in and the son of the house would be here soon. Eventually, but grudgingly, she'd showed him into a back bedroom furnished with mahogany and a Liberty print chintz. He said it was a bit of Olde England and utterly perfect. Then he dressed and made himself up with intimidating perfection before coming down. He introduced himself without a trace of awkwardness. 'I'm the advance guard,' he said. 'Euan will be along later. And you must be Tara. And where's your lovely husband? Alexander, is it?'

'Alastair. And I'm Tamara. He's stuck in South America.'

'That's an unusual one.'

'Unusual what?'

'Excuse.'

Tamara began to explain about Alastair's quest for medicinal plants, but Lezli wasn't listening. He said, 'I've been looking round, it's a neat little place.'

'Thanks to Vera.'

'Vera? Oh right, you mean the maid. She let me in. Now look, I've taken a look round, as I said, to see what to put on our list. I found one or two nice pieces. This little picture here, for instance, crying out for re-framing, but it's rather adorable.'

'I believe it's by Landseer.'

'Never heard of him. Or her. And that's mega-cute, that china figurine.'

'Meissen,' Tamara said.

'Look,' Vera said. A limo driven by a uniformed chauffeur had pulled up outside. A burly man got out, glanced up at the house, opened a large black umbrella and walked up the path.

'That's my boy,' Lezli said.

'Yes, we've met before.'

'Yo, lover,' Lezli called. 'Come say hi to your in-law.'

Euan came into the room and made straight for the desk. 'Now we'll see what the old boy was worth,' he said, opening the top drawer, which contained nothing but pencils and pens.

'It's Tara, Euan, she's Al's wife.' Alastair was never called Al.

Tamara said, 'Tamara. Hullo, Euan, I'm sorry Alastair can't be here but I'm glad to see you.' Actually, she wasn't. Euan looked disconcertingly like Alastair. It's like the good and bad twins, she thought.

'Ducked out, has he? Can't say I'm surprised.' The accent was mid-Atlantic, the voice harsher and higher than his brother's.

'Hardly. He's—' But it didn't seem worth trying to explain. 'It isn't possible to leave his expedition.'

Euan glanced briefly at her, his dark eyebrows drawn together in a scowl. Then he obviously changed his mind about what to say next and demanded some whisky, adding that he'd have a sandwich, smoked salmon, or if there wasn't any, ham would do. Tamara was about to say 'Fix your own, you know where the kitchen is,' when Lezli offered, 'Let me do it, I know how he likes it.'

Tamara said, 'I knew you were back, they told me about you at the mortuary. But you didn't leave any details, I didn't know where to get hold of you.'

'Did you need to?'

'Well, there were all the funeral arrangements for a start.'

'I don't give a damn about the funeral arrangements. Up to you.'

'And I didn't know you'd be staying here.'

'Uh huh.' Euan tugged discontentedly at the other drawers, discovered they either contained useless things – telephone books, envelopes, Sellotape – or were locked.

'Where's the key?' he said.

'No idea.'

'Where would the old man hide the sodding key?' He left the room to go to the lavatory and peed noisily. Coming out, he slammed the door, and then was silent for so long that Tamara went out into the hall to find him. Euan had unhooked one of the pictures and was dusting the glass with his sleeve. 'Needs reframing, and ultra-violet proof glass,' he said.

Tamara paused, again taken aback by the sight of him. He really could almost be her husband. Euan looked older, which of course he was, but the hair, the features, above all the way he stood and moved – they were almost indistinguishable.

'What?' he said, having noticed her stare.

'Oh, sorry, it's nothing. Just that you and Alastair look so alike.'

'Still?'

'I never really noticed it before.' She didn't add that she hadn't had much chance of noticing it, having met Euan so seldom.

'Well, it's old news,' he said.

'Your sandwich is ready,' Lezli called. He had done it properly, using a tray, putting a mat under the dish, and garnishing the food with parsley and lemon. 'Someone's cooked a ham,' he said.

'That's for tomorrow,' Tamara said. Euan grunted and started to eat, with big, greedy bites, chewing very briefly and then gulping down lumps of food.

'You know, Euan baby, there's lots better stuff here than you ever said. Quite a few pieces we could live with.'

'Need the will,' he said through his full mouth. 'Who's the lawyer?'

'It's still Wootton Hardman.'

'Slow and bloody expensive, you'd have thought someone could have told the old man where to go. It will be weeks before that dozy lot do anything.'

Tamara did not tell him that his father had given Alastair a copy of the draft will. She hoped to be safely elsewhere when Euan read it.

Discontentedly, Euan muttered, 'We need to know who the executor is. Or if the old man left it all to a cats' home.'

'His prerogative, if he did,' Tamara said.

'His duty was to pass it on to the next generation. Let's hope he didn't come under undue influence,' Euan said, staring at Tamara.

'From me?'

'Or my little bro. The good son who never puts a foot wrong. And always put up with anything his father chose to do. Let the old man wipe his feet all over him.'

'He didn't.' She was damned if she'd stand by while this rude carpetbagger cheated her husband out of his inheritance. 'He wasn't.'

'My brother the doormat.' Before Tamara could answer, Lezli

31

stood up and held out her hand to Euan. The hand was very large with prominent knuckles; a part of the anatomy that plastic surgery couldn't feminize. She/he said, 'Bed, lover,' and Euan immediately stopped talking, took the hand and left the room like a small child with his nanny. Tamara called, 'Goodnight,' but neither answered.

THE WEATHER HAD deteriorated by the time the rugby team's bus was approaching its destination. It didn't dampen their spirits. They had all stuck to the no-drinking-before-a-game rule, but it had been a cheerful journey all the same, with a couple of camera-laden supportive fathers in the bus, and when Coach got up to deliver his pre-match pep talk, they listened to what he said. When he finished with the question, 'So who's taking the trophy home?' the roar was loud enough to be heard outside the sealed windows and pneumatic doors. Several passersby, and people in the ticket queue, waved in support. In through the wide entrance and there they were: the best, the fiercest, the quickest in the business.

Towards the end of the first half, Davy neatly fielded the ball, collecting it and cutting inside with an unprecedented speed. He ran down to the 22-metre line. Without anyone laying a hand on him, he was through and under the sticks.

At half time the two teams were level pegging. Coach gave them another rousing speech. The fathers insisted on a quick group pose for the camera and one of them enthused, 'Brilliant! I'd say you were playing some of the best rugby I've seen all season. Is that how it felt to you?'

The only answer was a kind of group grunt.

Then it was time for the run onto the pitch, to a torrent of shouted encouragement and applause. But the magic ingredient had evaporated. The home team was regaining its advantage, the tourists' fightback was ineffective.

From the kick-off the fullback mishandled the ball and gave away a knock-on. The referee immediately spotted the infringement and blew for a scrum. The two packs faced each other, eight big strong men bound together by their interwoven arms. The scrum-half put the ball in and the men pushed and swayed until one of them kicked the ball backwards to a team mate and the scrum broke up.

One player was not playing any more. He was lying face down, flat on the muddy grass.

'Dave?'

'Hey, Dave, come on, get up.'

'There's something wrong!'

'Coach! Steve, here, Dave's—'

'Someone call an ambulance. Hurry!'

The St John Ambulance people reached them, panting. 'Clear a space, please.'

'Come on you lot, out of the way.'

'Don't just stand there gawping.'

Gawping or not, they stood there, dead silent except for one chap who was sobbing loudly.

One of the first aiders asked, 'What's his name?'

'Dave. David Canning.'

'Right then, David, don't try to turn your head or nod. We're just going to immobilize the spine.' A board was slid in under David's head and neck, and strapped firmly in place. As they watched in horrified silence, they heard the approaching sirens. A police car. An ambulance. Completely immobilized, David was lifted onto a stretcher and into the ambulance. Coach stood on the back step and said, 'The bus will be ready in ten minutes. Collect your stuff, get on board, go home. Got it?'

'Yes, Coach,' they muttered.

Coach got in to the ambulance and, siren blaring, it was driven away.

THE FUNERAL SERVICE was designed to be a cheerful celebration of a life well spent, with tuneful hymns belted out by a large congregation, optimistic verses touchingly read by grandchildren and the church deliciously scented by flowers that Tamara had ordered in her absent husband's name, *soleils d'or* daffodils from the Scillies. Propped against the pulpit was a portrait in oils labelled 'Dr Gordon M. Hope'. It showed him in late middle age, wearing a scarlet academic gown over a grey suit, and beside it a rather formal photograph of his wife as she was when Tamara first met her, before she showed any signs of the wasting disease that had later blighted their lives and eventually, only a couple of years ago, killed her.

Some of the congregation remarked on the love they had somehow discerned in the atmosphere. Others, having sensed the tension in the front pews, refrained from comment.

The church was full, the atmosphere steamy and damp. At the very back stood buckets full of dripping umbrellas. When the coffin was carried in, the wreath of white flowers already looked bedraggled, and in the quiet moments of the service, one could hear the rain battering against the post-war stained glass windows.

Tamara recognized very few people in the congregation, perhaps only those who had called at the house while she was in it. Sitting near the back so as to be able to make a quick getaway, Vera was quietly weeping, and Tamara watched as the dark-haired girl in the next seat drew her into a consoling hug. They both left the church before the procession of coffin and mourners came down the aisle, scuttling unobtrusively out, presumably to put kettles on and remove cling film.

Tamara had elected not to accompany the coffin to the crematorium afterwards, and it did not seem to have occurred to Euan to go with his father either. On the way back to the house he chose to travel with the grandchildren so Tamara was alone in the car with Lezli, who began, 'I sure hope the old guy did right by Euan.'

'Sorry?'

'In the will.'

'What do you mean, did right?'

'That he left him his half share after all.'

'After all?'

'He talked about disinheriting him when Euan saw him last.'

'Did he? When? Why?'

'Before my time. Back then Euan was still with Noreena.'

'Has he had many ... relationships?'

'Hey, what d'you think, a gorgeous guy like him? Three wives and you'd lose count of the lady friends.'

'Has he any children?'

'Not that I know of! Not that he knows of either.' Lezli laughed long and loud, and then, panting slightly, added, 'We're so together, me and him, we're all in all to each other, don't need anyone else. I don't know how you can stand having your beloved far away. But of course not many people have a great love like we do.'

'Have you been together for a long time?'

'One year and one-hundred and sixty-three days. But as a matter of fact he's still technically married,' Lezli said in a quieter, confidential tone. 'He's got to get free of – I call her "the third Mrs Hope". Kylie, that's her name – clings like a burr, she's always trying to wheedle money out of poor Euan, or getting her shyster lawyer on her case. You wouldn't think a woman could sink so low, trying to keep a man when she knows he doesn't want her. But I tell you what, it's a bit of luck you reminded me. We've got to make sure she doesn't get her claws into any legacy. This is all Euan's.' They were drawing up at the house and Lezlie gathered up his gloves, his ivory prayer book and his bag. 'God knows he's earned it,' he said.

Help! Tamara thought. Whatever's going to happen when they see the old man's will? Her father-in-law had repeatedly said that Alastair was getting the lot. Once he said that he was disinheriting his elder son. Another time, in a better temper, he was adjusting the proportions that individuals would inherit. In fact, Tamara realized, he played the will game throughout the last years of his life. And the last thing she heard him say on the subject was that he had left to his son Euan the family Bible and his mother's wedding ring and nothing else.

Vera had organized a massive spread, saying that people were always starving after a funeral. She'd put out tea cups and hired an urn, and on another table arranged glasses and bottles of sherry. There had been a plan: the deceased's elder son and his younger son's wife, Tamara, should have greeted acquaintances and friends and welcomed strangers together. But Euan, having limply shaken a couple of hands, turned away. Without apology, he pushed his way through the polite scrum and holding his phone to his ear, went out into the garden. The grass too high, the borders shaggy, it was blatantly neglected. Tamara glanced coldly at her brother-in-law and set herself to greet a congregation of strangers.

'Yes, it was a dreadful shock. The medics hadn't expected it. Of course, at his age you never know. But Alastair would never have gone this year if he'd had the slightest idea....' Gordon Hope's unexpected demise was one topic of conversation. The other was his elder son.

'Euan? Yes, wasn't it lucky that he got here in time to say goodbye. He's staying here just now, yes ... I'm sure he'll come in soon, I think he had to take an urgent call.'

She repeated this polite fiction, until an old man, whose name she hadn't heard, said in a pronounced Northern accent, 'Don't bother, love.'

She fixed her blue gaze on him, eyebrows raised. He went on, 'Anyone as knew anything about Gordon knew the boy was a dead loss. Was and is. Calls himself a doctor.'

'Well, he is, isn't he? I thought he had a practice in Oregon.'

'Oregon! I ask you! Enough said.'

'What do you mean?' Tamara asked. She had already spoken to nearly all the other guests and felt she could take the opportunity to find out something about Alastair's family, and in particular its black sheep.

'Look it up, girl. And you in a family of medics!'

'Are you talking about assisted suicide?'

'That's one name for it. I call it murder.'

'Was he doing that?' Tamara asked, actually rather shocked.

'He was. But the boy left that job, he's been working in a clinic, terminating pregnancies. From the very old to the very young, bringing death.'

'You know, Mr ... Mr – I'm so sorry, I don't know your name.'

'Bannister. And it's doctor. Dr Bannister. I was with Gordon at med school and we've been friends since he settled here in the south, and that explains why I know more about your in-laws than you do. A word to the wise. You want to be careful of Euan. He may look like your young man but that's as far as it goes. He's bad news, that boy. Always was, always will be.'

Surely not, Tamara thought. But then, she had never known why the unknown brother-in-law had disappeared, nor why she must remember not to mention him to Alastair's father.

'I realize there have been problems,' she began.

'Problems! Problems, is it? Just as well he didn't get here in time for my poor old friend to see him, he'd have died all the sooner.'

'I think he did see him actually.'

'In the hospital?'

'Yes, I thought it was so lucky that he got there in time.'

'Is that so?' The information seemed to surprise and even worry the old man.

Tamara said, 'Is something wrong? Can I get you anything?'

'No, no, all is well.'

'You look a little upset.'

'No. Least said ...'

'Soonest mended?'

'Exactly,' Dr Bannister murmured, putting his forefinger to his nose in a gesture so old-fashioned as to be of historical interest.

I must remember to tell Mo, Tamara thought. Her friend Mo was collecting material for a social history of British morals and manners.

What had he just said? 'I'm sorry, Dr Bannister, I missed that.'

'I said, Alastair getting on all right, is he?'

'As far as I know. It's a pity he couldn't get back, but ...'

'Gordon was right proud of Alastair, that's for sure.' Dr Bannister put his glass on the mantelpiece and held out his hand for Tamara's. 'Don't you worry your pretty head about it,' he said.

'Must you go already?'

'I must. Now that I know – yes, I must. Good afternoon.'

What was that all about? Tamara wondered. Then she turned back to the other guests.

Euan was somewhere out of sight by now, but his partner Lezli, at the centre of a fascinated group, was loudly describing the farewell ceremony for his/her own father whose body had been committed not to the earth, but to a cryogenic tank, to await resuscitation in some technologically advanced future.

Tamara was cheered by glimpses of her sons as they squeezed between guests offering plates and bottles. At first Tamara had been dismayed at the sight of the laden tables, thinking 'We'll be eating this for days!' Now, seeing the appetites that had been gingered up, she wondered whether the food would run out. Apparently some friends and neighbours had contributed to what, according to Tamara's worldly sixteen-year-old Duncan, ought to be called Funeral Baked Meats, adding that there should have been a black-draped, horse-drawn hearse to complete the picture.

M _Michell_
HAS AN APPOINTMENT WITH
ON

MON. _____ AT_____

TUES. _____ AT_____

WED. _____ AT_____

THURS. _____ AT_____

FRI. 6/21 _____ AT 11:40

SAT. _____ AT_____

We reserve the right to charge for appointments cancelled or broken without 24 hours advance notice.

: son Colin's gruff whisper tickled brother? The wicked uncle? He came didn't say a single word.'

an.'

ets his share I expect. Actually, Mum, s get – OK. Sorry, sorry.' He slid away him off. Though he had, of course, question.

d had been demolished people began ly to say goodbye to Tamara, asking kindest regards to be sent to Alastair. rking on autopilot: thank you so much; n your love, of course; send me an email, and I'll let you have his full address tomorrow.

When a tall man with a ruddy face and unusually large hands stood before her, she smiled automatically and held out her hand. He shook hers, but said, 'I'm not a guest, Mrs Hope, I'd like to have a word with you.'

The room had emptied quickly, and girls in black dresses were clearing the last of the food. Tamara said, 'Of course, but why?'

'I'm Detective Constable Gilbert, Thames Valley Police.'

'Oh. How d'you do.'

'I can wait until you have found someone to be with you.'

'I'm fine, absolutely fine. What is this about?'

'We'd like your agreement to our conducting a post-mortem.'

As he said the words, post-mortem, Vera came into the room. She said, 'What's going on?' A little surprised by the tone of voice, Tamara said, 'Would you mind just giving us a minute, Vera?'

'I heard you say post-mortem,' Vera said, staring at the police officer, who looked at Tamara as if for guidance. 'Were you talking about Dr Hope?'

'Yes.'

'But his body's been cremated.' Vera sounded angry.

'Not yet. There was a queue at the crem.' He said the last words as if they were the title of a crime novel, and quickly corrected himself. 'They are very busy at the crematorium just now.'

'Do you actually need our agreement?' Tamara asked.

'We can get an order, obviously, no need for an exhumation order in this case. It's all obviously easier if the next of kin consents.'

'You can't do that! It's monstrous! It's out of the question!'

'Vera. Please.' Tamara didn't know how to deal with this interruption.

'What?'

'I think, actually, you'd better leave this to me. If you don't mind.'

The woman obviously did mind, her face flushed, her lips quivering, her gaze fixed angrily on the police officer. Tamara held the door open for her, and she did leave the room, a bundle of resentment, grief and anger.

'I was hoping to keep this to ourselves,' Tamara said. 'But now ...'

'Difficult,' the policeman agreed.

'You must be acting on information received.'

'Certainly.'

'I quite understand.' And so she did. Dr Bannister had suspected Euan of killing his father, the moment he realized that he'd had the opportunity. And Dr Bannister had passed on his suspicions to the police. He must have influential strings to pull, to get so immediate a response.

Wondering what Euan could possibly have done in the past, to give rise to such distrust now, Tamara said, 'As far as I'm concerned, go ahead. Though given what we've just been doing—'

'You mean the funeral.'

'Exactly. Might be best to keep this quiet, if that's all right by you.'

'Agreed. If you'd just sign this release....'

It was a standard form, printed out from the gov.uk site. Tamara signed it without comment. She handed it back to the policeman. 'If it's allowed to let me know the outcome....'

'I'll get back to you. Thank you, Mrs Hope.' He left her standing in her father-in-law's front room, wondering quite what to say to Vera. She had sounded positively aggressive, and had been butting in to a private conversation. Was complaining or reproaching her worth the effort? No, surely not. Once dealing with Gordon's affairs was done, there would be no need to see her again. No point in making unpleasantnesses, then.

She found Vera angrily stacking plates in the sitting room and began, 'Well, that was a surprise!'

'It's awful.' Tamara hadn't realized that Vera was crying, great bubbles of tears pouring down her cheeks.

'Vera ...' Tamara looked at her cautiously, and helplessly. Why did she mind so much?

'Don't you care?' Vera sobbed out, in a distinctly hostile tone.

'Of course I'm sorry – the implications ... but a post-mortem? No, I don't mind as such. I think I might see it differently because I've excavated so many skeletons. I don't care very much about the dead body when the person's gone.' As she spoke, in a dispassionate, ultra-rational tone, Vera calmed down. She scrubbed a paper tissue against her wet face, picked up a few discarded wine glasses and left the room. If she had been wearing anything more feminine than black trousers and a white overall, Tamara might have said she flounced out of the room. Somehow I've offended her. Too bad.

The boys were clustered by the dining room table, scavenging the remains of the food. They had been fond of their grandfather, but now seemed unaffected by his death. Like Euan; but, Tamara realized, he wasn't there. Nor was Lezli.

'Have you seen Dad's brother, boys?' Tamara called.

'He's left, Mum. Him and Lezli. There was a taxi. But he didn't say goodbye.'

'Mum.'

'Mmmm.'

'That Lezli. Is Lezli a man, really? Dressed up like a lady?'

'Oh Duncan.' Tamara hesitated. How to explain gender reassignment to her youngest son? And the others; she noticed that they had stopped what they were doing to listen. She stalled. 'Wait till we're in the car, I'll explain then. Just come and say goodbye to Vera before we go.'

Tamara was pleased to see that all three thanked Vera unprompted, and James added, 'Please will you say goodbye to your niece for me?'

'Was that your niece, Vera? I'd love to meet her. Is she still here?'

'No, she's gone.'

'I just caught a glimpse – lovely girl. How old is she?'

'Over twenty,' Vera muttered, looking uncomfortable.

'Oh – she told me she was nearly eighteen,' James said.

'So easy to lose track. I can never remember how old you lot are,' Tamara said, and added, 'Good to be at UCL, what's she doing?'

'As matter of fact, she's studying archaeology. She'd heard me mention you quite often over the years, and it made her take an interest.'

'Really? That's flattering!'

'It's only her first year, but she's enjoying it a lot so far.'

'What's her name?'

'Iona.'

'I love that name. That's what one of you boys would have been called if you'd been a girl. It was your great grandmother's name, Granddad's mum.' As she said the words, Tamara suddenly realized something, so plausible, so likely, that it felt like a fact not a possibility. Surely Iona must be Vera's own child, Vera's and Gordon's, never acknowledged, and brought up as her own by an aunt. It was a familiar scenario back in the days when people talked about illegitimacy, and 'the wrong side of the blanket' and 'little bastards'. Gordon must have started sleeping with Vera even before his wife started losing her mind. Whatever the reason for their remaining unmarried after Mary's death, it didn't change one so-far unacknowledged fact: Vera was the real bereaved person round here, the real mourner.

I ALREADY SAID that I am interested in death. I don't understand that some people aren't.

How can any mortal not be? And as an agency nurse I see a lot of it. I'm sent to a good many patients enduring their final illnesses.

The first time I watched what was apparently regarded as a 'natural death' I felt an intense curiosity. Not pity, though the dying man was pitiful; not disgust, disgusting though the smells and sounds undoubtedly were; but enthralled and mystified. Nobody had ever told me that the labour to leave this world could be as arduous and painful as to enter it.

I was nearly sixteen, nowadays still counted as a child, but as my granddad never tired of saying, he started working for his living at fourteen. I was at the local grammar school. In the part of Kent where I grew up, schools haven't all gone comprehensive. I wore old-fashioned uniform, a gym tunic over a striped shirt, a blazer with a coat of arms on the pocket, regulation lace-up shoes. It marked me out as the enemy to all the other kids I'd grown up with, but I was a fast learner and I'm not just talking about the subjects I took exams in. I was an ace at making myself inconspicuous, diverting attention away from myself and – when it couldn't be avoided – really vicious fighting.

I liked school. School liked me. They thought I was university material. Eng Lit maybe – I was always good at writing – or history. They were horrified when I got myself into nurse training, and I did regret it, but it was the only residential course on offer and I'd always promised myself that I'd leave home the minute I had anywhere else to go. And I'd done work experience in a care home. It hadn't been too bad, in fact in a way it inspired me.

John was eighty-eight and had lived in the home for nineteen years. He had a strict routine, always got up on the dot of eight, breakfast downstairs in the communal dining room (most of them were brought trays in their rooms) and after breakfast he always went into the conservatory where he would sit on a high chair with rollers, and scoot himself around to do his watering and pruning.

On this day John had skipped breakfast and tottering a bit more than usual, went into the conservatory. A little while later the other work-experience girl went to make sure he was all right, and came running out again. She was going to get into trouble. Running was a sacking offence. I was curious and went over to the conservatory.

John's eyes were fixed on something outside the window. His face was kind of rigid, set. I saw the secateurs slide from his hand and then he fell off the chair, like he was folding up, right onto the floor. He was breathing really loudly, in and out through the corner of his mouth, his cheek filled with air, up and down like a balloon. One side of his face was completely still, the loose skin was dangling off it. There was no problem making a diagnosis. John had had a stroke.

They got him carried up to the hospital wing – it was a very well equipped establishment. I asked if I could help care for him, and they were quite glad to send me up there to sit with him, it kept me out of their way. He lasted for nearly a week. He coughed and choked until the final couple of days. Drawn, dehydrated, his liver failed, so his skin and his eyes turned yellow ochre. He grew ever weaker.

At first I watched him obsessively, I wasn't going to miss the moment this time. But I'd no idea it would be so long in coming

– five days – or that it would be almost imperceptible. John lay in the bed, he didn't move, but always breathing very loud and with long silent gaps between each breath. I kept thinking that was it, he'd gone. But I thought it couldn't be long.

He breathed in, wheezing, then silence, then he let the air rasping out of his lungs. In, pause, out, pause, in – and no out. Somehow, suddenly, while I wasn't looking, the breathing stopped. I had missed the moment. Only seconds later I bent over the body and it was still. In that little time, it had shrunk. The soul, the life force, the spirit – whatever it is that is life – fills out a face and a body. Without it, the human remains are diminished.

I was kicking myself for that momentary inattention. Next time I'd watch more closely. No, I'd film it. That would catch the vital second, the moment when the body was parted from – what? If I knew the answer to that question, I'd know all I needed to know.

ON THE WAY home Tamara had to stop for petrol. The boys went into the shop while Tamara did the self-service of fuel and paid for it. Then her sons came back to the car, each of them carrying rather a lot of unnecessary loot: chocolate, magazines and fizzy drinks.

'James paid for it all, Mum!' Duncan, the youngest, sang out.

'Really, did you, James? Yesterday you said you were totally skint.'

'And so I was until the wicked uncle gave me a tip!'

'What, at the funeral?'

'Afterwards.'

'That's not fair,' Colin, the middle son, said. 'He didn't even speak to me, let alone hand over any cash.'

'He said not to tell you, Mum, but …'

'Did he now. And what else did he say?'

'He said if I had problems I didn't want to let on about to my cozy bourgeois family, to ask him. He said he'd had a knock-about life, and he knows more about the world than you and Dad. And to get in touch if I ever need to make a quick getaway.'

'How? Did he give you his address?'

'Email address. But I won't be using it.'

'Why not?'

'Oh, well....' Shuffling his feet and not meeting eyes. 'Actually, as a matter of fact, I didn't really like him very much. The way he talked to Miss Fleming!'

'What did he say?'

'I couldn't understand it, something about blackmail. Moral blackmail, he said, using paternal guilt as a big stick. I don't know what he meant and I don't want to go to stay with him, he's a bit creepy. I mean, he looks like Dad but different from him.'

'I know what James means, Mum.' Colin was jigging up and down, excited by some inexpressible discovery. Colin knew what other people meant even if they didn't express themselves clearly. He seemed innately able to read body language, to interpret tiny gestures, sometimes to pick somebody else's unexpressed thoughts out of their minds.

'He's remarkably intuitive,' an early school report had said, and added, 'but he needs to learn not to articulate others' thoughts to the world, or even to them. His ability is rare and will be valuable, but it can also be a shortcut to becoming an outcast, distrusted by his own contemporaries.'

Tamara had been upset by those words. Without ever thinking about it very much, she'd taken for granted that her boys would fit in, be popular with their contemporaries – in fact, that they would master their own worlds as she had. Colin, however, was what his headmaster had described as 'an original'.

'I know what James means.'

'Bet you don't,' James growled.

'When you said he was creepy. It's 'cos he looks like Dad, except it's Dad when he's really cross. Not friendly. Dad in a filthy temper.'

Later that day, while the two younger boys were watching a movie on television, James peeled off and joined his mother in the kitchen. She had unrolled a site plan on the big table, and was marking up the area she had examined.

'Found something interesting, Mum?'

'It's hard to tell, there's been so much later development on the site.'

He was quiet, watching her for a few minutes, then he said, 'Mum.'

'Mmmm.'

'About Uncle Euan.'

'Uh huh.'

'You did realize he was high.'

'What?'

'He was on something. Not just pot.'

'Oh God. Are you sure? How could you tell?'

'Oh, Mum. I just can.'

'James …'

'It's OK, don't get all fussed about it. I don't do drugs, I've told you millions of times, really I don't, but I know people who do. And one of them is definitely Uncle Euan.'

TAMARA HAD ONLY met Euan a couple of times before, the first being nearly twenty years ago at her and Alastair's wedding, when Euan had caused unforgettable offence by refusing to meet Tamara's family before the wedding day or even on it. He didn't attend the ceremony, had sent no present, but stalked into the reception, walking right past the receiving line without pausing. He grabbed two glasses, pouring the champagne rapidly down his throat, spoke to two or three people and then he left. Tamara's father had been amused but her mother was hurt and Alastair momentarily shattered because despite everything, he still admired and even revered his much older brother.

The second occasion was in Oxford when Gordon was collecting one of his half-dozen honorary degrees. It must have been – what? – fifteen, perhaps even more, years ago. The episode was burned into Tamara's memory.

Gordon had been pathetically pleased to learn that Euan intended to turn up, but there was no sign of him when they had to take their seats. Nearly two hours and four long speeches in Latin later, the audience and participants were spilling out onto the lawn in front of the Sheldonian, and even into the street. Gordon came towards Alastair and Tamara, his new scarlet silk gown billowing behind him like a sail, his arms wide, ready to hug. Then he caught sight of someone and veered to one side. Tamara moved towards him, and heard him begin, 'Euan! My dearest boy, you came!'

'And now I'm going.'

'Please stay. You haven't even said hullo to your brother – or Tamara. You know Alastair's wife, Euan, Tamara.'

'Hullo, Alastair, hullo, Alastair's wife,' he said. Then he pulled his arm free from his father's hand and started to move away, in a straight line, forcing everyone to step out of his way. Gordon looked regretful, but Alastair looked devastated. Tamara let go of his arm and set off to catch up with Euan. Behind her she heard Alastair calling, 'Don't, Tamara, don't!'

Euan had left indignant guests in his wake, and Tamara found herself apologizing to all these strangers. 'Excuse me, I'm so sorry, I beg your pardon ...' as she squirmed between broad, gowned backs, wide brimmed hats and the general obstruction of a large and polite gathering.

She caught up with Euan just as he reached the pavement and waved to a taxi. He opened the door and barked, 'Station.'

Tamara took hold of the handle and pulled the door open again. 'Euan, don't go without talking to your family, they are so upset.'

'Let go, will you? Driver, move on.'

'Please—'

'Shut the bloody door.'

'Euan, do please come, just—'

'Fuck off, damn you!' he shouted, slamming the door shut. As the cab sped away, breaking Tamara's hold on the door handle, she lost her balance and fell onto hands and knees.

'Are you all right?' Several people who had been at the ceremony were now gathered on the pavement looking concerned and rather disgusted.

What an un-British scene they had just witnessed, Tamara thought, standing up easily, patting her palms against each other to wipe off the grime and then smoothing her skirt which, luckily, was long enough to hide her grazed knees.

'I'm absolutely fine, thanks so much!'

She told Alastair and his father that she hadn't been able to catch up with Euan. She didn't know if they had discussed him while she wasn't there, but after murmuring 'He's an odd chap,' Gordon didn't mention his elder son to Tamara again that day or later.

It was Alastair who told her, not long afterwards, what he had heard on the medical grapevine: Euan was moving to a post in Boston.

Tamara asked, not for the first time, what had gone wrong with Euan's relationship with his family. Usually Alastair brushed the question aside so she was quite surprised when he said, 'Believe me, I don't know. I've never known. Because the odd thing is that it's just us, just his family. He certainly has the capacity for making and keeping friends. There are chaps he was at med school with who still visit him and go out with him and make him their kids' godfathers. But his own family? He can't stand us. God knows why.'

After all these years of silence, he seemed suddenly to want to tell her far more than she had expected. 'Of course the difference in age means that I never really knew him. Though I kind of worshipped him, you know. The dashing big brother. But looking back, it's as if he always wanted to upset my parents. The jobs he's had, always sort of on the edge, you know what I mean? For a while he worked in an abortion clinic and wasn't very careful about the dates. He'd do them late, much too late really. The act specifies a time limit.'

'I should think it's more honoured in the breach.'

'Maybe, but you know how scrupulous the old man is. So then he moved on to a job doing artificial insemination, the law is really precise about what is allowed and what isn't, and he did more than he should. I think the last straw was when he was working with people in the final stages of cancer. Terribly difficult job, such a fine line between giving enough to stop the pain and not giving enough to kill. He stepped over the line apparently. My father was able to stop him being hauled up before the ethics committee, but only on condition that he didn't work in this country any more. They said he couldn't have a practising certificate, but they didn't actually strike him off. Which is why he went to the States.'

'You haven't mentioned girlfriends – or boyfriends for that matter.'

'Oh, he's not gay. He's just … he has special tastes. Or at least, the girls he's brought home, they might have been chosen to dismay a conventional father.'

'Not the girl next door, then.'

'The first one I remember was a lovely girl, really pretty and affectionate, but she was a trapeze artist in a circus – you can imagine what my parents thought of that. Then there was the Serbian ex-fighter, terrifying woman; and a Sudanese who was terribly proud of her successful business, which just happened to be running a brothel. And so on.'

'Goodness darling, what a story!'

'You can see it upsets Father. He loves Euan, but hates what he does and he's terrified of what the next disaster will be. Actually, so am I.'

Tamara realized that Alastair had loved and hero-worshipped his older brother. She imagined the little dark haired boy chasing around after the big dark haired boy and being discouraged repeatedly. A mixture of admiration and resentment, exactly the recipe administered to most younger siblings.

OH MY GOD. Oh God, No. Don't let it – oh no! It's too late. I've left it too late.

Davy snapped into consciousness, not waking slowly as he usually did.

He'd got used to the gradual progress of his returning aware-ness. There'd be a dream. In the dream he was running, jumping, swimming, self-reliant, strong, young, healthy. And he'd notice some little symptom. The finger twitching. The foot cramping. Thirst. Pain. Itch. Pain.

At a snail's pace his nervous system would fire up. Eventually he would be able to force his elbows to push him up far enough to be able to reach out, then to force his hand to do so, to pick up the safe bottle with its one-way nozzle for him to suck the water out without the risk of spilling it. Then he'd pick up the closed container of the seven pills he needed to make his body start up, he would pour them into his mouth, pushing in the one that stuck on his lip, taking a mouthful of water, shaking his head to free the dry white disc that had stuck to his tongue, forcing himself to swallow the package of medication, gulping it down. Sometimes one of the tablets got stuck in his throat. Biscuits were on his bedside table for that very purpose, to push the pills down with them. It would take about forty-five minutes, and then suddenly he would realize that he was free. It had been a daily miracle. He could move. Not fast, not easily, and only from the waist up, but he wasn't completely paralyzed.

Paralyzed enough to be suicidal. Who wouldn't be? The things he had to do to keep alive! Putting a catheter in his dick to urinate, twelve inches of a foreign body forced into his most private parts; to defecate he had to put his finger in his arsehole and root around and around until the shit came out.

Davy had become a paraplegic. Could anything possibly be worse?

Did they know that he'd discover the answer soon enough?

Nobody ever specifically warned him that worse was to come. Until now, you wouldn't have thought anything could be worse.

They talked about hope, and regeneration, and the miracles of modern medicine. They read him articles about scientific and medical progress, amazing technical advances. They said he was doing well, he was a brave chap, things will improve. Unless ... they didn't talk about 'unless'.

But he knew. He'd had one stroke, like he was an old man. A consequence of the insult to the brain, they said.

'Will I have another?' They replied that they hoped not.

For a moment Davy had hoped it would happen – a massive stroke to kill him outright. He had feared it would happen but not kill him.

And here he was.

An hour had passed, an hour and a half, two hours. He couldn't move at all. That was it. Today for some reason, he went from unconsciousness to full and awful knowledge. It had happened.

From the very moment that he first woke in a hospital bed, he'd known what the end would have to be. And he knew how cunning he would have to be to ensure it was possible. The doctors had been candid as they were taught to be nowadays, not to offer false hope, not to pretend even to young patients. So one of the consultants had come to sit at the end of his bed, a younger man than most of them, chosen for that reason perhaps because he was closer to being able to imagine what Davy was going through, dressed in a carefully thought-out selection of the type of clothes that Davy would feel comfortable with, speaking slowly and clearly but in the kind of accent Davy's friends assumed to show they weren't just posh rich kids. Dave's dad called it Estuary English. The doctor talked about paralysis and quadriplegia and the nervous system and the developments in medicine and surgery, circling round the subject and gradually closing in on the facts of the case.

Davy had been at the bottom of the scrum. The weight of the others had pressed on exactly the point on his neck that most needed protection. It was a common accident. Many a rugby player had suffered the same fate, and lived useful, enjoyable lives in a wheelchair. Davy was less damaged than many others, he had the vestiges of movement, which was good. But he had to be prepared: it might get worse. He'd had a stroke. He was of course far too young, yes, it was an old man's problem – usually. But it wasn't unknown in young people and in this case it was all part and parcel of the original injury.

So I moulder away here until – until what?

The question wasn't answered directly. Instead the consultant sketched out a rough diagram. Where muscles and nerves, tendons and bones, should be, and where they actually were. Impossible to correct in surgery. So Davy was in a vulnerable position. Davy must be ultra cautious. Something might snap.

If you've had one stroke, you might have another.

Difficult to get your head round this. But try. Just listen and take in what was being said, there'd be plenty of time to ponder over it. Later.

And now, something had snapped.

This is the day. Today. This is the morning Davy wakes to the realization that he's in bed and can't move and this is where he'll be for the rest of the day, the rest of the year, the rest of his life.

'THE THING IS, Mrs Hope—' the policeman began.

'Dr Hoyland,' Tamara said. After the runaround she'd had trying to get an answer out of the Thames Valley Police, standing on her dignity seemed a wise precaution.

'Is that so? A lot of doctors in your family.'

'My father-in-law, my husband, my brother-in-law – but I'm not a doctor of medicine.' She handed him her business card, on which she was described as 'Tamara Hoyland, MA, PhD, FSA.' The address was that of the Archaeology Unit.

'You're an archaeologist! I love that *Time Team* programme. You ever been on?'

'I have, a couple of times.'

'I must have seen you, then, I never miss it.'

By the time Tamara reminded him why she was there, the official formality had melted. 'Acting on information received ...'

'From Dr Bannister.'

'I'm not at liberty to say.'

'No, of course not, sorry. Do go on.'

'A post-mortem examination was ordered. It revealed no grounds for further action, and the cremation will proceed according to the original plan.'

'Case closed, then.'

'Indeed. And the Thames Valley Police apologize for the delay in letting you know.'

'Thanks. Apology accepted. But now all that's done, are you allowed to tell me informally why it was thought that something else had happened?'

'Apparently the deceased was thought to be rallying, the medics even thought Dr Hope would be out of the high dependency unit within a day or so. So by some standards the death was unexplained.'

Tamara's blue gaze remained fixed for a moment as a mental picture she had been looking at for some days popped up into her consciousness again: Euan, a medic who knew all about the mechanisms of life support, standing beside the machine. He could have fiddled with the settings. He could have introduced or removed some vital gadget or ingredient. He could have killed his father. Perhaps, Tamara thought, we'll never know.

The police officer said, 'One of the nurses quoted a useful mantra: all you can predict is that events will be unpredictable. So no worries, the file's been closed.'

TAMARA HAD BEEN invited to make an appointment with Gordon's solicitor and had herself insisted that it should be soon. It proved difficult to find a moment that was convenient for Tamara, Euan and the solicitor, an associate in Wootton Hardman, a firm that had, coincidentally, been used by her family and, when she needed advice, by Tamara herself. But Ben Tiller, who was in charge of Gordon Hope's files, seemed amazingly elusive. He was in a meeting, in court, on his way, on his way out.... In the end Tamara had to pull rank – the superior status of the cash-paying client. 'If it proves necessary to move our affairs to another firm ...'

'Mrs Hope, Jack Hardman here from Wootton Hardman. What? Oh – yes, he was my great grandfather. Now, I'm so sorry we seem to have been giving you a runaround – crossed wires I'm afraid. Mr Tiller left the firm rather suddenly, and we've been trying to catch up. And now I'm entirely at your service. What can I do for you?'

As it turned out there wasn't much he could help Tamara with. The very first clause of Gordon's will said it was to be read in the presence of his two sons.

'I've got Alastair's power of attorney.'

'You have?'

'I brought it. Here.'

'Thank you. Let me just … mmm … mmph. It's quite, what can I say – informal.'

'But legal? Effective? You know, it's likely to be some weeks, maybe even months before my husband gets home.'

'I sympathize, believe me. Look, let me just … I'll be back in five minutes.'

'He's gone to ask Daddy,' Euan said. 'You'd have thought the old man could have run to a qualified attorney. He always was a cheapskate.'

Young Mr Hardman returned, pink faced. Had he been running? Or bawled out by a senior lawyer?

'I've discussed this matter with one of my partners. We feel it's permissible to divulge the principal legacies, particularly as the post-mortem examination showed no problem,'

'Stop right there,' Euan snapped. 'What post-mortem?'

'I don't know any more than that there was one. I'm afraid.'

'Tamara?'

Tamara's smooth face showed none of her preoccupations. She said, 'I was told it had taken place, and nothing was found amiss. So it doesn't matter. If everything was all right, let's forget it. The will, Mr Hardman—'

'It bloody does matter. When was the post-mortem carried out? And why? And who gave permission?'

'I'm afraid I haven't the information.'

'Well who has? Tamara, what do you know about it?'

'Nothing, Euan. But why are you so upset about it?'

'I'm not upset about it, except that it was bloody unnecessary. Someone suspected that one of us had knocked the old man off.'

'It's OK, I'm sure it was just routine. Can we get on now?'

'As I said, Mrs Hope, we can reveal the main points, but not make the whole document available. Would that be acceptable, Mrs Hope?'

'Better than nothing,' she said.

'Before you go any further, how much is there?'

'As a matter of fact, there is rather less capital in the estate than we'd recently supposed.'

'What d'you mean?' Euan snapped.

'Your father made some sizeable disbursements in the last months of his life.'

'Sizeable? How sizeable?'

'Ball park – six figures.'

'Six – I don't believe it. Who to?'

'I don't know. And if I did, I couldn't tell you.'

'That bloody woman! I knew she was on the take from the moment – it's Vera. The so-called housekeeper.'

Tamara said, 'It was his to spend as he chose. Can we get on, please?'

'Of course. Let me see … Yes, here we are. The principal legatee and the sole executor is the deceased's son Alastair. I think that's about as much as it's proper to divulge.'

'The house?'

'I shouldn't …' he began, but quailed at the sight of Tamara's direct blue gaze. 'Yes,' he said hastily, 'the house and the money.'

'Right.'

'My God, the old bastard,' Euan exclaimed. 'The utter shit! He actually wrote me out of his will! The elder son, completely ignored – it's unbelievable. And God knows what you lot were doing, letting him – it must be breach of your duty to … or professional negligence. Or something.' His face was purple with emotion, his voice hoarse.

Tamara said, 'Euan, you know that Alastair won't—'

'And you can shut right up too, you – you … I simply don't believe it! I'll fight it, of course. I ask you, post-mortems! Disinheriting his eldest son! I know who's to blame. I know you're poking your nose in to my affairs and that can bloody well stop. In fact, fuck off, why don't you, just fuck off.' Fortunately he plunged out of the room himself at that point, and within a couple of minutes a young woman put her head round the meeting room door and told Mr Hardman that his client had left the building.

'Ought I to apologize for my brother-in-law?' she said.

'Oh no, not at all.'

'I expect you've seen worse.'

'From disappointed legatees? Yes, frequently.'

'And I sympathize with him, it must be horrible to know that one's own father ...'

'Yes.'

'Actually, I'm pretty sure that my husband will go halves.'

When she next reached Alastair on the sat phone, Tamara told him about the will. He didn't sound terribly interested. 'Oh, did he? I'll divvy it up with Euan, of course. We agreed on that when I was about eight.'

'That's fine, darling, but meanwhile, till you get back, what do you want me to do?'

'We don't want the house. Do we?'

'Swallows? Certainly not,' Tamara said with a shudder.

'You could get an estate agent, put it on the market.'

'Oh could I? And what about the things in it?'

'Well, we don't want them either, do we?'

She started to tell him that Euan had quite calmly, as if by right, taken up residence in his father's house, but before she reached the end of that sentence the phone connection failed. She'd been about to say that she hadn't tried to evict him, Alastair must do that himself, if he chose to. She thought of the gewgaws and memorabilia, the paintings and the furniture, listed them in her mind and visualized Euan and Lezli selling everything off. She would have to psych herself up to confronting them.

Really, this should be Alastair's job. If he decided that his

Indians and their medical secrets were more important, and if Euan took the opportunity to help himself to everything valuable – well, tough! But in fact, Tamara knew that Alastair really wouldn't mind, whereas she felt rather self-righteous about it all. Gordon had intentionally disinherited his elder son; he must have had a good reason.

Tamara had kept clear of Swallows since the funeral and didn't feel at all eager to go back. But she was going to have to.

Not today. Not this week. But soon.

'WE NEVER USED to quarrel,' Polly said sadly. 'Never a cross word, or hardly ever. But now ...'

'Oh I know,' her sister said. It was an all purpose reply and could have meant she wasn't really concentrating, But actually she was trying so hard to be strong for Polly, not to give way to her own grief for her favourite nephew, that she could hardly get even those three words out without sobbing.

'Robert just won't listen. He's given up, he's resigned himself. He thinks he knows that there's no hope ... but I still think my Davy could improve. Robert says he, his body, is an empty shell. Robert says he should be allowed to – I can't say it. I just can't—'

'Oh Poll, don't cry again.'

'Someone told me that he might have something called locked-in syndrome. It means that his brain's working but he can't show it.'

'Come on, wipe your eyes, here, take one of these. If Dave's locked inside his body, he needs you to be strong for him, you have to be his spokesman, his advocate.'

'You know what they said, Janey? They said he could stay like this for years. Literally years. Can you imagine? My lovely boy, trapped somewhere inside that useless body. Or his body, with him almost gone. I don't know what to do. I really truly don't.

And the girls. They've become so angry. Rude. Unkind.'

'It's because they are so upset, too.'

'I know, I do try not to ... But Dave was always the one who made peace. Oh Janey, what am I to do? How do we ever get over this?'

'Get over it? You can't. One couldn't. You find a way to live with it, that's all you can do. If that's what Dave has to do, then so do you.'

'And Robert?'

'Oh Polly, God alone knows. He'll learn to live with it, like you, or he won't. That's all.' Janey suddenly realized that she no longer wanted to cry, she wanted to kill someone. Why did they let boys play – *play! What a word to use!* – that dangerous game? Shouldn't it be illegal? The carnage of young men ... she had looked it up of course, and found that Dave had been hurt in a predictable accident, one with numerous precedents. Many, many boys and young men had been left paralyzed by an accident on the rugby pitch. They knew what could – what often *did* happen. And they let Dave risk everything all the same. It was unbelievable. It was wrong. It shouldn't be allowed.

TAMARA WONDERED WHETHER there was a usual age for making the changeover from going to lots of weddings or christenings, all cheerful tunes and colours, and finding that most services one had to attend were farewells.

Today's service ought not to be too melancholy. It was several weeks since the death, because it had been decided to await the return of a sailor son stationed in the Antarctic. His father, Tamara's mother's distant cousin Peter, had been declining for years with nothing left to hope for in this world, but being firmly convinced that heaven awaited, had often referred to 'welcome death'. Tamara didn't think she could have set eyes on distant cousin Peter for more than twenty years, or, as a matter of fact, more than a couple of times in her life. But he and Tamara's mother had been close as children. Tamara's big sister Alexandra, who couldn't make it herself, was firm that the Hoylands had to be represented.

The service was at eleven, and Tamara arrived a little late. She slid into a chair beside her mother's old school friend Bessie Woods, who hugged her and said, 'You're a sight for sore eyes.'

'Really? Oh good.'

'Such a pity we only meet at funerals.'

Evelyn Cattermole twisted round from the row in front and said, 'It's an epidemic, we're all dropping off the perch in turn.' Her deep voice, projected to be audible from the far side of a theatre, was followed by the much less clear tone of the local parson.

The service was one of those awkward compromises, in which familiarity alternated with formality. Distant cousin Peter had a devoted family who spoke about him in intimate terms. But he also had numerous relationships based on a shared interest in – of all things – travel and transport. His bookcases were apparently filled with obscure railway timetables, albums of never-realized designs for urban buses or North Sea ferries; and the best holiday of his life had been spent shovelling coal on an obsolete steam engine that pulled a single passenger coach to and fro between tourist attractions only three miles apart.

As four of the deceased's grandchildren played a movement from a string quartet, and even while another two read aloud a dialogue from a classical author, Tamara couldn't help overhearing whispered and muttered discussions about Peter's death. Apparently it had surprised everyone, even the GP, although he had been summoned by the carer and made a house call twice in the last week of Peter's life.

'Bit of luck, that was, I must say.'

'Luck? Why?'

'It meant the doctor could sign the death certificate, no post-mortem.'

'So what did the poor bugger die of?'

Shushing sounds were directed at the chattering pair, who muttered 'Sorry, Sorry' and lapsed into silence. After the service, huddling out of the wind, Bessie was approached by a red-haired young woman.

'Oh my dear, the glorious Gloria! How are you?'

'I'm very well thank you, Mrs Woods.'

'And working where?'

'In hospital for the moment.'

'Tamara, this is Nurse Gloria.' A few nods, murmurs and smiles, and Nurse Gloria had moved on to another group.

'She's brilliant, you have to get her via a nursing agency, so it costs a fortune, but she's so good. She was with Peter at the end. Good of her to come back for this.'

Bessie sat down on a low brick wall that ran round a formal flower bed, and absent-mindedly pressed her hand against the small of her back. 'All this standing!'

'Shall I fetch you a chair?'

'No, no, I'll be off in a moment. Just tell me first, how are the boys? And how is Alastair?'

'As far as I know, he's fine. He's still in Brazil.'

'Brazil? All alone? Without you?' Bessie exclaimed, as though Tamara had said her husband was on Mars.

'He's got a team of scientists and medics. They are hunting for medicinal plants.'

'Team ... it makes me think of sleds and huskies.'

'You don't think that's just because it's so cold here?'

'Perhaps you're right,' Bessie agreed, but she had already moved on to her next thought. 'It's silly of us to be standing round in this freezing weather. Let's go, and why don't you come with us, Tamara? We're going to lunch at Elspeth's club. You'll already know almost all of us.'

The pompous crimson dining room which until very recently had admitted no women, ever, was noisy with chatter, very unlike the old 'gentleman's club' it had been until so recently. Bessie led the way to a corner table where several of Tamara's mother's friends were sitting. Though well past pensionable age most members of this group were as busy as they had ever been, with their portfolios of boards, committees and quangos. Tamara had to suppress a bubble of grief and resentment. Why was her mother losing it, when her contemporaries were still going strong?

Many of these women had come to stay in Devon. As a teen-ager, Tamara, text in hand, had stood in for a National Theatre audience to hear Evelyn Cattermole rehearse Lady Macbeth's lines. She had been convinced by the then Shadow Home Secretary, as he practised a speech about capital punishment and the inadvisability of reintroducing it. She had been invited to contribute her own opinions when the motherless and child-less expert on childhood, Dr Fidelis Berlin, discussed her theories about maternal deprivation.

Now middle aged herself and the mother of three hulking boys, Tamara was amused to find herself representing the younger gen-eration. It was still, or again, her place to listen politely without joining in as the grown-ups talked about grown-up things, just now euthanasia. No discussion of rights and wrongs. Tamara was genuinely shocked to hear these self-determining women taking it for granted that they would make their own decisions to the very end.

'Can you imagine, lying there helpless, entirely dependent on someone like one's poor benighted spouse, or some agency temp like that girl who looked after poor Peter at the end ...'

'But she's lovely.'

'Absolutely. But what good's that if you can't read or talk? You'd be begging her to finish you off. Not that Peter could speak, by the end.'

'Such a dreadful fate, I do hope to die before I come to that.'

'I've got a stash of co-proxamol though I'm not sure how many it takes.'

'Somebody told me that anti-malarials are the answer.'

'I've still got some barbiturates left over from when they were legal – must have been back in the seventies. But the trouble is I don't know if they go off.'

It turned out that most of them had squirrelled away a secret stash containing what they believed, or hoped, would be a fatal dose. One said it was in her washbag, in case she was taken into hospital. Bessie's was in a locked drawer along with her will, premium bonds and the deeds of her house, another kept hers at the back of the bathroom cupboard in a plastic pot under some HRT pills left over from the days when she needed them.

'Pretty well everyone I know has made their own escape plans,' one woman claimed. 'But whether we'll have the nerve when it comes to the point – that's quite another matter.'

When Tamara said she had to leave, Bessie kissed her and said, 'You've been very quiet, dear.'

'I couldn't join in that conversation, Bessie.'

'Shocked?'

'Yes, frankly. And distressed. What one of you said about the doctor who murdered his own patients ... Harold Shipman.'

'I didn't hear it.'

'She actually said, I couldn't believe my ears, she said "I wish he were my GP".'

'I expect I would have been shocked at your age too.'

'It's shocking at any age, can't you see that? Honestly, Bessie, I'm appalled.'

Bessie, who had been Olga Hoyland's lifelong friend since they met aged eight in junior school, looked remorseful.

'I didn't mean to upset you, I'm so sorry.'

'I have to run, I'm late. Goodbye, Bessie,' Tamara turned in the direction of the Tube station. She found herself walking with Evelyn Cattermole. As always in this part of London there were a lot of people about. Most of them kept their eyes fixed on the ground or the shop windows or some inexact spot that enabled them to avoid personal interaction with any of the strangers crowding the pavement. A few, usually men, boldly looked at oncoming faces, their gaze sliding automatically away from invisible old women and unpromising old men. Some let their eyes meet Tamara's. From behind she looked exactly the same as she had twenty years before, a little above the average height, still wearing size ten clothes, her blonde straight hair swinging as she walked. The front view had matured but seemed unchanged in a kind light: blue eyed, rosy, in fact, *innocent*. Tamara's face had been her passport into and safely out of many a dangerous situation.

A window cleaner, poised on a high ladder, whistled as she went by.

An elderly man in a navy blue suit and striped tie glanced incuriously at the older woman, looked with more interest at Tamara and then, his eyes swivelling back to Evelyn's face, did a kind of double take.

'It's Dame Evelyn Cattermole!' he exclaimed. 'I saw you at the National, you were wonderful.' Evelyn made her usual practised response, signed her name on the back of a Sainsbury's till receipt for a Dutch tourist who had been listening and walked a little less briskly on.

'What did you make of all that talk at lunch?' she said suddenly.

'What talk? There were so many conversations,' Tamara replied.

'All that stuff about taking one's own life.'

In fact Tamara knew exactly what she felt, or believed, on that subject, but she had refrained from saying so during the lunch, and thought she'd better go on hedging now. 'It was interesting.'

'I thought it was disgusting. Shocking.'

Set free by the older woman's candour, Tamara said, 'Oh,

Evelyn, so did I!'

'I'm ashamed of my friends for saying such things. I wish your mother had been there, she wouldn't ever have put up with it. Well, I mean, she wouldn't have, in the old days, before—'

'But Bessie said she agreed with them.'

'Do you know, Tamara, I'd never suggest that Bessie was telling an actual untruth, but she has been known to embroider.'

'I was so surprised, it was the last thing I'd have expected my mum's friends to say. She'd never have sat there without arguing!'

Evelyn pronounced, as if from a pulpit, 'Life is so precious, a gift, to hear them making plans to commit – I can't even say it – I can't bear it.'

The beautiful and famous voice was getting louder with each phrase.

'It was just lunchtime chitchat, they weren't being serious,' Tamara said.

It was what she had told herself while listening to the offensive – and she couldn't think of any more apt adjective – discussion.

'That lot doesn't go in for idle chitchat.'

'That lot? Evelyn, they're your lifelong friends!'

'Ex-friends if that's what they really believe.'

They had reached Green Park Underground station. 'You're going by Tube, Tamara? Then I'll say goodbye.' A cool cheek-to-cheek, none of the hugs Tamara was used to. At least the delicious smell was as she remembered. She looks her age, Tamara thought. Evelyn swivelled on her high heels, put out her hand and a taxi slid to a halt beside her. A tiny wave, no smile, and Dame Evelyn Cattermole was driven away.

IF ONE UNLIKELY day he got out of this prison, Davy would have learnt more than he ever wanted to know about a wide variety of subjects. At first people had been a little careful of what they said given that they weren't quite sure if he could hear them, or if he was going to recover and be able to quote them.

By now there was little hope of that. Little or none.

The nurses talked across him as they made the bed or dealt with his uncontrollable body fluids. They'd talk about their boy-friends, their evenings out, their kids, their periods, their chatter full of an awful lot of things he'd never thought about before. And that was a fine waste too.

Today there was one agency nurse and another regular staff member whose name he could never remember. The two of them positioned him on the hoist and moved his inert body around as if it were a package to be wrapped or unwrapped.

'Careful,' the familiar one said.

The stranger replied, 'But he can't feel anything. Isn't that the whole point?'

'Yeah, but the skin shows bruises.'

'Oh well then. OK.'

Lucky he couldn't feel it, as a matter of fact, but he could tell that they were being pretty rough. The newcomer finished scrub-bing at his skin and said, 'I dunno, what's the point? Why do they bother with all this? It's like washing a cabbage or some-thing, wasted effort.'

'Much better to be dead.'

'Ain't that da troof.'

'I bet he'd kill himself if he could.'

'Have you ever finished one of them off?'

'What?' the nurse gaped, as if she couldn't believe she'd heard that question, but the other woman repeated it.

'Done for a patient? Killed one. On purpose, I mean.' Davy thought she'd asked it as casually as if enquiring where to find the lavatory.

'Killed – what, me? No, of course not. What a thing to say! Why ever would you think...?'

'Just wondered.' The women were both silent for a moment.

Then, holding the clean clothes they were going to put on him, the real nurse said, 'Pretty peculiar question if you ask me.'

'You'd feel like it was an hour-long orgasm. All powerful, like I'm the queen or something.'

'D'you mean you really have? Killed someone?'

He couldn't see her, only her reflection in the window, her head nodding up and down. She muttered, 'Put them out of their misery, you know? Like dogs.' After a short silence she burst into peals of laughter. 'Oh Hailey, look at you! Can't you take a joke?'

'So you haven't really?'

'Of course I haven't, you are funny. Though I wouldn't mind if someone did, when they're incurable. Like this one.'

She means me, Davy realized. That's what she's working up to, she's going to put me out of my misery. So why am I scared? Why aren't I grateful to her? I should be oozing enthusiasm, she's going to get me out of here. Instead, I'm lying helpless in this canvas hoist and willing the door to open, calling for rescue, only nobody can hear me. Help. Help. He thought the words so vehemently that he could hardly believe there'd been no sound. And then the door was swung open and his mother came in.

'IF YOU WANT to represent my brother in the division of the spoils, it's then or never.'

Euan had made the unilateral decision that his father's house would be cleared out the following weekend, which happened to suit him.

'But Euan, we can't do it without Vera.'

'Bugger Vera, she's been treating the place like it belonged to her for quite long enough. The house won't ever sell unless there's vacant possession. You don't have to be sorry for her, she's had a cushy little number here. My father could have been getting a proper rent for that flat, and, you might like to know, it's stuffed with family things. I'd been wondering what had happened to some of them.'

Vera lived in the housekeeper's self-contained flat above the garage.

'Alastair would never turf her out till she's got somewhere else to go, she was so good to your father. Anyway she has rights, some sort of protected tenancy, if you've been snooping round – and some of the things in the house must be hers too.'

'Too bad. She's not a beneficiary and neither are you for that matter.' Her brother-in-law had never been known to surrender in an argument, at least not in Tamara's experience.

She said, 'Nor are you.'

'Maybe, but I've spoken to him.'

'Alastair?'

'Who did you think I meant? Of course Alastair. We spoke the day before yesterday.'

'But I tried that day and couldn't get through.'

'Maybe he was scared to tell you. He's going to go halves. The old bastard was probably pissed when he signed that ridiculous will. Alastair says it's cool, I can go ahead sorting stuff out as far he's concerned.'

'You do know I've got his power of attorney?'

'You do know,' Euan replied, mocking, 'you know that he doesn't give a damn about the house or its contents.'

'Oh Euan, that's so not true. He gives lots of damns when he's here, it's just he can't think about home when he's out there.'

'He won't be back for weeks, we can't wait that long if it's going on the market. Anyway, he isn't interested.'

And nor he was. Tamara reached him later that day. 'What does it matter?' he shouted across thousands of miles. 'I don't want any of Dad's gewgaws, we've got too much stuff already. You should see how the Amazonian natives live. The idea of personal possessions doesn't come into it.'

'Alastair – did you tell Euan he could stay in the house? And get rid of things, or take them?'

'Well, not exactly … But I don't care if he does.'

'You gave me your power of attorney.'

'Don't get all legalistic. I told you, it doesn't matter to me.'

One of the problems with modern communications, Tamara realized, was that they didn't break up. And the idea of having a fluent trans-continental argument with her husband was too exhausting. She knew him in this mood. He'd be admiring the innocent tribespeople and feeling ashamed of his own extravagant European lifestyle. The fact that his hosts would be wise and ancient elders at thirty-five and would be lucky to live to the great old age of forty, didn't matter; nor did the exhaustion of the women who reached that age, with crippling prolapses after multiple pregnancies, with inner organs hanging down between their legs and naked breasts dangling like empty gourds. In Alastair's eyes these people were the salt of the earth and perhaps even the future of the human race. And when he was with them he certainly didn't have time to think about legacies.

Which meant that Tamara felt it was her duty to protect Alastair's interests however little he wanted her to. She would have to go down again on Saturday, and while there try to do her best for Vera too. What a perfectly dreadful two days awaited her, Tamara thought.

NEXT CALL: VERA FLEMING, housekeeper – and presumably more – to the late Dr Hope. She had first come to work for them more than twenty years ago.

'Vera, hi! It's Tamara. Is the cruise fun?'

'Yes, it's lovely, thank you.' A reserve in her voice?

'You certainly needed the break. Away from it all.'

'But it isn't, I haven't got clean away – oh Tamara, he's awful, really awful!' Vera was almost crying, her complaint hiccupping through the air. Tamara sighed.

'Euan I suppose?' she asked.

'It's always Euan. How could such lovely people have had such a ghastly son? He was difficult even as a child, his old nanny told me so. She said that when she first saw him, he threw his toy engine at her, one of those wooden trains with rails you fit together like a jigsaw. Gordon was so apologetic. Nanny was sure they gave her the job because they felt so guilty. You know, I really think he must have been a changeling.'

'What's he done this time?' Tamara asked. She could believe anything of the aggressive man who had dissed his own father's funeral. She pulled the phone cord as far as it would go, to reach the newspaper's puzzle page, and started to do the soothing super-fiendish Sudoku while conversing.

'I mean, Alastair wouldn't ever have even dreamed of going down to the house and sneaking things out of it,' Vera said.

'He didn't! Really? But how do you know?'

'The cleaner rang me. You know, that nice girl from Indonesia, you've met her.'

'I thought she was a Filipina.'

'Could be. I don't know. Anyway, she'd had such a shock I thought she was giving me her notice. Did Euan think to warn her he was coming? Oh no. So when she found the front door unlocked and lights on she nearly had kittens. And then she was dialling the police when Euan gave her the fright of her life by popping his head up through the trap down to the cellar.'

'It sounds like some kind of farce.'

'I wonder if that's what you'll think when you get there and find all the good things have been spirited away.'

'Honestly, Vera, I won't mind about that. We're drowning in stuff as it is.'

'But I can't bear to think of Euan making off with everything, it's not at all what his father would have wanted. Mr Big marches round the house without a word, just grabbing what he fancies the way he always has. And I can tell you now, Tamara, when he comes back, Alastair's so like his father, he'll give in to anything rather than fight.'

'What did Euan want?'

'Oh, ridiculous things but including things you liked, Tamara, anything you might have wanted.'

'That doesn't matter.'

'I know you don't care, Tamara, and anyway what does it matter, it's not the objects that I'm upset about, it's the principle of the thing. His father was always picking up the pieces after him, paying people off, putting things right. You've no idea … And when I asked him, asked if he was allowed to take things, he told me to shut up and said it was none of my business.'

'Oh Vera, I'm so sorry.'

'He took some crates of wine too, he said that nobody else in the family could appreciate good wine, it would be wasted on them. On you.'

'He could be right about that.'

Vera laughed unwillingly. 'Well … even so …'

For a moment the two women were silent. Then, 'What else did he take?'

'Oh yes. He's walked off with the *Naked Venus.*'

'I love that picture.'

'Well, you've probably seen the last of it.'

'What's he doing with it all? I mean, as he's living in the house.'

'Selling it, of course. He's always broke, that boy – I mean, that man.'

'Turning it into money. Interesting,' Tamara said.

'And he tried to take the inlaid table but it wouldn't fit in his car.'

'The chess table?'

'You might have wanted it for your boys. Or for Alastair – what will he say when he gets back and Euan's bagged so much more than his share of the loot?'

'Alastair won't mind.'

'I know. He'll probably say keep it, and take more with my blessing.'

'It's just not the kind of thing he cares about,' Tamara said.

'Look Tamara, I know you've been putting off the big sort out ...'

'But it's got to be done. I know. Euan wants it to be this coming weekend.'

'That's fine, I'll be in, let's see, the Aegean by then. No, wait a minute, let me look at the programme ... well, wherever I am, it won't be Oxford. But you can manage without me. Don't let your brother-in-law bully you.'

FOR MOST OF Tamara's life Olga Hoyland had been the sharpest, most perceptive person her daughter had ever known. Impulsive and a little disorganized, certainly, but so clever. They had discussed the mystery of Alastair's brother. In fact Euan had been the subject of conversation so many times that Tamara could have talked about him in her sleep – and, she thought, probably did.

'It's perfectly obvious that he hates the lot of us. Did I tell you what happened in New York?'

'If you did I've forgotten. Tell me again.'

'Alastair said we couldn't be there without at least trying to see him, so we walked up to his apartment block, it was on the Upper West Side. I thought he'd be away or out, I wasn't actually expecting to see him, but Alastair asked the doorman, and quite by chance he'd just gone to the shop round the corner and was coming back, and at that moment Alastair saw him. Alastair looked so delighted, Mum, it was simply pathetic. Tragic, even. Because Euan took one look at him and me, and bolted for his door, and when Alastair called his name he turned round and shouted at us to go away. Actually, he shouted "Fuck off". And I asked Alastair when he became so hostile, and he said he'd always been like that, full of hate. He certainly resents me, and Alastair once told me that whenever he mentioned his father and mother he'd be quite savage. But why? His father's so sweet.'

'These things are rooted deep, very deep in childhood.'

'So I believe.'

'He went to boarding school very young didn't he?' Olga Hoyland remembered.

'They had to send him, you couldn't have taken a little kid into that part of Northern Ireland, not just then. Gordon was taking his life into his hands as it was.'

'And Mary's life.'

'Well, yes, except they were working together. Doctor and handmaid. She wasn't a nurse, you know, she was trained as a teacher. I think she went back to teaching later, too.'

'You can see that a small child would think he was being sent away because he had been naughty or because nobody loved him. Especially if it was one of those dreadful boarding schools where the little boys get interfered with. Where was Alastair?'

'He was seven years younger. Which must be why he worshipped Euan. Still does, in a way.'

'And Alastair wasn't sent away to school.'

'No, because by the time he was old enough his parents were back on the mainland so there was no need. He went to day schools all through.'

'Poor little boy,' Tamara's mother said. 'Euan, I mean, not Alastair.' She got up to inspect the progress of her cooking, and a rich, enticing smell of fruits and spices was released into the room.

'Why poor?' Tamara asked, sniffing luxuriously.

'Well, first you take a child away from his parents and he thinks he's being punished for something. And then you send him to one of those schools that were designed to toughen up empire

builders, prep school and public school as bad as each other –
they were invented in the first place to destroy a child's natural
affections; and then every time he sees his little brother it's at
home so his subconscious is telling him that Alastair is always
there while he's been cast out into the cold himself ... he probably had the feeling all his life that he'd been less loved and less
favoured by his parents.'

'Well, it's an explanation. Logical, plausible, could even be
true.'

'I suppose it might explain his unusual girlfriends too,' Olga
remarked. 'All chosen to upset a conventional parent.'

'He might have grown out of wanting to upset them by now,
don't you think?' Tamara said.

'He hasn't given himself much chance. He ran away to another
continent instead of confronting his emotions head on.'

There was another question Tamara should have asked, if
only she'd thought of it when there might have been a sensible
answer. Was Euan so damaged that he would do something to
cause his father's death? Could he have maliciously fiddled with
the settings of the machinery keeping Gordon alive? Impossible
to prove, presumably, unless the guilty man had left fingerprints
on part of the machine he shouldn't have touched, and any medic
would know better than to be so careless.

Patricide; one of the most awful of crimes. Could Euan be
guilty of that?

I'M TEMPING AT the hospital again after a live-in stint with a bed-
ridden oldie. Having some fun with the boy on the seventh floor.
The long-stay wards are mostly full of wrinklies being ware-
housed 'cos nobody else will take them. How does that work?
You might well ask. The trick is to get your old person taken as
an inpatient. Doesn't matter what for. Say they've had a stroke,

or a fit, or some other agony, anything to get them admitted. Once they are signed in, you can be free. If you're the next of kin, give a false address. If you've been a Good Samaritan, get out quick while you can. The beds officer will do anything, literally anything, to move these people on from the hospital ward, but you can't just turn them out into the street and if nobody will take them in, then what are you to do?

You can see the family's point. They are so needy, these ancients, never a moment's peace, they need cleaning up and watering, feeding and exercise. Like dogs. You can see why nobody wants to take them on.

Anyway, going back to where I started, I've already mentioned this boy. He's quadriplegic, can't move a muscle for himself. He gets fed and watered and cleaned every day, his limbs lifted or shifted by hand like they were made of rubber. Sometimes he's sat in a wheelchair but he can't use his hands to move it, so unless someone like me gives it a twirl he spends the day staring at the same blank wall. All he's got to move is the eyes. And nobody else has realized that he's trying to make them talk. His parents were told he was brain damaged. His father keeps away as much as he can, and doesn't look at him when he has to visit. His mother feels a bit sick at the sight of his swivelling eyeballs and never quite meets his stare. Well, it's not my job to tell her where to look. But I can see it in his eyes, he's pleading, begging, praying to me. Me! Of all people.

Obviously I know what he wants. He wants me to bring him poison, or suffocate him. He wants to escape from this death in life. He wants to die.

I could do it. Nobody would suspect. The doctors have rather given up on him now that they've given up hope of repairing anything. They make routine, perfunctory inspections. His mother comes lots, but not at night. I could give him a jab or disconnect the life support just for a few minutes. It would be exciting to watch him die so maybe I will one day. But not yet.

I've got a plan. I'm going to tell the agency, no more hospitals, it's bloody hard work, not to mention thankless. And no one-to-one residential jobs either, the last one got too boring, even if there were rich pickings. They've got so much, those rich people, nobody ever notices. Next time I'll get them to send me to an oldies' warehouse, one of those homes where people get parked while they wait for death. But not a council home, nothing cheap and nasty. I want an expensive privately-run home full of rich people, and I'm going to stay on here till I find one. Anyway, there's no hurry because I'm really enjoying myself with the quadriplegic. The other day I made like I was talking to myself. I was preparing the hypodermics, and started muttering. *Got to be careful, just a tiny bit too much of this stuff and it would be curtains for the young master.* And so on. He was desperate for me to give him an overdose. I pretended I was fixing one. Actually, I think that scared him. Could be he hasn't really given up yet. We'll see.

It's really fun to watch him. You'd be surprised what a good time one can have in a hospital even at my lowly level. If you know what you're doing and know what you want.

BY THE TIME that Tamara arrived at the house in Oxford, having driven through slow and ill tempered traffic, the very last thing she wanted to do was start examining dusty papers and stuffy cupboards that had probably not been opened for years. Since Alastair was so uninterested in his inheritance, as he had confirmed when they last spoke, she felt very inclined to tell Euan just to keep the lot. But then she began to have remorse about her own sons who would probably like to have mementos of their grandparents, and about Vera, who had to be allowed to choose some things to remember the old man by.

She hadn't been in Swallows since the day of the funeral and was taken aback by the changes. Euan and his friend had been moving things out or around, but they weren't housetrained. Everything was covered with greasy dust. For a moment Tamara thought she was going to have to make a fuss. Then she decided that it really didn't matter. If Alastair didn't care, why should she?

'You've been raising money on stuff from the house?' she said mildly.

'We sure have,' Lezli replied merrily. 'Worth quite a lot, some of those dreadful little things. Oh!' Hand over mouth, eyes wide. 'You didn't actually want any of them did you?'

'Certainly not,' Tamara said, meaning it. 'To tell you the truth, all I do actually want is to get this over, as quickly as we can.'

In the role of hostess, Lezli stood up at once, and said, 'Kitchen first?'

Their meeting had been prepared for. A new Thermos pot, cups and saucers, milk in a pottery jug, sugar in a silver bowl and a tablecloth had been put out. There was a plate of elegant little biscuits; there were even tiny embroidered napkins. It would be too ungracious, in fact positively churlish to refuse, so Tamara sat down and decided to enjoy it. Lezli poured coffee, offered sugar and biscuits.

'Thank you Lezli. How nice you've made it all.'

'It's fun. I really like it here, like playing houses. I'm thinking we might stay in the UK for a while. Have to persuade Euan of course.'

Tamara said in a firm, uncompromising voice, 'You can't stay here. This house is going on the market. Unless you want to buy the other half-share.'

'Oh, not in Oxford, it makes Euan nervous, he wasn't ever happy here.' Both women were silent for a long moment.

Then Tamara asked, 'So what do you do, Lezli, when you're not here? Do you have a job?'

'I have a profession. It's death.'

'I – what did you just say?'

'I take a variety of roles. I'm an advocate for the desperate dying, I help them frame their petitions. Paraplegics who want to be taken to Zurich to end it all; and the reverse – I represent people who have been refused expensive medication even though it would give them another few months to live. And then I'm a doula.'

'Comforting women in childbirth?' Tamara asked, hoping she had not shown her horror at the idea of Lezli in the delivery room.

'Certainly not. I help men and women out of life.'

'Help them die?'

'Yes. I help them to plan where and how, and then to achieve their aims.'

'Like in a death café?'

'You know about the death cafés?' Lezli sounded quite taken aback.

'I've even been to one,' Tamara replied.

'I have the greatest respect for the death café movement,' Lezli began in speechmaker's mode. 'They are doing fine, taboo-breaching work. But as for myself and the doula movement, we are rather more hands-on. I help patients to take control of the last great event. It's very rewarding work.'

'Financially?'

'You know, Tammy, you don't look like a cynic, more like "Miss butter won't melt in your mouth" but you've got a dirty mind. I get paid, of course I do, the working woman's worthy of her hire, but I'm not in this for the money.' She didn't sound like an American, Tamara suddenly realized, spouting all those dusty old proverbs.

'Where did you grow up, Lezli?'

'In Brazil.' The answer was automatic. Then Lezli snapped back to attention. 'Why are you asking? What's that got to do with...?'

'I was just curious. But I'm sorry, I didn't mean to offend you.'

79

'So tell me, Tammy, have you made a death plan?'

'Frankly, Lezli, if it's like birth plans, I think it's a bit of a waste of time. The body hasn't read the plan. It does what it was always going to do. If the plan works it's pure coincidence,' said Tamara speaking from bitter experience.

'No no, you're wrong. One has to take control. Then, at the beginning, and later on too. You have to work things out, make the necessary preparations. For example.' Lezli pushed her chair closer to Tamara's and leant towards her like an intimate. 'For example, have you made your living will?'

'Informally,' Tamara replied, quelling the urge to tell Lezli that it was none of his (or her) business.

'Does an informal one have legal weight in this country?'

'I doubt it. In fact, no, it doesn't.'

'Why haven't you? Is it because you're too frightened of dying to think about it? But then what happens to your boys if you and Euan's brother get killed in a car crash? Have you thought about that?'

Tamara had naturally devoted sleepless hours to worrying about just that.

'I know. You're quite right. My late father was a lawyer, and he reminded me several times. But it never seemed really vital, I've got such a large family, all poised to rush to the rescue if necessary.'

'And Euan.'

'That's true.' Tamara said aloud, and silently promised herself that Euan Hope would never get his hands on her boys. She would deal with it the moment she got home.

'Here, this is for you.' It was a small version of what presumably was a big poster. It was headed 'Are You Afraid?' The text was about the fear of death and how a doula holding your hand would banish it.

'That's what I'm for. Let me help you, Tamara, I can see you're disturbed.'

'Not at all. I spend a lot of my working life dealing with death, you know, skeletons, relics – by definition really, an archaeologist encounters death all the time.'

'But not your own.'

'No,' Tamara said lightly. 'But I shan't have grave goods worth excavating either. Which reminds me why I'm here.' A clumsy connection, she knew, but it will have to do. She stood up and began to open and close cupboards.

'Euan's hoping you'll find some of the treasures,' Lezli said.

'Treasures?'

'He says some the things he wants have disappeared. Silver, glass, a Lalique vase, that sort of thing. I thought you'd probably taken them.'

'I don't think so.' Tamara's taste in home decoration was too different from her parents-in-laws'. She wouldn't have given houseroom to any of their 'treasures'.

In fact there was not one single thing Tamara wanted for herself even in the kitchen. Nothing Alastair could possibly want to see again. She filled a cardboard crate with useful objects; an ancient mincer, a kettle, a few saucepans, wooden spoons and sharp knives. Student lodgings were always missing something, so the boys could probably use the cooking gear.

The china was all busily patterned and delicately thin. There were genteel tea cups and saucers, but no mugs; salad plates shaped like a new moon but no cereal bowls. The silver was indeed silver, hallmarked. There didn't seem to be any everyday stainless steel. Tamara found paper and a pen in her bag, and sat herself back at the kitchen table to make a note. She drew two columns. To be auctioned: all the china and glass in the kitchen. To be got rid of, if necessary paying a contractor: all the food. The place was stocked as though for a siege.

'What would you like to see next?' Lezli asked in a hospitable voice.

'Oh, don't worry about me, I know where things are.'

'It's no trouble.'

Tamara looked at Lezli, suddenly realizing that Euan must have told her (or him) not to leave Tamara alone as she looked round the house. What was it they didn't want her to find? She said, 'Euan won't like it? Well, tough. I don't like the way he's been helping himself. When Alastair said you two could stay here, he didn't mean that you could take anything you fancy. I'm going round with the inventory now and we'll see what's missing.'

In fact, one and a half hours later, her eyes hardly focusing and her head pounding, Tamara caught up with Lezli in the spare bedroom, which was a perfect mid-twentieth-century survival, with faded pink velour curtains, a shiny eiderdown, also pink, and the wardrobe, chest, dressing table and chairs all in very dark coloured oak. Tamara thought the whole room should be delivered unaltered to a museum. She said, 'Where's Euan?'

'I think I just heard him coming in.'

'Well, I'm done, except for the attic.'

'The attic? I never knew there was one.'

'Really.'

'I'm just – Euan!' The banshee-shriek came suddenly, and so close to Tamara's ear as to hurt. 'Euan! Come and see this!'

Tamara led the way into a small lobby outside the laundry room. There was a six-foot long key which was supposed to fit into a hole in the trap door set into the ceiling, which it eventually did. There was a ladder to pull down and unfold. Tamara climbed it first, going up into an unimproved roof space, festooned with cobwebs and jam-packed with obsolete equipment. Years ago, when they were between houses, Alastair and Tamara had stored their own possessions there for a few months; it was the only occasion on which Tamara had gone to South America with Alastair. It was hard to believe, looking at the crammed space, that there had been room for the extra stuff.

'They can't ever have thrown anything away,' she murmured, and remembered her mother-in-law's voice, years ago, saying, 'It might come in handy one day.' Suitcases, a tailor's dummy, an easel, a rowing machine, an old-fashioned tent and some blankets that were more moth hole than fabric. It was a glory hole; the place superfluous household gear came to die. She returned to the open hatch, began to call down to Lezli, and then changed her mind and went down the ladder. She'd seen a torch in the main bedroom's bedside table. And here it was. Would it work? Yes, it shone with promising brilliance. Carrying it and a damp towel to wipe dust away, she climbed the loft ladder again.

Euan followed her up and started on the old fashioned tea chests. He squatted beside one, levered its lid off and exposed a pile of papers. He aimed a pocket torch at it, and said, 'Old utility bills.'

Tamara moved cautiously along the attic, standing only on the beams. If one put a foot on the dusty floor boards, it would probably go through the ceiling of the room beneath. There were more chests containing papers, one full of about five years' worth of a science fiction magazine called *Astounding*, and another with half a dozen women's hats, mid-twentieth-century style, wrapped in tissue paper. This one smelled powerfully of old-style, now illegal mothballs. Tamara set aside a couple of the magazines to show her sons. Euan was holding a piece of parchment and the cardboard roll it had been in.

'What's that, Euan?' Tamara asked.

'Junk, really, all junk. This one's my father's Edinburgh degree certificate. And his commendation from the church elders on the occasion of his marriage. That sort of thing.'

Lezli called anxiously from below, 'Are you all right up there?'

Euan didn't look up, but called 'A-OK.' He pulled a small briefcase onto his knee.

'Anything interesting?' Tamara asked.

'My old school essays.'

Tamara had not expected civil answers and was wondering whether to use this occasion to ask where certain treasures were – a pot by Bernard Leach, an oil painting of the Fighting Temeraire – or to try to build bridges with her brother-in-law, when she was overtaken by an uncontrollable fit of sneezing. 'I think I'd better go down,' she gasped. Stooping beneath the roof beams, she edged past Euan. Glancing down at the case, before he put the lid down, she had a flashing glimpse of a document with embossed seals and formal signatures. A prize certificate? Memorabilia of Euan's school days? He's welcome to them.

She was still sneezing intermittently as she looked through the cupboard in Gordon's bedroom, a beautifully ordered small collection of well cared-for clothes, presumably kept in such good nick by Vera. Tamara felt a momentary pang of guilt and anxiety at the thought of her own heirs trying to make order of the over-crowded jumble of her clothes cupboard.

'I suppose these go to the charity shop,' she muttered and then realized that somebody else had put a notice on the cupboard door which said, 'Oxfam to call for these on Friday'. I don't know why I'm bothering, she thought. This has all been done already, without me, and honestly I don't care. In fact, it was a relief.

As she went through the house it had become obvious that nobody had cleaned it for a while. Meeting Lezli on the stairs, she asked if Vera had come round at all.

'Yeah, she happened by last week. Actually, she came in through the front door, took one look and started crying. Then she left. Peculiar way of behaving, I thought, wouldn't you say so?'

'She'd been with Gordon for a long time.'

'As his cleaner,' Lezli said firmly.

'Well, perhaps a little more than that.'

'She's due back on…?'

'Next Friday.'

'I'm just going to have a quick look at her flat now.'

Swallows had been provided with one small garage by its original builders, and in the seventies Gordon had bought a larger one in the next street over, a converted stables with a loft converted into a small flat. There had been a varied series of housekeepers and gardeners living there. Vera Fleming had come to work for the Hopes eighteen years ago, stuck it out in the job as Gordon's wife became more and more ill, and then stayed on to look after the man alone.

Vera had not needed to be given notice. She had already decided to move before going away on her short break, and when she opened the door Tamara saw that she had packed almost all her belongings into cardboard boxes and plastic crates. Everything was sparkling clean, in marked contrast with Swallows itself.

Back in the house Tamara started looking for a suitable momento to give Vera. A picture? A piece of furniture?

'I'm trying to find something Vera would like to have,' she told Lezli. 'I want to offer her some thing of Gordon's.'

'Oh, I don't think that's what Euan would want.'

An angry speech sprang into Tamara's head. Euan could shut right up. Then she took a breath and reverted to her careful calm. 'He needn't know.' She went across the room to a big Spanish-looking chest of drawers that also served as a side-table and pulled open the two top drawers. They were both empty. Tamara said, 'Gordon used to lock valuables in here. His wife's jewellery, his own medals.'

'Did he?' Lezli sounded very bored.

'Do you think Euan has taken them? Did you sell them along with the nick-nacks?'

Suddenly furious, Tamara went to the bottom of the stairs and shouted, 'Euan, come down here right away please.'

'What's the matter?'

'Just come down. Now.'

'OK, I don't mind, I want a drink anyway. Scotch, Lezli, with plenty of ice.' He didn't meet Tamara's eyes as he came down.

'Where's the jewellery, Euan?'

'The—?'

'Don't try that on with me!' she snapped.

'OK, I won't. It's at Searle's shop in the High Street to be cleaned and valued.'

A little bubble of rage burst through Tamara's self-control. 'Look here, Euan. Damn it, I know Alastair says he'll go halves with you, which is his prerogative, but just now I've got the legal right to decide what happens here. And what's going to happen is that you'll go off now and fetch back those jewels, and don't try cheating because Vera knows exactly what was in there, and I'm going to get her to come round and tell me that they are all there, and then I'm going to put them in my own safe deposit till Alastair gets back. And another thing. The table in the hall is piled high with bills: water, electric, gas, council tax, Gordon's car – have you been using it? You must have noticed the tax disc has expired. And so has the insurance. You can't drive it. If you're staying here you'll have to pay those bills.'

'Why can't they be paid out of the estate?'

'Because they wouldn't need to be, if the house was empty.'

On the way back to London, Tamara felt ashamed of her outburst. Not like me to lose control, she thought. It's not as if I mind about Iona. Alastair would like the idea of having a sister. Poor Vera, ashamed where in the modern world there was nothing to be ashamed of. Poor Gordon – or no. Snobbish Gordon. He could have formalized his relationship with Vera if he'd wanted to. But she wasn't good enough for him.

No. Be fair.

If Gordon and Vera had married they would feel they had to acknowledge Iona as their daughter, which would mean admitting that they had been committing adultery for at least eighteen years, well before Mary fell ill. In Gordon's personal, narrow-minded world, how infinitely shaming that would be.

One can see why he couldn't face it.

After a day of drizzle, real rain had set in. Nasty driving

conditions, especially at dusk. Concentrating on the road, a series of items of furniture paraded through her mind, a mahogany breakfront bookcase, wide heavy dining chairs with leather seats, an infinitely enlargeable table, a sofa so heavy that once placed against the sitting room wall nobody had ever tried to move it again. They'd all have to go to the auction house. As for small and portable things – there weren't that many left. Annoying to realize that Euan had once again got exactly what he wanted.

YOU KNOW WHAT is the best fun. It's telling everything to someone who (I'm pretty certain) hears it all and can't do anything about it.

They've sent me up to the seventh floor again. The tetraplegic rugger bugger is still there, still alive and still, I believe, hearing and seeing without being able to show it.

So I started telling him about what happens when a person dies. The physical changes. The pain. The fear.

'That's what you want, isn't it?' I murmured. 'You think you want to die. Shall I turn off your air? I did that once. Not a pretty sight, a bloke suffocating in his bed. Actually I relented and turned it on again so he survived. Brain damaged, of course, rather like you Davy boy. You know, it's nice to have you here to confide in. Shall I tell you about the first time I adjusted the life support machine? That's something you'd like to hear, isn't it, mmm?'

I suddenly felt irritated beyond bearing by his motionless body and limbs and his flailing eyes. I pinched him really hard where it wouldn't show. But he didn't feel it. So instead I started turning the taps on the life support machine. I stood to one side so he could see what I was doing.

'There there,' I crooned. 'All quiet. This is what you've been longing for, right? You want to die. And I want to watch you die.'

Any second now there'd be an explosion of beeps and sirens, so I quickly turned the taps and dials back to where they'd been. 'Don't worry, I'll be back, we're going to have a good time, me and you. More fun for me, of course, not so much for you.'

I'd do it one day, he knew I would, but it would have to be a day when the technicians called to service the machine, and when other people had been to see him.

Treats in store, Davy boy, I promised. Treats in store.

IT WAS ONLY as an archaeologist that Thea Crawford was at all adventurous. Her clothes were elegant, but not at the cutting edge and if the designer said that a dress needed a red belt, a green one would not do. The food she served was traditional and never experimental. She had always been the kind of cook who followed every recipe exactly. No improvisation in her kitchen. If she didn't have the sugar, honey wouldn't do instead; no way would she substitute lime for lemon or peanuts for walnuts.

'You're such a conformist,' her son used to complain when he was a teenager, more than once adding that it had been a pity her conformity lapsed when choosing his name. He had endured the embarrassing 'Clovis' until he went to senior school when he announced that in future he was to be known by his second name, John.

'But there will be so many other Johns,' his mother protested and he replied, 'That's exactly why I like it.'

As it happened, Thea had chosen a profession in which caring about your appearance, let alone taking an interest in fashion, was so rare as to seem perfectly non-conformist. None of her colleagues, so skilled at identifying the evolution of material culture in the distant past, had the slightest interest in such developments in their own time. Some years ago Thea had presented an experimental study as light relief at the end of a conference about the genesis and development of grave markers in the post-Roman period. Her talk was called 'The Genesis and Development of Pockets in Women's Clothing.' She showed slides of embroidered purses dangling on cords around the neck, from the shoulder, or from a belt. She showed horizontal slits in a skirt's waistband, small patch pockets on large navy blue knickers as worn by schoolgirls in the first half of the twentieth century; she demonstrated how handkerchiefs would be crumpled up and shoved in a sleeve. There were contrasting slides of tight short dresses by Coco Chanel whose wearers were forbidden to spoil the line of the garment with any extras, and the wearer-friendly, woman-shaped clothes of the mid-twentieth-century designer Jean Muir, with useful pockets in every side-seam. It had come over to the audience of academics as quite entertaining but wholly irrelevant. In the audience there had also been a journalist with a serious interest in archaeology, who recognized an amusing story, and turned Thea's idea into a 1,500 word review front, in which she described Thea as 'The Dressy Don'. It was enough to make a woman wear denim jeans for the rest of her life, Thea had remarked. But she didn't; and it was in an ancient 'good luck dress' (successfully worn to bring her luck on several previous occasions) that she went to see the hospital consultant, to be told the results of the second lot of tests. He still addressed her with an authoritative manner, and pooh poohed her hesitation.

'It should be fine. And afterwards nobody will notice. Wear a dress like the one you have on – not too tight, with a bit of room in it, and then nothing will show, it won't smell, you will get used to it.'

'How long?' she said.

'How can I say? With secondaries ...'

'I've got a lot of work to finish off.'

'My advice is to get on with it, in that case.'

'While I still can?' That last remark, she observed, received no reply.

TAMARA STILL REMEMBERED exactly what her mother had said about Euan. Something lucid, perceptive and sharp – so like Olga herself. No, like the old Olga who no longer existed.

The thought was painful. Looking back, one could see that Olga had already been at the beginning of her speedy decline. She lost her specs a little more frequently. She forgot that Tamara was coming for the weekend. She left a cake in the Aga so long that when they took the tin out it was full of charcoal. But for a little while she was still the same person, if diminished.

And then, suddenly, shockingly, there would be calls saying she was out in the street naked, or in the middle of the night, or smoke was pouring from her kitchen, or – this one was the last straw – she was cross-legged on the sitting room floor, carefully, meticulously tearing up books. Tamara found her there.

'What are you doing?' she'd shrieked. 'All Dad's books! Mum, you're losing it.'

And momentarily a light turned on in Olga's head. 'Not losing, lost,' she said, her voice infinitely mournful. Where had she gone? What had happened to the lively, perceptive, interested mother? And where had she come from, that sad, whining, indifferent imposter? At first there had been a carer, then two carers, three, as the need to have Olga watched increased. She was still living in the family home at the time, a comfortably shabby, book and art lined house in which she had retreated into a kind of den, gradually and imperceptibly. But visiting family members began to notice that nobody had been in the drawing room, or their father's library, or even the big kitchen, for quite some time. Alexandra wrote her name with her forefinger in the dust on the grand piano. Tamara began to throw away mouldy food from the store cupboard, tins so old that the sides bulged outwards. Olga seemed to have made the smaller sitting room, the one with a television, into her bed-sitting room. Did she even climb the stairs any more to the bathroom? Or was she strip-washing in the downstairs loo? Or was she, in fact, not washing at all?

'It sounds so awful, putting our mother in a home,' Alexandra wailed.

'Not as awful as leaving her here alone.'

'She'd be better dead, wouldn't she?' Alexandra was weeping as they left the home, and wept even more when they got back to the house and found their brothers and several grandchildren chucking household goods onto a huge bonfire. The house had been sold, its proceeds needed to cover the expenses of Olga's new life. Or her new death-in-life. The family agreed that there was no point in having to make the long drive to the south west, and found a place for Olga in an up-market and very expensive care home in Surrey.

AT ONE TIME the partners in the Helleborean Nursing and Residential Home, in Surrey, had thought themselves quite well off, and so, comparatively, they had been. That was *then*, when people still respected doctors, and when doctors' salaries were well above the average even for professional people, at a time before the price of houses in central London started their inexorable rise, as zillionnaires from the Far East, oligarchs from Russia, oil-rich Arabs and gang leaders from the most dangerous parts of the world competed to buy them. The ripple effect brought changes throughout London and out in the suburbs, and even as far as country districts within commuting distance. What the older doctors remembered as a pleasantly relaxed village was changing, and not for the better. The neighbourhood was almost deserted by day, inhabited only by children too young for school and their foreign nannies, and by the infirm ancients occupying what had formerly been the local squire's residence.

Its days as death's waiting room were numbered. As soon as

the present owners of the building had found a way of getting round the contractual obligation to maintain the premises as a hospital, clinic, care home or sheltered accommodation, it would be sold to the highest bidder; and that meant a very high bid, a very large sum of money – it being not much more than an hour from the City and a remarkably pretty house, soft red brick, and symmetrical with generous sash windows and elaborate plaster work in the downstairs rooms. There was no way that any charity could possibly buy it.

Meanwhile, rich old people spent their final years, months or days there, making an extravagant down payment plus weekly service charges for their well-furnished apartments or single rooms, and for the promise that they wouldn't be turned out into a health service geriatric ward when ill. And a lot of them were ill, or ill-ish, a lot of the time.

Pressure of work was getting to the doctors in the local NHS practice. The senior partner was out of action having broken several bones in a skiing accident in February. Another partner was on maternity leave. When they advertised for a locum the responses were discouraging. One well-qualified applicant was, no doubt, an excellent medic but unfortunately couldn't speak or understand a word of English. Another was a woman with good qualifications who described how she always prayed with her patients before listening to or examining them. 'What if they refuse?' she was asked.

'Then they don't get well again.'

Back to the pile of applications. In the end they settled for an English doctor who freely admitted it was years since he'd looked after ordinary patients because he'd got completely involved in a research project. He'd worked in Europe and the United States and South Africa.

'The time has come for me to return to hands-on medicine,' he'd said. Not ideal; he'd be slow, and might not know his way through the labyrinth of committees that needed satisfying and placating, but presumably if he'd been doing research he had some brains, and he had sent in all the necessary certificates to qualify him for an immediate start.

THEY STOOD BESIDE his bed and talk-talk-talked. Jabber, natter, words, words. In the case of his mother interspersed with wails, sobs and tears. Sometime she'd lean across the machinery to press her cheek against his. Not that he could feel it, but he could just see the reflection, distorted by the curve, in the shiny steel of one of the gadgets that was keeping him alive.

'Oh my Davy, my baby, if only you knew ... Mummy's here.'

Sometimes she'd persuade herself that she'd seen movement and get all excited. He thought, this is shit, if you really love me why can't you fucking tell what I'm fucking thinking?

They talked about the machinery that kept him alive. Nutrients dripped into his body, air pumped into his lungs, two nurses and an electric hoist turned him regularly so as to avoid bed sores.

They talked about hope too, but it was the hope for a miracle, not the hopeful expectation of miracle-free improvement.

His father came, looked at him and looked away. Once he said, 'He's a vegetable.'

'No!' His mother's denial sounded like a wounded animal's squeal.

'If he was a dog you'd put him down.'

Yeah, right on. You've got it, Dad. Don't let them keep me like this!

'He's in there, can't you tell? Can't you feel him? He's trying to tell us something. Look, Robert, his eyes are moving.'

'They always do. It doesn't mean anything, you heard what the neurologist said, they've carried out repeated tests, he's not locked in, he's just not there, Davy's gone.'

'But how can you be sure?'

'Davy, Davy, blink, move your finger – anything – just to show you're listening. Davy?'

VERA RANG FROM Oxford some days later. Her voice sounded dreadful. She had lots to tell Tamara, but had to keep stopping to cough.

Firstly, she'd found a flat and in fact was moving there that very day; a tiny place, but really nice, and her very own. Right the other side of town from Swallows and not too far from the bridge club on Woodstock Road.

How can she afford it? Tamara wondered, having discovered that property in North Oxford fetched close to London prices.

Vera might have felt Tamara's unspoken question winging through the ether, because she embarked on a long explanation. The doctor had been very generous, he'd always said he would look after her and so he had.

The missing million, Tamara realized.

And now for the bad news.

Euan and Lezli had quarrelled. They shouted so loudly that the neighbours on both sides had heard them. Lezli had called Euan a murderer, Euan called her a ghoul, she complained that he was a parasite, Euan yelled that he couldn't have known there'd be no money for him when Gordon died, she announced that she was done with bankrolling him now, and Euan's final salvo had been about Lezli's gender. 'You'll never be a real woman whatever they cut off or sew onto you.'

Both had gone, leaving Swallows in a shocking mess. They had not paid the utility bills, so the services had been cut off and some of the furniture and pictures had disappeared. If the house were to go on the market, Tamara began, but Vera interrupted.

'I'll go over and let them in, I'd be pleased to, you can count on me.'

'Would you really? That's so kind.'

'It'll have to be repainted and even have new carpets. It was in such a state!' Vera was weeping into her phone. 'I always kept it so nice for the doctor.'

Family fall-outs returned one to the nursery, Tamara thought. She made soothing and complimentary remarks. She said she would pay the bills – privately reminding herself to do so out of Alastair's account, since it was he who had encouraged his awful brother to stay there. She told Vera to help herself to anything she wanted, and asked how she was off for furniture.

'Really, Vera, I mean it, take anything you like from Swallows. You'd be doing us a favour, really, take furniture and fittings, bed linen, china – absolutely anything you can use.'

'May I? May I really? I'd so love to have some things as a memento, it would be wonderful to have the reminders of – of your parents-in-law. He was such a wonderful ...' Vera, again, couldn't keep her tears at bay. She sobbed energetically into the hand set.

BACK TO PRESENT problems. Tamara metaphorically shook herself, like a dog coming out of a river, and went back to work.

Search online for a firm of industrial cleaners, arrange for them to scrub right through the house. Make appointment with three or four estate agents, fixing a time to meet them at Swallows. Arrange for Vera to come to the house and vet the estate agents, also to show them where everything is. I don't even know where to find the fusebox, Tamara thought.

This was all going to cost a pretty penny. Tamara told herself that the longer Alastair stayed away and maintained his lordly indifference to events back home, the more she was justified in throwing his money at his family's problems.

Tamara found herself absentmindedly washing her hands in

Fairy Liquid at the kitchen sink, twisting them over and over in the detergent as if she had to wash away the greedy, competitive possessiveness that she'd momentarily felt. She thought, I don't need stuff from our house to think of Mum and remember Dad.

Olga Hoyland always seemed and sounded as British as they come, having discovered how to blend in, and also acquired her cut-glass intonation and accent at school. Her own mother, Tamara's grandmother Anastasia, had just been starting out as a member of the Tsarina's court when the Russian Revolution began. Anastasia's father had been killed in the first year of the war, her only brother perished six months later so Anastasia was accustomed to acting as 'the man of the family'. She had gathered up her vague and anxious mother, her three younger siblings, the English governess and the family's pet spaniel, and through sheer force of personality jollied and bullied them eastwards until they reached sanctuary in China, joining a little enclave of Russian refugees in Shanghai. From there, after the war, the party moved on to San Francisco for a short while, before crossing America from west to east and eventually arriving in Britain in 1921. Tamara could just remember Grandmère Anastasia. Others thought she was a fierce and formidable presence, but she'd been charmed by her youngest granddaughter and never seemed frightening to her.

'You're so like your grandmother,' Olga would wail when Tamara gave trouble as a child. 'If your lives hadn't overlapped I'd say you were her reincarnation.'

Dad: Rob Hoyland, a country solicitor; who as a young man before the war had been an adventurer, going in to Nazi Germany to rescue Hitler's victims.[2] He'd been an active member of an undercover unit. Tamara was well into adulthood before she discovered that he had been awarded a British medal for 'conspicuous courage' and in France, the Légion d'Honneur. In Israel, he was included in the list of Righteous Gentiles. Conspicuous courage: a quality less obviously needed when old and at peace in

---

2 *Telling Only Lies* by Jessica Mann

a lifetime home in beautiful countryside with a loved and loving family. But he'd shown the quality again when diagnosed with an inoperable brain tumour. Three to six months, he was told. To his son, a colleague, the surgeon privately whispered a warning, 'It's not going to be easy.' The whole family knew that; seven years previously, Olga's sister Anna had received the same diagnosis and died, slowly, in mental and physical agony.

Rob neither talked about the diagnosis, nor kept it secret. He didn't need to be specially kind to his wife because he was always kind. She didn't need to look after him more carefully, because she took the utmost care in any case.

He didn't discuss the future. It was only after his death that they found the file labelled Dignitas. There was a cheque stub showing how much he had paid to join (thousands of pounds). There were copies of the organization's documents, the conditions for being accepted, with which he did indeed comply. In one letter, he'd written that he couldn't do it at home for fear of traumatizing whoever found him. But equally, it would be cruel to have his wife or children forced to watch him decline and die.

He was still living a relatively normal life when he decided the time had come. He was still able to walk alone, though driving was problematic because his eyes reacted slowly to light and shade. However he drove himself to Exeter station, saying he was going to his final reunion, an annual event, with wartime companions. In fact, as later became clear, on arriving at Paddington Station he had planned to board the Heathrow Express platform, and in a shorter time than it had taken him to get to London from the West Country, land in Zurich and, as instructed, would take a cab to the address Dignitas had given him. At just about the time that he would be lifting the fatal glass to his lips, his wife would be reading his final farewell.

We both know what's in store for me with your sister's tragic last days so fresh in our memories. In ducking out before reaching that stage, I'm sparing you and the family as well as myself. I believe that Dignitas will deal with many of the formalities, whereas if I finished it myself in England you would have to face inquiries and an inquest.

I've made arrangements to be cremated in Zurich, and you can do whatever you like with the remains. Have a party or chuck them in the dustbin, or just leave them for the clinic to dispose of.

These well-laid plans were frustrated when Rob Hoyland fell at Exeter station, not crumpling to the ground but falling straight, like a tree, to lie flat, staring upwards, conscious in the strict sense of the word, but momentarily taking nothing in. By the time the ambulance arrived and he was lifted in, Rob was properly conscious again, though his speech was slurred. He was taken to the Accident and Emergency Department where one of the doctors on duty recognized and admitted him and ensured that he was taken to a side room of the ward. He died three days later having been in a coma for two of them.

Rob's death came as a horrible shock to his family, although all of them had been told he was dying. His sons immediately understood what pain he had tried to spare himself, and his family. Tamara and Alexandra couldn't forgive him. 'If he'd got to Switzerland we wouldn't have had the chance to say goodbye.'

'My God, just listen to yourselves!' their eldest brother Peter exclaimed. 'Selfish or what? You think Dad should have survived in agony just so you could say goodbye?'

'And tell him we loved him.'

'You think he needed telling?'

'And thank him for being such a good father.'

The younger Hoyland son was called Paul. He was a doctor, in fact a senior consultant at a London teaching hospital. His specialism was brain surgery. He said, 'If you hadn't let him know all that before, it would have been too late anyway. But of course he knew. He made that plan out of altruism. Love. He loved you. Us.'

Peter, a solicitor, added, 'You're being idiotic, girls. Would you really have wished Aunt Anna's misery on him, just so that you could tell him something he always knew?'

'Well, if you put it like that ...' Alexandra and Tamara were both in tears by this time.

'What you should be thinking is that he was one of the bravest people you'll ever know. To set off alone to his death in order to spare us all ...' His voice broke and he mopped ineffectively at suddenly streaming eyes.

The news of Rob's frustrated journey got out when one of the passengers waiting on Exeter station for the London train told someone else who passed the information to a journalist, that a card had fallen out of Rob's pocket when he fell. It was a booking confirmation from the Zurich clinic.

The family organized a memorial service, to which far more people came than expected. The local MP asked a question in the House about legalizing assisted suicide. The bishop of the diocese preached a sermon on the subject of compassion for the dying not necessarily meaning to 'strive officiously to keep alive'. A pressure group trying to force the government into legislation permitting assisted suicide in the United Kingdom seized on the story of Rob Hoyland as a perfect example of why new laws were needed; and Olga Hoyland took her first step down the slippery slope to dementia.

THE MANAGER OF the nursing home, Mrs Bussell, had no actual uniform, but she invariably wore a dark blue skirt suit, thinner or thicker as the season dictated, with a cream silk blouse fastened at the neck by a round blue brooch, with beige nylon tights and black lace-up shoes. She was strict with the staff, on that subject at least. Pink overalls for the cleaners, light blue ones for the nursing assistants and navy blue for the nurses.

Compared with most care homes for the very old, the Helleborian was remarkably pleasant. The very high fees bought residents privacy – all the bedrooms were single, though there were two suites on the top floor for married couples; everyone had a private bathroom, telephone and, if they wanted it, their own furniture.

'This must cost a pretty penny,' the new visitor remarked, but not aloud. He looked round the flower-filled reception area and walked across to the desk, where a young pretty woman had been on the telephone for a long time. 'Free range eggs, of course madam, and organic vegetables, naturally.' She looked up at the visitor and made a gesture signifying apologies. 'You'd have to ask Mrs Bussell about that, I'm only the receptionist. Yes, of course, hold on one moment please and I'll put you through.' A moment's wait, and then a great sigh of relief. 'Sorry about that, I thought she'd be asking questions for hours. How may I help you?'

'I'm Dr Macintosh.'

'OK.'

'I was asked to look in.'

'Oh. I'm sorry, Doctor, I didn't realize – I'll tell Mrs Bussell.' She pressed some button on the phone, spoke into it in a low voice and then asked him to wait just a moment, could she get him coffee?

Dr Macintosh glanced at the headlines in the newspapers laid out on a low table, gulped down his coffee, and went back to the desk. 'Look, I've got a very busy day. I don't know what you're waiting for, but I must get on. What's the room number? The patient is a Mrs ... let me see.' He pulled out an iPad and flickered his fingers over the screen.

'Dr Macintosh, good morning. I do apologize for keeping you waiting, I simply couldn't get off the telephone, it was ... well, I'd

better not say the name, but quite a VIP who was making enquir-
ies for his wife. I really couldn't cut him short.'

'And I really can't waste any more time.'

'Yes, indeed, I apologize again.'

The telephone had been ringing continuously, ignored by Mrs
Bussell, but at this moment the receptionist said, 'Excuse me, Mrs
Bussell, but Mrs Hope just wanted to tell us that she'd be looking
in this afternoon on her way to ... somewhere. She wondered
whether there was anything her mother needed?'

Mrs Bussell was already almost out of earshot. 'That's fine,
tell her—' (calling over her shoulder as she clicked briskly away)
'tell her we don't need anything.'

'If you come this way, it's Mrs Peasgood we're a wee bit concerned about.' She marched down a long corridor, talking over
her shoulder as the doctor followed her. 'I'm afraid you'll find her
a little difficult, she's very confused, and not at all happy, and
I'm afraid she isn't easy with strangers. We have a new nurse on
that floor. I'm afraid you might frighten her a little. She's used to
seeing Dr James, Sarah – is she away?'

'She's moved, I think. Anyway, you've got me now.'

'Indeed, indeed and welcome. I hope you'll be happy in this
neighbourhood, it's a good place to live – where are you from
yourself?'

'London.'

'Ah, right. Well, here we are.'

The name on the door was Mrs Dora Peasgood. Mrs Bussell
made a perfunctory knock and then opened the door onto a scene
of struggle. Two young women were trying to restrain a fighting bundle of discoloured, sagging flesh. The old woman, naked
and almost bald, was emitting a thin sounding scream, all on the
same note. 'She won't stay in bed,' one of the nurses gasped.

'Now Dora, this won't do at all.' Mrs Bussell turned to the
doctor. But he had already opened his case and found what he
needed. Stepping round the nurses, so that he was behind the

ST. JOHN THE BAPTIST PARISH LIBRARY
2920 NEW HIGHWAY 51
LAPLACE, LOUISIANA 70068

hysterical patient, he dabbed cotton wool on her bare buttock and then sank the needle into the scrawny skin. The old woman didn't seem to notice, but the tranquilliser acted very quickly. The scream stopped suddenly, the wasted muscles relaxed. One of the nurses caught her under the arms as she started to collapse, and then the other helped by lifting the feet, and they laid her down on the bed.

'Good girls,' Mrs Bussell said. 'This is Dawn, Doctor, she's been with us ever since the home was opened, and this is Gloria who has come to us from Peterhouse Hospital.'

The doctor nodded at the young women and started to turn away. Then he turned back and said, 'Gloria? Do I recognize you? Have we met before?'

'Only in dreams,' she replied. When she smiled deep dimples appeared in her cheeks and her eyes screwed up into narrow slits. He stared at her for an appreciable moment.

Then he turned away and said, 'She should sleep for several hours now, I'll come back later when she's awake, and see what's going on.' He turned to the door, but Mrs Bussell was there before him.

She said, 'Now that you're here, Doctor, I wonder if you could take a look at a couple of other residents?'

'Are they urgent?'

'Not to say urgent – not yet – but I'm a little concerned about Mrs Hoyland and also—'

'In that case, you'd better ring the surgery.'

'Oh, but I shan't be here. I have one afternoon a week, you know, it's a life-saver considering …'

The doctor interrupted to say it didn't matter. 'Another doctor will see the patients, and presumably there'll be someone in charge in your absence. I'll make sure they let you know what needs doing. Now I must get on.'

❖

THERE WAS NO sudden rush of work at the archaeological con-sultancy, which depended on a thriving economy and a healthy building trade. The consultancy, or one of its rivals, was called in when some tiny snag had halted building work. A vole, a bat, a rare breed of frog; a worked stone, some Bronze Age metal, the fragments of a pot or decorated pavement would be unearthed, and unless the foreman was quick and cute enough to hide it, the information would reach the authorities and all work on the site would be stopped, often to be held up indefinitely.

Tamara's agency had acquired an enviable reputation amongst building contractors for its speedy and efficient rescue excava-tions, and with other professionals for the quality and promptness of the subsequent reports. One could almost believe, as a satisfied client said, that the firm really understood that time is money. The firm had thrived when building thrived, but in more austere times there wasn't enough construction going on to keep rescue archaeology going. And even if something interesting turned up, the builders and their employers and even the local authority planning departments sometimes connived to keep the archaeolo-gists out of it.

But at a time of slump there was very little work going. Tamara and Ivor Brooke, a university friend with whom she had set up the consultancy, had made the dismal decision that most of the staff would have to be 'let go'. Being responsible for that, having to conduct consultations, to inform people who had become friends if they weren't already, that they were losing their jobs, made Tamara tell herself, 'Never again.' She had enjoyed being the boss when things were going well but now made herself a solemn promise never to become an employer again.

'I SIMPLY CAN'T take a day off at the moment,' Tamara told Vera.
'I know, dear.'

'But I really do have to talk to an estate agent about selling the house. I found one who'll come in the evening, which is easier. Can you manage it too? You can? That's great!'

'Have you seen Euan, dear?'

'Not since he moved out. Why do you ask?'

'There's something on my mind, it's niggling me. It was that day you went round the house, and then you came to see me, do you remember you told me you'd been up in the attic? Well, I had quite a good notion of what's up there, there was an attaché case ...'

'Yes, I saw it. Looked like it was full of certificates.'

'Exactly, but the point is—'

'Dr Hoyland? Tamara?' It was the clerk of works for the building project that had been interrupted by the discovery of an almost complete mosaic floor, presumably from a Roman villa. 'Tamara, it's urgent. There's a statue.'

'Vera, sorry, I've got to go. I'll call you – or anyway, see you. Let's meet at the house a bit before he's due to come, OK? Great. Friday, then. It'll be lovely to see you.'

Friday turned out to be another hideously busy day. Tamara made it to Oxford on time by the skin of her teeth. Vera wasn't there yet. When Tamara unlocked the front door she was greeted with a great waft of industrial chemicals. The cleaners had certainly done a thorough job. But the sterility emphasized the destruction of what had been a comfortable home. There were un-faded squares and rectangles on the walls where pictures had been taken down, gaps on the dresser and sideboard, patches of rough floorboards that had been under Persian rugs. Tamara waited by the open front door to let the chemical smell evaporate.

'Dr Hope? I'm Ozzie, from the estate agency.'

'Oh, hullo. Nice to meet you. D'you mind if I wait for just a little while, Miss Fleming must have been held up. She knows the house much better than I do, so I thought ...'

'Yes, of course, good idea.'

'But do have a prowl round while we're waiting.'

Tamara hoicked out the phone, looked in vain for messages and tapped in Vera's number. Engaged. Still? She'd been on the phone for hours.

'There must be something wrong,' Tamara muttered. 'Damn damn damn.' She listened to Ozzie's footsteps as he tramped up the stairs and went into each of the first floor rooms in turn.

When he came down, clutching his smartphone, he said, 'I've taken measurements of everything except the attic.'

'Good, that's fine.'

'My advice? Redecorate! It's a good honest period house—'

'Not a very attractive period, the nineteen thirties.'

'It's coming into fashion, actually. Housewise, that is.'

'I don't think I can be bothered to redecorate.'

'Up to you, of course. But for a better price ...'

'I'd rather have a quick sale.'

I'm beginning to hate Oxford, Tamara thought. She had signed a whole sheaf of documents for the estate agency, locked up the house, thinking that with any luck she wouldn't ever have to go there again, and then got herself stuck in the mother and father of all traffic jams on the way to Vera's new home.

Tamara had personal academic connections with several universities, but Oxford was not one of them. She had done her first degree, in archaeology, at the University of Edinburgh, and her PhD at London's Institute of Archaeology. So Oxford had remained a place to have fun: parties and punts, hot dates, cool people. And once she started going out with Alastair her idea of the city changed again, no longer a place to go to enjoy yourself, but a duty; those interminably long weekend visits, trying to make the boys behave properly at lunch in the dining room with the grown-ups; the endless month of Sundays that the Christmas/New Year break turned into every other year; it became a place whose name made her shiver before her brain caught up with her instincts and she put a tight lid on her own emotions and reactions.

Alone in the privacy of her own car, motionless in the sprawl of traffic on the slow homeward commute, Tamara allowed herself a moment of the truth she could never share with her husband. She wasn't exactly glad her father-in-law was dead, but the consequences of his death took weights off her mind. Never again would she have to drag the reluctant boys to use up one of their few free days visiting Alastair's father (and, in earlier days, his mother). Never again would she have to watch her brilliant husband reduced to an embarrassed silence as his father denigrated his chosen career as a research medic. She remembered a quite recent Sunday lunch when the old man made a long, insulting speech about medics who never saw patients.

'I may not have much time for your brother, Alastair, but at least he's hands-on.'

'Yes, but what's he doing with them?' Alastair muttered. Aloud he said, 'Hands on in the sense taking life with his own hands, you mean, Father? Terminations? Or euthanasia?'

'That will do, Alastair.' The old man spoke to Alastair as if he were a child, though none of them dared to interrupt.

'Hands on in the sense that he interacts with his patients. Forms a human relationship. Which is more than you can say about your indigenous tribes.'

'Where is Euan working?' Tamara asked. Mentioning her brother-in-law's name was naughty, but it had served to draw the old man's acid attention away from Alastair, who minded, to her, who didn't.

Someone hooted, and Tamara realized that the traffic was moving. Another hundred metres and she could turn off the jammed main road. Of course when she did there was nowhere to park. In the end she told herself she could afford to pay a fine, and stopped on the double yellow line in front of Vera's door. Actually, Vera's and half a dozen others. Tamara shifted the bag of house-warming flowers (blue and white hyacinths) onto her other arm, pressed the appropriate bell, waited and pressed it again. No reply.

'It's open,' a voice behind her said. A boy with a stack of the free evening paper.

'I always go right in, they never lock it.'

'Thanks. I might have been stuck outside for hours.'

A lobby with a row of locked letter boxes, and a flier for pizza deliveries sticking out of the one labelled number six. The boy counted out six copies of the free sheet and put them on the floor. He said, 'And I wouldn't trust the lift.'

'Really? Oh, OK then. Thanks again.'

One flat to each floor so a long climb up to Vera's top floor door. A stack of plastic boxes parked on the landing. Tamara rang the bell, and rang it again. She knocked with the brass knocker and with her knuckles on wood. After a while she crouched to look through the brass letter box. When she pushed the tight-fitting flap open, a smell leapt out like a poised animal and Tamara jerked herself backwards, letting the thing close.

'Ugh, yuk – what is that?' She asked the question aloud, but knew the answer perfectly well. That was the smell of human or animal decay. Taking a deep breath and holding it, she bent to look again.

The light on the stairs illuminated only the hall, so Tamara took out her phone and used its flashlight. A tiny entrance lobby, with some broken china on the floor and removers' boxes stacked in a corner and reaching across half the doorway. From the angle visible through the letter slit, one could see very little. A pair of women's shoes, brown, sensible, highly polished, lying toe-up and a little apart; the stockinged ankle and lower calf of the shoes' wearer, perfectly still but at an awkward, in fact inhuman angle. Beside the shoes, a seething mound of black flies almost obscuring the substance they were drawn to, now drying and darkened, but unmistakable: blood.

Tamara called Vera's name, but more for form than with purpose. She told the woman who replied to her emergency call that she was pretty sure that the flat's occupant was dead.

Tamara sat on the stairs waiting for the police to come. When they did, she repeated, several times, her precise account of entering the building, peering through the letter flap and seeing Vera on the floor. She did not mention other details she had noticed. The porcelain shards were the remains of a frivolously flowery jug, that used to be displayed along with other pieces of china, on the sideboard in the dining room of Swallows. It was Meissen, and rather valuable. And on the wall facing the front door Vera had hung a mirror, antique, spotted glass in a carved frame: Chippendale, Alastair's mother had said all those years ago, when she was showing her future daughter-in-law the family's particular treasures. These two pieces had been gone a long time, three years, perhaps, or four, but Alastair's father never said anything about it so, assuming he had sold them, nor did Tamara.

She conformed to the official routine with determined patience; answered questions, refrained from asking them, gave a statement, made no comment on the awkward wording a police constable had used in preference to hers, signed it as a true record. She did not feel the sadness till she eventually got home that night. Death of a Good Woman, she thought. A heart attack? A stroke? What a pity, even a tragedy.

It was shaming to realize, as Tamara did realize when the police came calling two weeks later, that after so short a time Vera's death evoked only a feeling of mild regret rather than proper sorrow. Even after hearing what the officer had come to tell her, she felt more curiosity than horror. Given that the police now suspected foul play, what possible motive could there have been? Why would anyone want to kill, of all people, Vera?

'Are you sure?' Tamara had asked, incredulous.

'Forensics say there's no doubt. The blow to the cranium was not received in falling, nor made by any object that could be found in the apartment. We are treating this case as murder.'

'Do you want to interview me again?'

The news had been brought to Tamara by DC Gilbert, the officer she had met at the funeral reception. He said, 'I've looked you up.'

'Sorry?'

'You don't suppose busy detective officers usually deliver this kind of info? Or that you'd be giving a witness statement all comfy at home instead of coming down to the station? You know everything's different for a Double AF.'

'I'm a ... what do you mean?'

'Afford All Facilities.'

'That was ...' Tamara began, and then stopped herself saying any more. It wasn't her fault if the official database was years out of date so she might as well take advantage of it.

'I don't mind telling you, we were in receipt of information that cast suspicion on a member of your family.'

'Euan. My brother-in-law.'

'You got it.'

'But you didn't?'

'There's no evidence to support it, in either case.'

'Either case? What on earth do you mean?'

'In the matter of his father, the pathologist's window for the time of death is probably within the time Dr Hope the younger spent waiting in Oxford Police Station for the return of his passport and other documents. And we can't find any back-up for the idea that he went to see Ms Fleming. No scientific evidence, no fingerprints, no witnesses.'

'I'm rather glad to hear that,' Tamara said.

'Apart from the fact that we're left with two dead bodies and no notion who killed them.'

'Yet.'

'As you say, yet. So that's it.' He stood up, a very tall man with a rather small cranium and a downturn to his lips that suggested chronic disappointment.

'I'm embarrassed to admit that I don't know, but did Vera

have any family?'

'Well, there's her niece. Iona Harper.'

'Yes, I saw her at my father-in-law's funeral, she sat beside Vera at the back. Didn't have a chance to talk to her, though I think two of my sons did. Have you met her?'

'Spoken to her. And to her parents. They farm, in Cheshire.'

'I don't get this at all. Are you still treating Vera's death as murder?'

'We are, yes. But the girl's in the clear. She was off on a college trip to Spain,' he said.

'Thank you for telling me.'

'Any help or support you need ...'

'And thanks for that too,' Tamara said. 'I'm perfectly willing to come to your office if you want to speak to me again.'

'Ta.'

'And you'll let me know what the outcome of all this is?'

'That would come in the category of every facility.'

As he left Tamara was thinking, there's a catch in this story. It's nearly twenty years since I was with the department. Do they want me to ... what? Come back? What do they want from me? Or is it the usual explanation – pure inefficiency? My name could have been on their lists all these years.

She realized that was the likely explanation. Nobody had deleted her name from the list of AAF operatives; and as this was her first encounter with police or any other officials, she hadn't known. Of course she'd have had to get herself removed from that list, she'd have to do it now.

Or would she?

Must I really? she thought. It was useful to be taken into the police confidence. And one could be very glad to be afforded all facilities, in some – any – unexpected circumstances. No harm had been done in the last twenty years by her name on that list. Had it? No. Much better to let the sleeping dog lie.

Anyway, it didn't matter. It was all irrelevant. Think about poor Vera. That last conversation – what had she intended to say? Something about an attaché case? Irrelevant now. Poor Vera, killed just as she was beginning to enjoy her independence. Why? What possible motive could there be? Looking back, it was clear to see that Gordon had feelings for Vera, and that she had really loved him. But they had carried on with the housekeeper pretence, even after Mary died. The strictly Presbyterian elder of his church couldn't be seen as an adulterer. Which must also be why they hadn't gone public once Gordon was free. But it did explain why Vera was so proprietorial about Swallows and its contents.

Maybe, she suddenly thought, maybe Alastair knew about it all along! Or, come to think of it, not. He would never have let the girl remain a stranger to the family, even if she'd been brought up to believe herself to be the daughter of her adoptive parents. Tamara was sure that he'd be looking for her as soon as he was back. Poor girl, what a muddle. And was her existence anything to do with Vera's death?

TAMARA HAD BEEN counting the days till Easter when Alastair was due back. But as nearly always happened, his longed-for return was disappointing. He was inevitably short of sleep, and anxious to the point of obsession about his specimens. When at last he could sit down with his family, he was too exhausted either to tell them about his excursion or to be – or even pretend to be – at all interested in what they had been doing.

This happens every time, Tamara reminded herself. Why on earth don't I learn from experience?

This homecoming was the worst of all, because no sooner had he unloaded all the specimens than he began to collect the gear he would need for the next expedition.

'I was seriously disappointed that the team was so inflexible. They all insisted on coming back on the agreed date. Now I'm kicking myself for not staying on even if it was going to be on my own, I could swear that one of the old women was finally going to show me how they ... but the others weren't having it. The girl Myrtle had booked her wedding – which reminds me, Tamara, can you do something about a present for her? Something handsome, she was worth her weight in gold with the women, and while I was laid up. What? Oh, it was nothing, just a few days of taking things easy. But the point is, darling, that I think this may be it. The jackpot. The Holy Grail.'

Alastair's endlessly-discussed final expedition, following quickly on without waiting for the usual twelve months, was to be the biggest and longest of all. By its end, his particular area of rain forest would have yielded all its pharmacological secrets, or at least as far as contemporary science could tell. In the future, who knew? But for the time being, that was it. The rest of Alastair's career would be spent on experiment and analysis in a comfortable laboratory. This expedition would be his final fling. And he couldn't wait to get going.

Euan had not reappeared, though his bank account remained active, a greedy ever-open mouth waiting to be fed.

Having been warned that it could take years for Gordon's estate to be settled, at last Alastair decided to divvy up as he had promised, at least those things that were in his possession. He scrupulously made over the fifty per cent share that would have gone to Euan if his father had divided his worldly goods equally between his sons. Alastair made a transfer to his brother's account at Barclays Bank. There was no acknowledgement. Alastair sent a letter to Euan care of the Oxford branch of his bank, but it was returned with a scribbled sticky attached to the envelope. It said that they were unable to forward correspondence or to give information as to Dr E.G.M. Hope's current address.

At one stage in her life Tamara would have been well placed to trace the missing brother. Department E had access to a good deal of varied information and Tamara had access to its data. Perhaps she would have asked a colleague to help. But, she reminded herself, that was twenty-three years ago, and it was a good decade since she'd had any contact with anyone from Department E. In some ways that was just as well since she had come to the conclusion that there was something so dodgy about Euan Hope that it would be better for the world to forget that he had any relationship with the explorer/healer/idealist Dr Alastair Hope.

THE HELLEBOREAN WASN'T exactly a care home, which is why Olga's oldest friend Rosemary had felt able to move in to it long before she really needed to. She and Olga had lived very differently. Rosemary had married almost as soon as she left school and was a full-time wife and mother or grandmother. She never earned a penny in her long life. But the two women seemed bound together by their memories. They had started at nursery school together in 1942, held each other's hands in air raid shelters, shared the occasional apple, and the first post-war banana, and although Olga started at university when she was eighteen, and Rosemary called herself a debutante and went to dances and tea parties while also learning to type and write shorthand, they still saw each other in the holidays. Olga was Rosemary's bridesmaid, and godmother to her first child. Rosemary came to Olga's rescue when she had post-natal depression and was afraid she'd harm her baby in a bad moment.

Rosemary, widowed a little before Olga, and with her two sons in, respectively, Townsville, Australia and North Carolina, had decided to settle in sheltered accommodation. At the Helleborean the stables and an adjoining barn had been converted into tiny cottages for old people who still needed some independence, and one of these suited Rosemary perfectly. She passed the time playing bridge and Scrabble with other residents, and was thrilled to think of Olga living under the same roof.

'Alzheimers? Dementia? Not my friend Olga,' she'd said, when told, and after Olga moved in spent time with her almost every day.

'She's still here, her spirit, her personality, she knows who I am.' Olga would be propped and secured into a large chair, and Rosemary would sit beside her, holding hands, and gently chatting about what it said in the *Mail* today and what Nigel had written from America, and what a lovely man the new doctor was, so good-looking, so kind, never seemed in a hurry, she burbled on and on, apparently indifferent to Olga's lack of response.

Rosemary was mentally sound but had a lot of physical ailments, always apologizing to the doctor when she turned up at the surgery with a new one. When her legs became so swollen that she couldn't go out, or even walk round the house, she graduated to visits in her cottage. The doctor who came to see her was only an assistant (at least, so the local gossip maintained) but she thought he was gorgeous. Sympathetic too; he understood what it was like for her, living alone in sheltered accommodation trying to maintain her dignity and independence.

'But you've got to take it easy. You're a candidate for a heart attack. Remember please, lots of sitting down and resting.' It was nice, Rosemary thought, to be spoken to with such kind care. I think he really likes me. Next time he called in, the following week, she had a tea tray and a luscious cake ready just-in-case. And the week after that ... which is this week, she thought. Easter Week: a festival for the Church. She posted a birthday card to Tamara's brothers, for Olga's sake, and Easter cards to her own sons, simply to be in contact with them. And Alexandra and Tamara sent Easter cards to Rosemary, and to Olga even though she wouldn't know what they were. Olga was in excellent physical health, the new doctor had told the care home's matron. Her body seemed immortal, even if her mental powers had expired. You didn't need to be married to a medic, Tamara thought, to foresee the inevitable course of events. But there was still some hope. Someone might invent a miracle cure. Life is precious. Tamara was still convinced that 'any life is better than death'.

PROFESSOR EMERITA DAME Theodora Wade Crawford turned up, a little late, for the monthly lunch in the club dining room. She was pleased to see the right number of people at the big circular table where they always sat, not too many for comfort or too few for conversation. She greeted her friends affectionately. Only some of those who might have been there had actually come that day and when Thea joined them, the others were talking about Absent Friends.

One had bowel cancer, another had emigrated to live with her daughter in Sydney, Fidelis Berlin was in Germany, visiting places mentioned in her late mother's diary, Anne was spending the winter in Mauritius, Tamsin had surprisingly become the principal of her own former Cambridge college and was in America drumming up donations from insufficiently grateful alumnae; Olga Hoyland had dementia.

'Really? How very sad, I'm sorry to hear that.'

'It's hit her terribly quickly. Just a few months. She's in a home.'

'I know her daughter Tamara very well, she's a colleague of mine,' Thea said.

'Actually she joined us here a few months ago – very good value I thought.'

'We might ask her to take Olga's place. Or would that be tactless?'

Thea didn't say much that day. She was, as always, perfectly dressed and made up, with newly manicured nails; when she opened her scarlet briefcase Bessie Woods, who was sitting beside her, noticed a package labelled 'Baby Dior'.

'I forgot, Thea, congratulations on the new grandchild, how many does it make?' she said.

'Two, plus three steps,' Thea replied. Bessie looked sharply at her old friend. Her voice had been thin, the intonation flat. Something was wrong. Like nearly everybody in this loosely-knit group of successful women, Thea was still as busy as ever. She had retired from her university post a year early, because she wanted to get back to her own work, finish her magnum opus on the subject of 'Amulets, Charms and Magic Tokens in Antiquity'. Inevitably she was bombarded with invitations and requests but was run off her feet with lecturing, external examining and writing.

'You sound tired,' said Honor, a bulldozer of a woman for whom nothing was better left unsaid. 'What about cutting down a bit? You're not getting any younger you know.'

'Look who's talking,' the woman on her left whispered in Bessie's ear.

'I've got to go, I have an appointment,' Thea said, putting a couple of twenty pound notes on the table to cover her share of the bill. She looked from face to face, catching the other women's eyes one by one. 'It's been lovely,' she said. 'Really. All of it. Always. Lovely.'

'See you again soon,' Elspeth said. It was only later, thinking back to that day, that any of the women realized that Thea Crawford had not echoed the prediction.

Two MONTHS AFTER his return Alastair was off again. And this time he wouldn't be feeling anxious about his relations. As a matter of fact, with his father dead and his brother having again gone off into the blue, the only family he had was Tamara and the three boys. When Tamara had suggested that Vera Fleming might have had Gordon's child Alastair was outraged. 'Don't you dare say such things about my father! It's out of the question. No, Tamara, no no no. Don't suggest such a thing, not to me, not to Euan.'

Tamara thought Euan would turn up again, sooner or later. Not long before, at a private view party for the work of a cerami-cist and his painter wife, she had met a man she knew was one of Euan's friends and asked if he'd seen Alastair's brother. The man looked nervous, his body and feet visibly poised for a quick getaway. Tamara filled his embarrassed silence. 'It's just that Alastair gets worried about him, that's all. So do tell me, have you seen him? How is he?'

'Fine, fine,' she heard.

She asked, 'Still with Lezli?'

'Oh that was just one of his wind-ups—' He stopped talking, making a motion with his arm that looked as if he was going to clap his hand over his mouth but stopped halfway.

Edging very slightly to her left, so as to make it difficult for him to get away, and lying blatantly, she said, 'That's what I thought. He really enjoys shocking his family, doesn't he? From the trapeze artist onwards.'

The man looked relieved but embarrassed. 'I thought he was rather unkind in that way, to his parents. But it was his secret to tell, not mine.'

'Actually I thought Lezli was terrific.'

'I rather liked her, too.'

'Where did Euan find her?'

'Actually at her partner's private view – he's a painter. Terribly good, I'm sure our descendants will be looking at pictures of Lezli at every stage of the gender re-assignment process. But just now they are broke, so when Euan suggested ...'

'Arriving with Lezli as his partner to upset the grown-ups.'

'Exactly.'

'And where is Euan now?'

'He's still in England.'

'Alone?'

'Oh Lord no, old Euan's still got it in spades, he was hardly on his own for a week before he set up with a ... but I really shouldn't ... I've got to ...'

Tamara thought it was fascinating that Euan was capable of keeping loyal friends who wouldn't gossip about him or tell his secrets.

'Thanks,' she said, dazzling the man with her brightest, most artificial smile. 'And don't worry, I shan't let on that you spoke to me.'

'He is so very set on his privacy, you see,' Euan's friend explained apologetically. Tamara said how well she could understand it (which was not true); and that she hoped they'd meet again some time, which wasn't either. She decided not to mention the conversation to Alastair until he was back home again, safe. When, occasionally and for as short a time as possible, he emerged from the deep jungle to see a dentist, or send images of some plant to a colleague, he would also ring home. But conversations from afar, by phone or Skype or any other of the high-tech communication methods were always unsatisfactory. Tamara would tap on his name optimistically, eager for the sound of his voice, hoping for moral support and practical advice. She was left jittery and irritable, every single time, forced to remind herself that she really didn't mind doing things for him, selling his father's house, doing all the family admin – though, as it happened, doing the admin unsuccessfully. The most recent request had been to collect all the documents he'd need to show to get his licences renewed.

'Why do you need them, darling? Do I have to send them to you?'

'No, but have them handy for when I'm back.'

'Are you planning to go back to hands-on medicine?'

'I don't know. I just want to be ready for whatever turns up.'

Tamara had not found them yet. She knew he'd be cross on the phone, wouldn't show interest or gratitude.

And, she thought, he never asks what I'm doing. Of course I want to hear about his adventures, but he might take a bit of interest in mine.

Then she laughed at herself. She was being ridiculous. Adventures? She'd had her fair share of them, years ago, but they didn't go with motherhood. Instead of adventures, she'd had twenty years of being responsible for three other people, ensuring they reached the end of each day.

And now? The children had gone. One was at college, one travelling in his gap year and one had moved from a London day school to spend his teenage years at a boarding school in Cornwall because it offered a course in surfing, theory and practice. No more rushing to get them to school on time, no more nagging about homework. It seemed to have happened quite suddenly.

'You'll be OK on your own, Mum, won't you?' Duncan had said just before he left, and Tamara had instantly assured him she would be fine. 'And I am fine,' she said aloud. 'Fine and free. What shall I do with my newfound liberty?'

The day stretched ahead. She didn't have to go anywhere, even to the office, which was in a business park just outside Oxford, carefully distinguished from a longer-established archaeological services supplier based in the middle of town. In good times there was plenty of work for both.

These were not good times. Tamara was on a work-from-home day, a money-saving mechanism eagerly embraced by the accountants of Archaeological Services, the independent firm of which she was joint director, in charge of the professional services. The founder and other director was a businessman. Tamara directed the archaeological work when there was any. But when money is short, adding to the sum total of human knowledge is a luxury. The only digs going on at present were last-minute rescue excavations conducted when a contractor turned up a treasure and wasn't quick enough to hide or destroy it. In the present economic climate there wasn't much private building, still less private archaeological excavation.

Tamara rang the two permanent staff members to ask what they were up to. One was busy updating the list of potential diggers, marking those who would do it for free, and in a different colour those who had to be paid. The other wasn't answering her phone. She'd probably skived off to buy yet another new dress to dazzle her colleagues.

THIS WON'T DO, Tamara told herself. The phone rang: Alexandra. She didn't actually have anything to say, but took a long time saying so. She had taken to telephoning quite often, perhaps trying to make up for the absence of their mother. Alexandra was seven years older than Tamara and for much of their lives they had been at the wrong stage for each other; their periods of being students, of starting careers or rising up in them, or newly married, or new mothers, or women coming to terms with their empty nests had never coincided. As adults too their lives were very different. Alexandra was a full-time wife and mother, her husband making megabucks in a merchant bank. He didn't have much time for Tamara's idealistic medic. Alexandra's children went to expensive schools, Tamara's to the local comprehensive, until this year when Duncan had miraculously won his scholarship to the school in Truro. The conversation ended as it always did. 'Seen Mum recently?'

Alexandra had visited her the previous day. 'There's a new doctor. I didn't see him, but all the old biddies think the sun shines out of his ... well, you know.'

'Did they tell you what he said about her?'

'No, not really. To tell you the truth, Tamara, I don't think there's anything to say. She's just not all there, not even a bit there.

I don't feel that it's Mum I go to see in the home, it's like there's a changeling in the room and the real person has disappeared.'

'I do know what you mean.'

'Listen, I've remembered what I wanted to ask you. Have you heard any more about that woman – I forget her name – the one who was your pa-in-law's girlfriend? Have they found who did it?'

'If they have, nobody's told me.'

'I've got to fly, speak soon, love you, byee....'

It was some days since she'd heard anything. The number was on her speed-dial and miraculously, DC Gilbert was picking up. He sounded dejected.

'I'm sorry, Dr Hoyland, I have nothing to tell you.'

'Because you haven't got anything? Or it's confidential?'

'The lab hasn't come back with anything yet.'

'Are you any closer to finding a motive?'

'No progress there either.'

It was Euan, Tamara thought, but I can't shop Alastair's brother. He's quite clever enough to have killed Vera with some vicious weapon, hit her hard on the head, see her fall to the floor, but all without crossing the threshold of the flat at all. He'd have stood in the outside hall muffled up in a protective coat, and used a weapon that was easy to dispose of. There'd be no evidence of him being there at all. And then he'd probably scuttled back to the United States.

DC Gilbert was down-hearted, but it was only about a professional setback. Tamara felt disconcertingly depressed and ashamed on personal grounds. Did I say the wrong thing to Euan? Was I supportive enough to Vera? Did I make her believe that she'd be a really welcome addition to the family? And the girl too – but Iona didn't want it, and can you blame her if she's heard what a quarrelsome, jealous lot we can be?

'DC Gilbert, are you there still? Oh good. Look, what's the position about a funeral?'

'Can't be done. Not until the case is settled, file closed.'

'But Vera's family…?'

'I did hear something about a memorial service up north.'

To which not a single member of the Hope family had been invited.

'Can you let me have contact details for the niece – Iona? Her email address? It's a facility I would like you to afford,' she added, and the words were like magic. She could almost hear DC Gilbert leaping to attention. But then he replied, 'I would if I could, but we haven't got it.'

QUITE OFTEN IN her life Tamara had made decisions by working out, or guessing, what Grandmère would have done, or at least advised. In this case, get up, go, *do* something.

But what shall I do? she asked herself.

Where do I go from here?

As a practical archaeologist Tamara knew she would never make an academic. What other jobs were there in her field?

After university and two years of postgrad work, she had become a civil servant dealing with ancient monuments. But that had not been her only occupation. She had another, secret and unadmitted employer. Her job as a practical hands-on archaeologist had been a useful cover when she was investigating a recalcitrant civilian. Her misleadingly innocent appearance had been an equally invaluable attribute.

Somehow, in the busy years of small children and big work projects Tamara had lost contact with Department E. Now, in calm waters, and bored, she no longer knew how to get in touch with it or with Mr Black.

Dad would have known, she thought. But I haven't a clue. Advice needed. Help! And as that word came into her mind she found herself uttering an actual sound, a muted, closed-mouth squeal. What's wrong with me?

Too much time on my own.

Missing Alastair.

Missing the boys.

An empty nest.

Worrying about Olga. Oh, Mum, if only ... Enough!

Tamara sprang to her feet. I'll go mad if I just stay at home, she thought.

The weekend loomed before her but there was no need for her to be here.

I could go anywhere, she thought. I'm completely free. It's like before I met Alastair, I did exactly as I chose. I didn't need to fit in with other peoples' arrangements, and I never had to worry about his dinner being late or if there was enough food in the house. I lived to please myself.

I'm not really sure I can do that again, she thought. If they did offer me a job would I say yes? Not sure. But there's no point in thinking about that until I've tracked down Mr Black, or Department E, or whatever it's called now and whoever replaced him. And get fit again. She pulled off her clothes and stood in front of a full-height mirror. Distastefully she prodded at her arms, her hips, her thighs. Not fat – she was still the size she'd been in her twenties – but yielding. Feminine, if not quite flabby. 'You've let yourself go soft,' Tamara told her reflection.

A resolution: a daily visit to the gym. Swimming. It wouldn't be easy on her own, without the old instructor who had taught her before going active with Department E, and she certainly didn't expect to return to 'active service condition'; in fact it was very unlikely that Department E, or whatever it was called now, would expect her to. In fact it was pretty unlikely that they would want anything to do with an operative who had been on the retired list for nearly twenty years. But getting fit and strong could only be a good thing, no matter what happened next.

Second resolution: get advice. What to do next as an admissible job? Life advice.

Career advice. But whose?

IT DOESN'T NECESSARILY happen quickly. It's also fascinating to watch it coming gradually, inevitably, like standing at the top look-out corner of a medieval castle and every morning seeing a hostile army with its knights on fast horses and its gear piled on slow carts, its dust cloud rising above the desert, moving not far in one day but inexorably, still coming. For every little hitch on that journey there is the little physical episode on this one. The patient's future, like the castle's, can be foretold: both will succumb.

I have already told you that I am interested in death. Knowing that, you will understand why I've chosen to temp in this care home. Nearly every inmate is old, in fact ancient, and they have come here to die. And so they do. At night in their sleep, by day, attended by professional staff, suddenly or leisurely. You would think that I would have more opportunities than even I could want to see that moment. But the chances of my being in the right place at the right time seem to be sadly small.

Take, for example, today. I was just too late. It can have been only a little moment before I entered his room that the 'oldest inhabitant' died, but dead he was. His eyes were open, glassy and sightless, as they would only be for a very few moments after death. Indeed, as I stood there the sheen dimmed, the pupils dilated, the eyeball flattened. I pulled the lids closed. The face was taking on the dingy pallor of death. The body was already shrunken.

In the accounts of 'good deaths' – or for that matter bad ones

– people who write stories build on other novelists' descriptions, which of course are traditionally wrong. Have you, for example, ever read a deathbed scene that includes the fact that the bowels open and urine flows? Deathbeds stink.

And you've heard of the death rattle. Well, when you hear it you'll realize what a misnomer that is. No, take it from me, death isn't pretty. But witnessing it is beyond exciting. It's a privilege. In fact, for me it's a turn-on.

I washed the body, but wasn't gentle with it, for he had cheated me. This old man was beyond my punishment. Luckily there will be other bodies here, other opportunities. This is a useful place for me. When I discovered where Dr Gorgeous had moved to, I looked round the neighbourhood, there's always a good job for people with my skills. There were three establishments that were little more than warehouses for surplus-to-requirements human beings. They are called 'care homes'. But I've learnt that when there's little care for the inmates there's even less for the staff. So I kept my eyes open, cased the joint carefully, and soon discovered that the Helleborean was where I needed to be. I told you there'd be no trouble getting a job, and nor was there. They leapt at me.

He hasn't seen me yet. I look a little different from the nurse he met on the high dependency ward when his father died or to be accurate, was edged a little prematurely into his death. But he'll remember me from there, and he'll remember our encounter by the morgue too. This is going to be fun.

THEA CRAWFORD. THE DISTINGUISHED old archaeologist had become more a friend than a mentor, but she knew Tamara and was one of the few people who also knew about her former, secret occupation. Who better to suggest which direction to go in?

She tried, several times, to catch Thea on the phone.

Having been in two minds about contacting Thea, Tamara at

first took her inaccessibility as a sign that she shouldn't; in fact, she almost persuaded herself that it was a message: that it was time to do something new. But archaeology was more a calling than just a job. I need to be re-enthused, Tamara told herself. I need to speak to someone whose lifework it's been, and who thinks her life well spent. Or his.

Thea Crawford didn't call back. Tamara tried the number again. No answer, again.

I'll go and see her, Tamara thought.

'Get that,' she said aloud. Then she thought, can I really just get up and go? When did I last do that? She was so inured to a mother's life, in which one was never free to go anywhere without making arrangements for the family, that the idea of impulsively getting into the car and driving off seemed at once exciting and naughty.

She found herself, almost without having noticed what she was doing, on the top floor of the house, methodically locking windows and pulling electric plugs from their sockets. She watered plants lavishly. She and Alastair had bought their house, a semi-detached Victorian villa in Putney, when he landed a senior post at the Hospital for Tropical Diseases, luckily just before prices begun to rocket. Even with two good incomes, and Tamara's legacy from her grandmother, it had been a stretch, but she loved the house with its tiny stained glass conservatory, period tiles round every fireplace and distant views from the attic, between other roofs, of the trees in Kew Gardens.

She felt a curious fizzing in her body, as though her blood were somehow aerated, an excitement recognized physically before her brain had processed her thoughts. Tamara walked across the room for her bag, and took out a small folding mirror. Do I look any different? she wondered. Two decades of being a good mother, a good wife, a good professional; two decades living a calm and sensible bourgeois life, of bringing her children safely to the end of each day. Two decades of suppressing her adventurous, anarchic impulses. I've been content, she thought. Calmly, sensibly comfortable and satisfied.

But now it's time. All change.

Number one: call the original Department E number. The digits were engraved on her memory. But she was not surprised to find that the number was 'not in use'. Who might know what had happened, who was there to ask? Tamara's father had known Mr Black. One of Dad's surviving friends, perhaps? Or perhaps one of Mum's. Her gang.

Well, that couldn't be done in a hurry. Next: Thea.

Having retired from her professorship in London, Thea had been made an honorary fellow of the Institute, partly to honour her achievements, but as far as she was concerned, so that she remained entitled to use the library and could get access to journals online.

Tamara rang the secretary to ask where Thea was, and got a quite rude brush-off. 'You can't honestly think that we give out information about our staff to any Tom, Dick or Harry on the phone.'

'I'm Dr Tamara Hoyland, I've lectured to your students several times and I use your library. Hardly what you'd call any Tom, Dick or Harry.'

'Maybe. But I'm still not breaking the rules.'

Grumpily Tamara went there in person that afternoon. In fact she needed to consult some books about Roman period hoards because something was nagging at her. Had she been too quick in dismissing that metal detectorist in Gloucestershire? Even if most of the site had been built over it might have been worth having a look. The voice of good sense told her that hoards, almost by definition, were buried away from any settlement, so there wouldn't be anything to find. The voice of neurosis whined away like a dentist's drill: suppose you've missed something mega?

Tamara went into the Institute, swiped her access card and

walked past the obstructive secretary without a glance. The library was busy and it took a little while to find someone she knew. Meredith had been in her last undergraduate year when Tamara started at Edinburgh University.

'Tamara – hi. It's been years! Oh God, you still look marvellous. I bet you've got a portrait in the attic.'

'What?'

'You know, like Dorian Grey. It's up there getting the wrinkles that should be on your face, dammit.'

It was difficult to answer because Meredith did have a lined face and her hair was going grey. 'It's all genetics,' Tamara said.

'Ssssh.'

Justly rebuked, Tamara whispered and gestured, and Meredith understood and left the room with her. When they were out of the library, Tamara said, 'Listen Meredith, where's Thea? She's not answering her landline or mobile.'

'I think she's gone to ground. Hiding. Away from it all.'

'Do you know where?'

'I do actually, I happened to see a forwarded letter that someone was putting in the post box. She's in Cornwall.'

'At Buriton? She had a chair there once – her first one.'

'Did she? I don't really know much about her as a person. Her books are pretty good though. Someone told me she was writing her memoirs – some archaeologists I have slept with, he said it should be called.'

'I hope you kneed him in the goolies.'

'I let the copier lid fall on his hand,' Meredith said with pride.

'Really?'

'Really.'

'Was he hurt?'

'He made as much fuss as if it had been amputated.' Meredith began to giggle. Actually, it was funny, Tamara thought. The two women were momentarily helpless with laughter, which, Tamara thought, certainly made a change. And the excellent Meredith not only knew Vera's 'niece' Iona Harper, who was described as a very promising first year student, but was perfectly happy to pass on her email address.

IT HAD BEEN the wettest winter for more than 250 years, or so at least the news media were saying, and it wasn't over yet. Much of southern England was literally underwater and much of western Britain was cut off by the failure of public transport links. The saturated soil could absorb no more, which left water lying on the land, muddy and soon polluted with sewage. At Dawlish, in south Devon, the railway line into west Devon and Cornwall flapped in the wind, for all the stones and soil that supported it had been washed into the sea. In Somerset the Levels had turned into an inland ocean, the pretty villages almost as drowned as Atlantis. Householders, evicted by natural forces, camped out in village halls. The Thames had burst its banks and flooded the expensive homes of Berkshire and Surrey. Cliffs and beaches were battered by record-breaking waves which carried away familiar geological and historical features.

So many people had lost the use of their landline telephones that it was not unusual for a call to be answered with nothing but a sinister buzz. Quite a few mobile phone masts had also been damaged. Tamara couldn't get through to Thea Crawford. She rang the University of Buriton central switchboard and asked to speak to Professor Crawford.

'We've been asked not to put calls through to her rooms,' a very young woman's voice replied. Tamara, politely thanking her, briefly wondered whether to add a warning that she shouldn't let her reply confirm the fact that Thea was in Buriton, decided not to interfere and rang off.

She went to the cupboard under the stairs, heaved aside skis, surf boards and cricket bats to get at the suitcases, and chose a waterproof one. Then she sent a text to Duncan ('Coming Cwll w/end, take u out supper?').

The travel warnings were being ratcheted up into a kind of hysteria. Any fool who ventured onto 'the roads' could expect to be in serious trouble; they would be stuck in record-breaking water-splashes; they would skid off the road and fall down a mountain or cliff, over and over until the vehicle hit solid ground and burst into flames; a young woman would snuggle into the warm cab of the kind lorry driver only to have trouble beating him off because he wasn't kind after all, just ardent.

Tamara packed a bag with a Thermos full of hot coffee, added a tartan blanket and a powerful torch. She put in a bottle of water and a book, and as a final afterthought, a pillow.

Then she spent more than half an hour putting on clothes and taking them off again, in the hope of not catching a disapproving or disappointed glance. At least, Tamara thought, her hair was good. The hairdresser was adept at matching the original bright blonde, and at giving it a sharply-cut swing when Tamara moved her head.

I'm not that different twenty years on, she thought, at least to look at. But I've lost something. Zest? Self-confidence? Unguarded, her mind went a step too far and made an inadmissible final step: my husband?

MY DAD WAS the first to give up.

'Can't you see it's pointless?' he'd demanded. 'The fact is, Polly, it would have been far better if our boy had died, if he'd been killed outright.'

'Don't say it – how can you say that?'

'Face facts. Not something that you've ever been very good at.'

'That isn't a fact.'

'You've heard the medics.'

'There's still a chance, there's still hope.'

'I wish you'd just stop with the endless hope, trying to sound upbeat – as if he could hear you!'

'Sometimes I really think he can. Look, his eyes follow me, he can see me!'

'No Polly.' Gentle now, sorry for her. 'They explained it to us, don't you remember? It's an illusion, my dear. I wish it wasn't.'

He puts his arms round her and her head lies on his shoulder and they stand like that, very close, for a long time. Then his phone rings and he lets go of my mum and has a long, angry conversation with someone, and when he rings off his bad temper is back.

'And all this junk, this room's a tip! Take it away, get rid of it all, and the pictures, get them out of here, there's no point and you know that perfectly well. Oh damn it Polly, stop crying for God's sake.'

She's taken to bringing in objects, things I'd used or liked. My surf board, and a week later my wet suit, a cricket bat, my iPhone. She'll hold them in front of my staring eyes and beg me to react. The next thing was music. She brought speakers and plugged the iPhone in and eventually – it took her a whole day – worked out how to make it blare out my playlists.

Most of the time there's no point in thinking I can make her understand me. If she could read my thoughts, or hear them ... but life's not like that. Nor is this death in life.

Some days I feel more optimistic – this has to be some kind of cosmic joke, they aren't really going to leave me like this for ever, I can't believe it. It's not funny any more, I want to shout it, let everyone know. Joke's over.

That was the first thing Helge said when my mother brought her into my room. She stood there gazing at me like she could see through the bedclothes and the machinery, like she could actually see me, Davy, a real person inside this disguise. I'd seen her there when I woke from – well, not a nap. I wasn't asleep, so I should say, from a brief period of unconsciousness. Another nurse. They change them often enough to make it seem like they don't want us getting too friendly. Just as well. It means I haven't had the one who looked like she was going to kill me, she hasn't appeared for weeks.

I like the look of this one. She picks up my left hand from the bedclothes, opens the fingers one by one and looks with great concentration at the palm, tracing some pattern with her forefinger on my skin. For a moment I believe I can feel it. Wasn't that a warmth on my palm, an area of sensation? But it fades, and within a moment I know that there was no miracle.

'So what do you think?' my mum asked.

'I think we should get on well, your poor Davy and me.'

'You mean you'll take the job?'

'Yes.'

Interesting. Apparently I'll be leaving the hospital, though that was the first I'd heard of it. Going home? Maybe not, after what my dad had said the other day. But anywhere would do. Since willpower was the only thing left to me, I'll concentrate on willing my mum to do it. Just get me out of here.

SINCE OLGA HOYLAND was living in an institution that was not more than a couple of miles detour from the main road south and west, Tamara stopped off on the way. The gardens, or grounds, were as spectacularly pretty as on her previous visit, although the last few months had been so wet.

The house did not smell of shit and piss; the chairs were not arranged around the wall facing into a blank space in the middle of the room; everybody was fully dressed in clothes that looked as though they were their own. Inevitably it was overheated – people feel the cold when they are very old. But as homes for the very elderly go, this was a good one. And actually, if one were to stop pretending to oneself and everyone else, and instead to be completely honest, Olga Hoyland was no longer in a state to notice whether it was good or bad.

It should not feel any more daunting than visiting one's mother in her own house, but every time Tamara went to The Helleborean (Sheltered Accommodation) Home she had to force her feet up the steps to the front door, and, her shoulders rigid, her smile fixed, to go upstairs and along the corridor to the room on which a neatly painted plaque announced in white letters on a red background, Mrs Olga Hoyland.

She would go in, notice with approval that the flowers were fresh, the bed was made, the furniture had been polished. 'Hello Mum,' she would say without expecting any reaction and without getting one. She'd walk forward on the comfortable brown carpet, bend over and kiss her mother's cheek, observe that the smell in the room was of furniture polish backed up by disinfectant and a faint reminder of Chanel No. 5; she would say in as normal voice as she could, 'This all looks very cozy, Mum. How are things? Is everything OK?'

On a good day there would be an answer. 'Very well thank you.' Or perhaps, 'How kind of you to come.' On a bad day there simply would be silence, no reaction. And on no day would there be enough loosening of Alzheimer's disease's grip for her to hear her mother's real voice saying motherly, welcoming words.

Alexandra and Tamara had drawn up a timetable, arranging that there should never be more than three days without a visit to their mother by one of them or their brothers. It was not for Olga Hoyland's sake precisely or at least not directly, but for the staff, so that they should know that this patient's care was carefully overseen. Every few weeks one of them made a point of having a chat with Mrs Bussell, just a tactful reminder that their mother was protected.

'Actually they do look after her beautifully,' all four of Olga Hoyland's children had observed. Three of them sometimes added, 'They're very kind, and very concerned, one couldn't ask for better.'

The fourth, the youngest, Tamara, could ask for better. Would death be better? No! Not that!

But what was all this for? Olga was never going to get well again, rather, as every day went by, she lost more and more of the intellectual power that had made her human. And yet ... And yet ... Weakly, thinking in cliché because really this was more a feeling than a thought, Tamara would tell herself that while there was life there was hope. Perhaps a miracle cure would be discovered, regenerate those atrophied brain cells, return to her the clever, perceptive, funny and always loving mother whose ghost was surely in the failing machine of her body.

This was a bad day. The nurse said Olga had been overdoing it the day before when they had a party for another resident's 100th birthday. Everyone came and had a lovely time. Even the new doctor had briefly looked in. There were frequent changes of medic, as the doctors in the local practice took turns to look after the four care homes, two hostels and a boarding school in the neighbourhood. Dr Macintosh was lovely, the nurse said, Tamara should meet him, specially as he said he might be able to help Olga with new techniques. He had a special interest in the very aged.

When Tamara went into the room she found Olga lying on her side, knees pulled up towards her chest, her thumb in her mouth. She had no apparent reaction of any kind to Tamara's appearance or to her greeting.

There wasn't the slightest point in being here, but she couldn't walk straight out again. Tamara fidgeted around the room, picking things up and putting them down. A hairbrush. A small stone, perhaps one that had been in her mother's shoe. A cotton wool pad. Her mother had not moved. Her regular but rough breathing rasped in and out.

Tamara sat down on the chair placed to the side of the bed.

Poison? she thought. A pillow? A pillow over the face.

No! No no no no no. There's life here, it might change, she might come back.

Oh Mum. Where are you? Where are *you*, not your body, you, yourself, the person?

I can't do this any more, Tamara thought. She walked out of the room and fast, faster until she was almost running, along the corridor, down the stairs and across the hall and out. But I've gone wrong somewhere, this isn't the way to the car park. She was standing at the edge of an old-style kitchen garden, with fruit boughs trained across its rust red walls, and stone-edged beds, some of them full of early vegetables. There were daffodils, there was blossom. There was also a great deal of mud. And it was still raining.

Seeing a door in the wall to the left, Tamara squelched her way to it. When she opened it she found herself at the far end of the car park and walked quickly across it. She was wet through after even that short exposure, and, concentrating on changing her jersey for a dry one out of her suitcase, didn't notice a car parking quite close to hers, its driver getting out and glancing in her direction. Then he leapt back into his driving seat and roared across the pebbles and off up the short private driveway, and away.

Did he go because of me? she wondered. But no, surely not. How could I scare anyone off, and anyway, why? No, he must have forgotten something.

Tamara turned the engine on and backed out. As she swept forward again her eye was caught by writing on the parking space beside the one she had left. It said, 'Doctor'.

PROFESSOR CRAWFORD WAS almost single when Tamara, a still gauche and countrified student, had first encountered her in

Edinburgh University's Fine Art and Archaeology Department. Technically she was still married to a journalist, a well-known voice from the world's trouble spots, but they had parted shortly after that. Thea was a role model: clever, decisive and original.

Thea had become a professor unusually young when, back in the early seventies, she had applied for the Chair of Archaeology at the University of Buriton, in Cornwall, and had been amazed to be offered it. As a woman, in that still unliberated decade, as a mother, and as the wife of a notorious foreign correspondent, she had expected automatic rejection. Being invited to the interviews had been surprising enough; being offered the job seemed astonishing. It was also, in some ways, disastrous.

If Thea's husband had taken a job so far from home, she would, in those days, have been expected to up sticks and move no matter what that did to her career. No such assumptions were made when it was her job that required moving. Her husband simply refused to come, so they met only during the vacations. Thea's next job, in Edinburgh, was no more convenient for a Londoner than Buriton, and by then the relationship was pretty half-hearted. They separated, without quarrels or disagreements, and said they were still each other's best friend. In Thea's first term at Buriton[3] she had found the dead body of one of the college's stalwarts. Dr Helen Eliot, supremely compos mentis at nearly ninety, had apparently slipped on some spilled polish and fallen hard with her head hitting the fender-corner. One of the eulogists at her carefully non-religious funeral service had suggested that Helen herself would undoubtedly have chosen that quick death rather than lingering, increasingly dependent and infirm. 'Euthanasia is illegal,' he affirmed, 'thou shalt not kill.' Then, after a pause, he added, 'We need not strive officiously to keep alive.' There was nobody left at the university to remember any more about Helen Eliot than her name, which was inscribed on one of the honours boards, but somewhere there must be a record

---

3 *The Only Security* by Jessica Mann

of her death and the events surrounding it, because when Thea arrived for her first term as honorary research fellow, the porter made a long speech, mostly incomprehensible, explaining that the domestic bursar had tactfully chosen to give Professor Crawford an apartment in the newest building on campus. The architecture was experimental and right-on. Waste water was recirculated, waste everything else sorted into minutely defined categories; they tapped the earth's heat and grew grass, a natural insulator, all over the flat roof.

At that time Thea Crawford was in her late sixties, healthy and busy and looking much younger than she really was. When she returned for her third and last spring term at the university the work had gone well and would be finished as the timetable required, by Easter, and published within a year. One of Thea's more unusual attributes was that she had never been late in fulfilling any obligation; she was always on the dot even for social engagements and in all her life had never missed a train.

She'd come by train this time, a composed, elegant figure seated in the first-class coach. In front of her on the table an iPad, an advance copy of a not-yet published biography of a famous soldier/archaeologist, and a bottle of still water. It was a long journey, nearly six hours from Paddington to West Cornwall, during which she did not open the book or the computer but stared out of the window, apparently fascinated by the changing countryside. As it happened, everybody else was looking out of the window too. It had been raining for weeks, heavily and unrelenting, soaking into the already sodden ground until the saturated land could take no more. The train crawled across the Somerset Levels, the tracks slightly elevated above this inland sea. It edged slowly between the sodden water meadows outside Exeter, tiptoed along the track between the cliff and the sea at Teignmouth and Dawlish. This day was calm, although still raining.

'If the wind gets up, if there's a southerly gale ...' A fellow passenger seemed to know what he was talking about. 'Marooned.

That's what we'll be. Cut off from the rest of the country. An island.' It sounded as if he looked forward to it.

A cab had been ordered to meet Thea at Buriton, the terminus, and the gate warden was waiting for her when it reached the college.

'Good to have you back again, Professor Crawford – sorry, Dame Thea I should say,' he said, waiting to hold out his hand to shake hers until she had begun the movement, since he was not sure whether she would embrace him or nod and smile or shake his hand. Thea held out her right hand. Small and cold, it disappeared into the porter's massive paw.

'Professor will be fine,' she said. 'I'm not used to answering to the other yet.' It was nearly four months since the announcement in the New Year list: Professor Theodora Veronica Wade Crawford, for services to archaeology. She hadn't wanted to accept it. Dame was such a dreadful title, like some freak from a pantomime, she said. But of course, in the end, she took it gracefully and gratefully, saying the honour was not really hers, it was for the team. A symbol of their industry and inspiration.

The gate warden crooked his little finger to summon an underling to carry the cases, opened a large umbrella and began to walk with Thea, his proudly prominent stomach leading the way.

They were walking towards the old college. 'Hope you don't mind, Professor,' he said. 'There's this conference going on in the new buildings, every single room occupied. I don't mind telling you, it's well weird. Fortune telling, reading the tea leaves – they say it's about probability theory but you wouldn't think so with all those sideshows. Oh well, mustn't grumble, that's the way we keep the old place going, conferences. Doesn't matter how nutty if they pay!'

Thea did not answer and he sneaked a sideways look at her, thinking that for the first time she looked as old as she was. Must be pushing seventy, he thought, or even more. Seventy-two? Seventy-three? Not looking her best.

They haven't really gone and put me in Helen Eliot's rooms, she was thinking. Surely not! And they hadn't, not quite. Two doors along, a corner suite, with the sitting room looking out over the college garden but the bedroom and kitchenette with windows looking over the roofs of the town to the sea.

'This all you've got, Professor? Or is the rest coming separately?'

Thea glanced at the two suitcases. 'No, that's everything.'

'I suppose you don't have to carry books and papers these days, not like you used to. All on here, isn't it?' He placed the iPad on the desk, and stood there for a moment lining it up. 'Not like the old days,' he repeated.

He wants to chat, Thea thought.

The sound of an alarm pinging quietly interrupted his words. Then he said, 'Got a bomb in there or something, have you?'

She went and stood by the open doors, and said, 'Thank you, I'll be fine, I can manage now.' Once she had closed the heavy wooden outer door, and the cream painted inner one, took a pillbox out of her handbag and swallowed a couple of tablets. Then she sat, or perhaps collapsed onto a green sofa and closed her eyes while she waited for the medication to take effect.

ANOTHER ARGUMENT. His parents, back again. His father had only just heard of his mother's plans. He didn't even bother to keep his voice down.

'How much, did you say? I don't believe it!'

'It's my own money.'

'That's right, and it'll be your own bankruptcy too. You'll be cleaned out in no time – do you know what it costs to have full-time care?'

An inaudible murmur. Then his mother's voice again.

'I think she'll make a difference. She's very experienced—'

'With geriatrics.'

'Not only that. She's been with two other paraplegics.'

'And where are they now?' his father demanded.

An inaudible mumble from his mother, but it was easy enough to work out what she'd said, because his father, now a little less aggressively, said, 'I suppose that's the way all her cases end. No miracle cures in this game.' A pause. Click click – high heels moving towards the window. The sound of sobs. His father's voice again.

'Here, it's a clean one. Let me just ... hold still, your mascara's running ... there, that's better, now have a good blow.' Sniffs, snuffles, a long sigh. What were they both doing? Davy couldn't see that side of the room. You'd have thought someone would have had the idea of turning him, or the bed, to give him a different view. His father said, 'I've been a right bastard haven't I? It's only because I'm so bloody miserable.'

'I know. So am I.'

'Our lovely boy.'

Now they were crying, both of them. He could see just a tiny part of them reflected in the shiny instruments. They were hugging one another tightly. Before, he'd have thought them embarrassing and soppy. Now he felt sorry for them, in an abstract, unfocused way. Not much fun for them either, all this.

Door. Footsteps, creaking, not clicking on the hard floor.

'Mrs Canning. Mr Canning. Good afternoon.'

I know that voice. Slight accent, deep, trustworthy. A 'lean on me' voice.

'You wanted to see me?'

Father: 'Good of you to come down. Yes, we wanted to thank you for what you've done for Davy—'

Oh, it's the big cheese. The consultant. Davy had only seen him at the centre of a crowd, students, nurses, patients' relatives, waiting for his precious words.

'Not at all, not at all. I'm only sorry that our efforts haven't met with success.'

'We've got the impression that there's no more to be done. You've tried everything there is to try and then some, but ...'

'The results have been disappointing, I must admit.'

'So give us a candid opinion: what actually, is the prognosis?'

'Very hard to say. So much depends on these artificial aids, to keep him breathing and ingesting nutrition ... it can be many years. But then there are other cases. Survival can be for a very limited period of time.'

'So there's no hope, really.'

'It's a mistake to cherish unrealistic ideas. It's tough love, you have to be realistic, in fact hard, brutally hard, if you are to cope. And help your son to cope.' It seemed to be a remark this medic had made often before. He sounded, actually, brutal.

Too restless and agitated to sit, Davy's father was walking round the room. From time to time he came within Davy's vision. Was it good that he could see and hear, he wondered? Would it be better to be in a coma?

Dad said, 'The thing is, we're thinking of taking him home.'

'Oh! Really?'

'What would you say to that?' his mother asked.

'That would be ... well, it's a major undertaking. I don't think – forgive me – I wonder whether you realize quite what you'd be letting yourselves in for? To do for Davy literally everything, every single day. For the rest of his life. Or, of course, yours.'

Can't see it happening, Davy told himself.

'He needs such a lot of personal care,' the doctor said.

Too right. A catheter in his dick, a napkin round his bum and absolutely no control of his bodily functions.

'My wife has a carer in mind.'

'May I suggest a compromise?'

'By all means.'

'A kind of halfway house. I quite understand your desire to get him out of here, but why not find a suitable care home? I know it's usually the elderly who live in them, but there's actually no age barrier, they are meant for everyone who needs care. And of course, you'd be free to pay the salary of a personal carer if you choose to go down that road.'

'Do you mean that we should start looking at old people's homes for Davy?'

'You could do that. But as it happens I know of one that might be very suitable. If it would be of any help, I'll give you the number.'

THEA CRAWFORD HAD read enough to have given up hope. But she was not, conversely, in despair. Intellectually she knew how limited the time left to her would be – and what would happen to her in that time. Emotionally she couldn't feel it. The information she had acquired seemed to have nothing to do with herself. A kind of automatic self-protection, she guessed. Or numbness.

All the same, she wasn't going to sit around waiting for fate to take its course. She'd finished one of her projects, her contribution to a multi-authored excavation report. It might need amendment when the bone analysis came in, but the general editor could do that.

Then there was her autobiography to complete. The trouble was, she could no longer remember why a memoir of her life in archaeology had ever seemed like a good idea. The publisher must have been dazzled by her name-dropping. As a teenager, she had spent one term at the Institute of Archaeology, then housed in a splendid villa in the middle of Regent's Park. She'd seen Gordon Childe and Mortimer Wheeler, Kathleen Kenyon and Max Mallowan. She had even set eyes on Sir Max's wife, Agatha Christie.

At Cambridge, she'd been taught by Grahame Clark and Glyn Daniel. She had worked on historic excavations: Masada, in Israel, the theatre at Epidaurus, a season at Stonehenge with Stuart Piggott, Avebury with Richard Atkinson, at Gwithian with Charles Thomas. Little interested in gossip though Thea was, even she could see that younger archaeologists would be interested in eye-witness, personal memories of the subject in its academic infancy, when there were very few jobs for archaeologists, and excavation was not yet regarded as a synonym for destruction.

Right. So she really needed to hurry up and finish that work before ... before taking other action.

And what about personal considerations? Clovis – no, she silently corrected her own thoughts – John and his children. No doubt they would be sorry, but the death of a grandparent was in the normal course of events. As was the death of a friend. The picture of her friends at lunch flashed into her mind. Chatty, funny, concerned, supportive women whose company had enhanced her life; but the gap would close up quickly.

As for private life in Buriton, so interesting and zestful during her previous sessions in Cornwall: this year she hadn't even called the architect from Truro who had become a good friend last year, or the ancient local landowner who still hoped she would succumb to the temptation of becoming a countess. She didn't have the time or the energy for socializing. Getting herself to the library was about as much as she could manage. These days she was always utterly worn out when she made it back to her set of rooms. No question of going down to dinner in Hall and sometimes she couldn't be bothered even to assemble a snack in the 'kitchen in a cupboard' built in to her living room. The unlabelled box file she had brought with her was in full view in the book case. Where do you hide a leaf? In the forest. None of the team of cleaners would think of looking at a box file of papers. They wouldn't be interested, and if one of them happened to wonder about her, she'd look for information on her laptop. Everyone in that generation, just like people ten years older such as her son

John Clovis, lived in an electronic world and believed implicitly in an electronic future. It must be years since he had handled an actual letter, or put down coins to buy something as old fashioned as a printed newspaper. It was certainly a cheap and simple way to live, if also a cheerless one. Thea had refused even to toy with the idea. 'I like materials,' she'd said. 'Paper, wood, metals, fabrics, stones, pottery – things I can touch and shape. Anyway, think of the archaeologists of the future. What evidence will survive for them?'

She jerked awake, still on the sofa where she had collapsed after supper. 'Three o'clock in the morning,' she murmured, her intonation half aggrieved, half surprised. Pitch dark outside, no street lights visible on this sea-facing side of the old college. 'And I've still got my jacket on! Again! Really, I don't know what's come over me.'

She took off her clothes, pulled on her pyjamas and dressing gown, switched on the electric blanket to warm up her bed. Then she made a pot of herb tea and sat down with it and the box file. It contained not papers but books. Books on a particular subject.

At the top was an annoyingly cheery paperback about cancer. The author had written much more about breast tumours and the ever-improving odds of surviving them to lead a long and healthy life, than about diagnoses that were death sentences. But perhaps what I've got would have been curable too, Thea thought, if I'd gone to the doctor when I first ... No. That was not a profitable train of thought.

She picked up instead a text book on 'self-deliverance'. She had read some of it before, dismayed at the mental images evoked by the advice. Not much dignity in a death that involved some of the gadgets described. A hosepipe to the car's exhaust, for God's sake; or some Heath Robinson device involving children's party balloons!

She murmured, 'Razors pain you; rivers are damp; acids stain you; and drugs cause cramp. Guns aren't lawful; nooses give;

gas smells awful; you might as well live.' Who said that? she wondered. Never mind, look it up tomorrow. You brought these books, Thea, jolly well look at them. The voice in her head was her own, forty – no, fifty years before, high, bossy. That girl's too clever by half, someone nearby had muttered, and then she heard, 'And doesn't she know it!' Where was that? She'd been wearing a green and grey dress, Horrocks glazed cotton, with a wide, tight patent-leather belt and a full skirt held out by a crisp, many-layered net petticoat. The material batted against the back of her legs when she walked.

Four o'clock in the morning. Still pitch black outside. Thea went into the bedroom and slid onto the welcome, warm smoothness of the clean white sheet.

If I can still enjoy this, for example, if I take pleasure in this physical comfort, then surely I'm not ready for any of those gruesome methods of what the death industry calls self-deliverance. Go to sleep.

Why aren't those authors prosecuted – isn't aiding and abetting a suicide a crime any more?

Count sheep. List prime numbers.

She turned on the bedside light and picked up a notebook that lay beside it. She'd started it on the day of her first tests, never imagining that they would reveal anything important, let alone fatal. In it she'd made notes at every consultation, knowing how the doctor's words would disappear from memory. Then she added doodles, made when bored in the waiting area ... oh, what hours she had spent waiting, waiting. And she had copied out quotations. Perhaps she should publish it. *Crawford's Cancer Collection*?

'I don't think so,' she said aloud, surprised by her own thin, cracked voice. She cleared her throat energetically, and then said the words again. That's a relief, back to normal. Leafing through the little volume, she paused to read a speech she had cut from a newspaper and stuck in the notebook. It was the report of a

House of Lords debate on 'assisted dying' in 1986. A peer who was a concentration camp survivor described what lengths inmates would go to, in order to acquire the means to kill oneself, and how it gave them the strength to carry on. The conclusion he drew was still relevant. 'Is it not time not only to stop making the ending of one's life a crime, but to establish it as a right?'

THEY'VE GOT ME working all over the place – feeding one inmate her slop with a baby spoon, remaking soiled beds, reading to a man who's had an eye operation. I don't really mind, because it gives me a chance to take a good look round and that could prove useful because I've already found several cubby holes and unused spaces which might well come in handy. And that tetraplegic boy I was having fun with in the hospital has turned up here! That's a stroke of luck.

But the really good thing has nothing to do with luck. It was judgement – my own judgement. He's the real reason I came here. The medic is Mr – or rather, as it turns out, Dr Gorgeous – the man I saw a few months ago in the hospital basement. He remembered me. Took one look at me and that was it!

We had dinner at a pub called The Anglers Arms, about half an hour away as his super vintage sports car goes. We talked and talked like we were intimate friends who'd been parted for too long. He told me about his childhood, how he always felt like he was surplus to requirements in his parents' house, too big and brash and noisy for them. Then he asked why I was a nurse, he said I wasn't like most of them and I told him I knew that. 'They think I'm a snob because I keep apart from them and read books and talk properly. Actually I could have gone to uni, I got a place at Newcastle to do Eng Lit, but I really wanted to get clean away, earn my own living and never have to see my family again.'

'That bad?'

I said yes, but didn't tell him about the old man – even mentioning him makes my skin crawl – or my mother who should have, no actually who must have known what he was doing to me. She knew and she didn't make him stop.

I'll never forgive her for that. She can send me emails and letters as much as she likes, but our relationship is over. Mac wasn't shocked. He doesn't get on with his family either, so he quite understood what I was saying.

DUNCAN WAS MILDLY pleased to see his mother, and extremely pleased to be taken to a restaurant in Truro, plus three of his friends, for a blow-out meal. The friends, another boy and two girls, seemed almost unnaturally polite and sophisticated. Tamara wondered what had changed young people since her own rebellious and argumentative teenage years. She wouldn't have dreamed of introducing her parents to her own friends. She remembered giving her parents hell. Now here she was, a parent, mortified to think of her younger self.

'We can't stay late, Mum, we're down for helping out at a lecture.'

'Oh? An interesting one?'

'Dunno.' He held out a flyer.

It was called 'Crime and Punishment, Our Changing Values', and pictures of an actual hanging were promised. Tamara was about to say it was disgusting when she noticed the name of the lecturer – an old acquaintance from before she was married.

'Are you allowed to bring a guest?'

'Absolutely!' one girl said, and the other one added, 'We've been trying to get more punters to come, but most people have other things to do on a Saturday evening.'

THE LECTURE HALL, on a Saturday evening, was half full, if that. The Head of Languages, who had invited Jonathan Solomon, broadcaster turned academic, made no allusion to the empty seats in his introduction of the speaker.

Seated in the third row from the front Tamara looked at him with surprise, even incredulity. He'd been an aspiring journalist/TV star when she had last met him, the son of a writer with whom she'd made friends during a rather dramatic Egyptian holiday. Now, not quite quarter of a century on, she saw a different person, one who didn't give a damn what he looked like. So he looked exactly what he was, a provincial professor whose mind was on higher things than his appearance. Patchily shaved, with old style unimproved teeth and wearing unmatching dark blue trousers and jacket, a crumpled shirt and a time-expired tie. The young Jonty Solomon would never have recognized himself.

I don't even know if Max is still alive, she thought. Max Solomon, first met on that action-packed trip, had been a writer though when she met him, used the past tense about his calling. He had been unable to write for a long time and even given up hope of doing so again. As it turned out, the excitement of those ten days in Egypt had a dramatic effect on him. Words poured over the psychic dam behind which they had been penned up: poems, essays, polemics and pleas for peace; a novel. Tamara had been dismayed by her own inability to read Max's work. She didn't doubt its merit, so unanimously proclaimed, and once or twice found herself re-reading a line or a paragraph to remember it, but the language was heavy with decoration, the narrative not so much driven as gently escorted down rambling by-ways. These unreadable (at least, by her) books were shortlisted for every conceivable literary prize, and had won several of them.

Jonty began his talk.

'I may be a professor now, but I started my career as a TV journalist, and that taught me how to catch an audience's attention. So, take a look at this.' He clicked the gadget in his hand

and the screen was filled what looked at first like an abstract painting, Gradually the lines and colours rearranged themselves in the watcher's eye. It was the face of a man, or perhaps woman, tongue protruding from the drawn back lips, face engorged with blood, eyes protruding from their sockets. A rope was tightly twisted round the neck. As the audience realized they were looking at the dead face of a hanged man, the sound of disgust swelled in the lecture hall. But as they looked, it became clear that it was a painting, not a photograph, which made it less appalling though no less gross.

'This is a portrait, dating from the late nineteenth century. It shows the last moments of a man who was hanged for trespass. A harsh punishment for doing something we no longer regard as a crime. And that's what I'm going to talk about this evening: our changing view of criminality. There's a lot of history about the punishment of actions and behaviour that we don't consider criminal at all. For instance, this picture of the Martyr's Memorial in Oxford shows the site where four men were burnt at the stake for their religious beliefs. This was five centuries back – and it was not an era when people were respectful of other peoples' traditions, customs or religions. If anyone had ventured to suggest any anti-discrimination legislation, he or she would have been regarded as dangerously insane.

'In this next picture you see a perfectly ordinary public lavatory. In 1954 a peer of the realm, a homosexual – which wasn't yet called "gay" – was sent to prison for having sex with another man in this place. It was against the law to be gay right up until the 1970s.'

Up flashed a photo of a dumpy little housewife with a shopping bag. 'This respectable looking woman was sentenced to imprisonment because she had performed abortions – which until the 1970s was a breach of the law in all circumstances.

'This notice advertises a hanging. Executions were public events until the nineteenth century, and hanging was the sentence for surprisingly many crimes. Trespass, witchcraft, blasphemy – did you know that blasphemy was a crime right up until 2008? And so was witchcraft until the middle of the twentieth century.

'Back to this invitation to a hanging. The condemned man had tried to take his own life, but it didn't work. In some countries, in some societies, taking one's own life was and still is seen as virtuous and honourable – think of the Japanese Samurai, or Socrates in ancient Athens. In our country, suicide used to be a criminal offence. So this man was nursed back to health simply so that he could then be flogged and after that, executed. Hanged by the neck until he was dead.'

All this is just the sort of thing the boys enjoy, Tamara thought. But a few rows in front of her several girls were saying 'Gross!' and 'Yuk' and other disgusted monosyllables. One of them, a tall thin blonde, rather ostentatiously got up and pushed her way along to the centre aisle and then out of the auditorium.

Jonty was saying that the hangman was kept busy. 'For instance, in 1723 Parliament passed a new law known as The Black Act which created fifty – five oh – new hanging offences. Very few of them would be regarded as criminal or even wrong nowadays, and they certainly aren't illegal. Now, you could just tell yourselves that society was more primitive and we are more civilized. Or you could ask, if we are shocked by the past, what will our descendants think of us? What do we forbid that they will take for granted as a normal, accepted and legal part of life? Or what do we take for granted that will shock future generations? Any ideas? Anyone? Yes – you in the third row at the back. Tell us your name.'

'Morwenna Trembath.'

'Good Cornish name. All right, Morwenna, shoot.'

'Eating animals.'

'Good one, Morwenna – you could very well be right. Though I doubt if it will become a crime in my lifetime. Anyone else?'

'Wasting natural resources like fuel and water,' an un-named youth called.

'Very likely, I'd say. Good.'

'Corporal punishment – smacking kids,' a boy's breaking voice contributed.

'Not yet a crime in this country, but certainly disapproved of.'

'Sending little kids to boarding school.'

'That's more a social than a legal question, but I take your point.'

The lecture was turned into a discussion, a technique that Tamara admired since it meant that by her reckoning the speaker had needed to prepare no more than ten or fifteen minutes, after which his audience did all the work. His subject, of course, was one that was likely to excite interest. Not so easy in her own case. All the same, it was worth thinking about. As was the original thesis.

The speaker had carefully and cleverly enthused the young audience, which went on talking and arguing even after he had stepped down from the podium.

'Illegal to be gay – how dumb is that?'

'Or terminating a pregnancy!'

'Or forming a trade union.'

'Well, what about ...'

'Tamara Hoyland, as I live and breathe! D'you remember me? What are you doing here?'

'Of course I do. And one of my sons is at school here.'

'Can we have a drink or a sandwich or something? I'm catching the sleeper train so there's some time to fill in.'

It wasn't the most gracious of invitations, but it was too late for Duncan to be allowed out of school now, so there wasn't anything better to do.

Jonty Solomon had been rather attractive when younger and had a job that required him to take an interest in other people. But it seemed that he'd given up TV for academia quite a long time ago. He gave her a move-by-move account of his career, a title-by-title account of his publications. He listed the names of his wives (three, so far) his four children and his dog.

Then, in the tone of a man doing his duty, he said, 'What about you? Do you ... do anything?'

Now that he'd asked, she couldn't be bothered to tell him. She sipped the warmish Chardonnay and said, 'Just tell me first, how's your father?'

'He's happy as a pig in shit,' Jonty said. 'He loves being lionized. And he's won enough prizes to be comfortably off.'

'I'm glad. I really liked your father.'

'He liked you. Did you know he'd gone to see your boss to say how wonderful you were?'

'No, I'd no idea. My boss? Who d'you mean? At English Heritage?'

'I don't think so, was that where you worked? I thought he said something else, department of ... I don't remember.'

'Environment.'

'I knew it began with an E.'

Neatly bringing the conversation back to himself, he started to complain that his father had never made a similar effort for him.

Tamara left as soon as she could, explaining that she had to check in at the hotel she'd booked in Buriton before they locked up for the night.

The weather was wild. Heading towards Buriton, directly into the storm, Tamara didn't dare to drive fast and even at a steady slow pace it was something of a fight to keep the car in its lane. Luckily nobody else seemed to be out, the road was deserted. As she progressed slowly westwards she found herself thinking about Jonathan Solomon's list of forbidden behaviour. It was long and looked at from this vantage point irrational, and the punishments specified had been cruel. It was hard to believe that it was so recently that many of them had been enforced. Equally, it was amazing that in such a relatively short period of time nearly all the taboos once taken so seriously had disappeared. Something was bound to take the place of those obsolete prohibitions – but what? And what customs taken for granted now would seem equally oppressive and foolish to posterity?

It was getting on for eleven o'clock as Tamara drove into Buriton. The place was like a ghost town apart from the usual gang of bored youths hanging around the war memorial in the central market square. Otherwise Tamara saw nobody on her way to the hotel. It was the one where visiting lecturers and visiting parents were usually housed by the university and Tamara, who had visited Buriton several times when she was working for English Heritage, had stayed there before. Pulling up in the car park she noticed a nearly full moon, and its restless reflection in the choppy sea below. There was the eighteenth-century observatory and lighthouse, the building whose picture symbolized Buriton, a light on in all but the top floor where dedicated scientists still watched the universe. And here, thank goodness – Tamara heaved a big sigh – here was the hotel, a receptionist, the door key. Suddenly she was completely exhausted.

Tired or not, she had to make sure about her mother. 'Just checking that she's OK,' she said to the night nurse who answered the call. Uncomprehending sounds were the only reply. Night nurses never had English as a first language. 'My mother,' she repeated patiently, clearly. 'Mrs Hoyland. Room 226.'

'OK.'

'D'you mean she's OK?'

But that was not what the woman had meant. Another buzz, and another receiver picked up. 'Yes yes yes yes ...' Not stopping. Unstoppable. Her mother's voice.

After several minutes Tamara put her phone down. Presumably the dozy night nurse, or somebody would go along and deal with it. With the vacant mind and persistent body. With her mother.

The comparisons made earlier in the evening came into her mind. Who was to say which laws and customs were right?

In Lapland the very old members of a tribe walk away into the snowy distance and are never seen again. In Japan honour attaches to suicide, not shame. Even here, animals are put down in old age. It was thought cruel to keep them alive, with no hope of improvement in their condition.

Was it cruel? To her and Alexandra, to their brothers, yes it was cruel. But to Olga herself? Tamara realized that she had no idea what her mother would have wanted.

But she was perfectly certain about what she would not have wanted. Olga would not have wanted this.

Tamara was tired. The day had not gone exactly as planned. She'd intended to drop in on Thea, and if she was out just sit there until she came back. But it didn't matter, tomorrow would do fine. After all, it wasn't as if she was expected. Or as if Thea was going to be very pleased to see her.

Her room looked towards the bay, with the lighthouse in the foreground. It was brilliantly white, extremely picturesque and featured in every guide book to Cornwall, but simply by remaining standing, it had turned into a fake. It was several years since the announcement had been made that the lighthouse was obsolete. There was no longer any need for its sweeping light, or for the rhythmic beeps of its foghorn, since all had been superseded by digital technology. It was sentimentality that kept it going. But even the least sentimental of visitors might take pleasure in the pattern of light sweeping rhythmically round the bay, might watch and count it, be almost hypnotized ... be sent to sleep by it.

DISCUSSING THE STAFF was inevitably part of the daily programme. Not much to do except gossip, when you're old and it's cold outside.

Most of the residents liked the new doctor – not that it would matter if they didn't. Take it or leave it; these days you thought yourself lucky if any medic had time for you.

'Macintosh listens to me. The others always make me think I'm holding them up from more important patients than me.'

'That little redhead was all right.'

'Doctor James, if you please! Sallie, she's called.'

'She meant well. But she was always in a hurry, always chasing her own tail – I don't think she ever finishes a sentence, in and out like a hurricane. She's gone to work in A and E!'

There was competition between the residents for the attention of the more interesting or attractive staff. The man settled back in his wing chair and said, 'I don't know about that, she's a sensible little thing really. We were discussing Northern Ireland the other day, over a cup of tea in my room.'

Tea! Political discussions! Those were trump cards. Rather weakly, the woman reminded him that they had seen the last of his sensible little thing.

At the same time as residents discussed the staff, the members of staff were having a similar conversation. One of the health-care assistants said it wasn't good for patients – 'sorry, I mean residents' – to get too fond of a doctor because the medic would move on. 'They always do.'

A colleague disagreed. 'Love them and leave them.'

Another said the new broom swept clean. Doctor Macintosh, for example, had realized that Mrs Olivieri had a problem with her vocal chords and was sending her for tests. Dr James had accepted the huskiness as natural to the old woman. New eyes, new insights.

Dora Peasgood died in her sleep that night. She'd been in her late nineties, and had seen a doctor within the last two weeks, so there was no need for an inquest. Dr Macintosh wrote 'heart failure' on the death certificate and handed it to Mrs Bussell, saying 'I always wish that I could simply say the cause of death was "old age". Her brain and body were worn out. Please send her family my condolences.'

Dora had not been one of the more popular members of the community, and there was on average a death a month, but the loss of one of their number always led to an atmosphere of fear and despondency. Who's next? the other residents wondered, knowing that none of them would be leaving except by dying. One of the residents had tried to get a sweepstake going. He'd got very few takers before the management heard of it, and swooped right-eously down on the old man. Having been a colonel in an infantry regiment he wasn't accustomed to being foiled or rebuked, but he took it like a lamb and after that kept his speculations to himself. Which was a pity, since he'd settled on Mrs Peasgood as the next and would have won a tidy sum if they had managed a wager. In fact, as often seemed to happen in this and other care homes, one death led to another. The croaky Mrs Olivieri's cold became pneumonia. Her living will expressly forbade the use of antibiot-ics, a surprise to her friends, but apparently not to the staff. 'Her life was hanging by a thread,' one of the nursing assistants said dramatically. 'It's a miracle she lived so long.'

GOOGLING MAX SOLOMON brought up a great deal of informa-tion about the Nobel Prize. Tamara was pleased to think of her melancholy companion on the trip to Egypt becoming rich and presumably more cheerful.

She had enjoyed Max's company in Egypt, as he'd seemed to enjoy hers, but it was a real surprise to learn that he'd identi-fied Tom Black as Tamara's boss, and known where to find him. Perhaps, she thought, they knew each other already? Maybe they were old friends?

She was in the kind of hotel that did not provide charging points for guests' electronic equipment, but did supply a large leather folder containing, amazingly, blotting paper, which Tamara had thought long since extinct. How long since I wrote and posted an actual letter? she wondered. She pulled the paper (Wedgwood blue, with deckle edges) towards her, and began trying to compose a request to the Nobel Laureate.

Dear Max,

You will be surprised to hear from me after so long but I hope you remember me from our Egyptian adventures more than 20 years ago.

I had the pleasure of meeting your son today, and he told me that you were (or are) acquainted with my former boss, Tom Black of Department E. I would very much like to see him again, but he seems to have disappeared without trace, as indeed has Department E itself. Is there any chance that you could let me have his contact details, or put me in touch with him in person?

I would love to see you again too. Meanwhile, all best wishes from Tamara Hoyland Hope.

How cross Alastair would be if he discovered that she was even thinking about going back to that secret work. They had originally met when she was on a case, but he didn't like her connection to an undercover world, and had once told her that she was at her worst when working for Department E. He much preferred her public face, the archaeologist, wife and mother.

Tamara had never replied that she much preferred his conventional face, as a lab bound scientist, to that of the distant explorer who was saving the world thousands of miles away. But these last few days a revelation had been creeping up on her. She said aloud, 'I know what's wrong with me. I'm bored, bored – bored through and through. I've had enough of security and domesticity and being a good wife and mother. It's time to let out the adventurer. Adventuress? If I don't run Tom Black to ground, goodness knows where or how I'll do it. But it's time for me to get back into that world.'

'It's called locked-in syndrome,' Helge said.

'I've never heard of it.'

'Are you sure? Someone must have mentioned it, surely.'

'I don't think so. Darling, come over here a minute – have you ever heard of this syndrome that Helge's talking about? Locked-in syndrome? What is it exactly, Helge?'

'David is a tetraplegic. That means that all four limbs are paralyzed, so is his torso, so is everything on his head. The facial muscles cannot move, the tongue, the vocal cords, everything is disabled, turned off. But in some cases, and I think your boy may be one of them, the brain is not disabled. Locked inside the useless body, someone is still there.'

'But that is terrible, dreadful, it's even worse than we've always thought! It can't have happened to him! You mean that my boy's brain is still working in there, he's asking me to help him, that is so dreadful.' Tears were pouring down her face, her body shuddered, almost in convulsions of misery and pain.

'I'm afraid you're mistaken, Helge,' Davy's father said. His voice was level but he was obviously furious. 'Don't get your hopes up, darling, he was tested for exactly this, several times. The specialists found no sign of comprehension.'

'But his eyes move.' Helge murmured. 'Look. I believe there is hope of establishing some kind of communication with him.'

'Oh, if you could do that ... If only he could tell me what he's feeling.'

'There are precedents, it has been done. I'll recommend the book to you if I may, it is an extraordinary memoir originally in French. The author was a journalist, he'd been the editor of *Elle* magazine and was absolutely top of his profession when he had something like a major stroke and woke up to find himself in a hospital completely paralyzed. Eventually somebody realized that there was one tiny part of his body that could still move, his left eyelid. So someone devised an incredibly labour-intensive method for him to communicate, they would hold in front of his face the letters of the alphabet one by one, and when he blinked that left eyelid it meant that was the letter that he wanted. Almost unbelievable that he wrote a whole book in this way. It's called *The Diving Bell and the Butterfly*.'

'Davy, Davy – blink now my darling, blink to show you understand.' She leant over the bed in a frenzy of eagerness, scrutinizing his face, ready to catch the tiniest movement. But none came. It gradually dawned upon her that it wasn't going to happen. Disappointment flooded through her.

'It is likely to take a very long time. Don't be too optimistic at first. Look, why don't you leave me with him? We might as well start getting used to another. And don't give up hope, I still think we should be able to communicate in some way with the poor boy.'

WHOEVER SAID WE weren't supposed to enjoy our jobs? Working in the Wrinklies Warehouse, I'm happier than I've ever been. It's unexpected. It's luck. Pure luck.

I met Mac. And Mac met me. Apart, we're just ordinary people with big ideas.

Together, we make the ideas come true. We make each other into the people we were born to be. Just as there are chemicals that are absolutely innocuous on their own, and absolutely lethal if combined with one other substance, so there are people who would fantasize and imagine but never actually do anything until they meet the one person, perhaps the only person, in the world, who enables or encourages or inspires them to make their most secret dreams into reality. Examples? There are lots; let's start with the Moors Murderers, Myra Hindley and Ian Brady, whose mutual egging on empowered them both. Or what about Bonnie and Clyde?

I'm not sure that I or Mac would ever have actually done much alone. It would have gone on being fantasy-time for ever. Which is what Mac says too. TBH, neither of us is very brave on our own, and neither are we very clear about what we want. But together we take off, we fly.

Of course we've both taken tiny independent steps. I've adjusted the odd dial on a life-support machine. Mac's put some wrinklies out of their misery. He was surprised by the high it gave him.

But the excitement of a joint enterprise – that's something else. Somehow, quite naturally we enthuse each other, ideas sparking between us like I was the match and he the box. Ingenious notions that begin by seeming completely impractical and fantastic and after we've thrown them back and forward between us come out sensible and do-able. So we've got exciting plans. And here we're in the best possible position. No shortage of potential clients round here, all that's necessary is to be clever and brave – and to make sure that anything written down isn't incriminating.

But Mac says we have to wait. His next priority, he's going to need my help, is an inmate who used to know him in another life. He's wants her gone before she recognizes him in this one. Or before one of her family does. I don't ask him why 'cos I know he'll tell me when he's good and ready, and when he does, I'll reciprocate with my own confidences.

And it's not as though we'll be doing anything wrong. It's like abortion, as he explained to me. That used to be a crime and any medic doing it would be struck off, tried, imprisoned, disgraced – not so long ago, either. Right up till the 1970s. Mum was a girl then, it's not like it was the Dark Ages. And now nobody thinks twice about it.

Or being gay. Look how that's changed.

Well, it's only a matter of time till wrinklies will be allowed to choose to go. All we're doing is anticipating the legal reforms. And if we happen to enjoy it – well, would the world be a better place if we were unhappy in our work?

'NOW THEN DAVY, you show me. You can move your eyes. Or not move them. Now, listen to me. Move them as far as you can to one side, just to show you're hearing me. Nobody else is here, it's just you and me. Do it for Helge, you can, I know you can.'

The eyes had a squint. The whites were bloodshot, and also not really white. They looked dirty.

Helge stared and waited, and then she saw the iris, a faded blue, push itself to the side. And stay there, fixed, as she counted, one second, two seconds, three – in six, they relaxed. Whispering, she said, 'You did it, Davy, you really did it. Inside this, you're still there! Oh my God, I don't believe it! After all this time.' There were tears in her own eyes, which, after a moment spilled out down her cheeks, so she let herself slide down till she was kneeling on the floor, and buried her wet face in Davy's bedding. All those months, conscious, hearing them talk about him, it didn't bear thinking of.

LIKE MOST NON-MEDICAL people in modern Britain, Thea Crawford had had very little experience of other people dying. Her father, aged eighty-seven, had a stroke on a Monday and died on the Tuesday, before Thea could get to see him.

Eight years later her mother had tripped and fallen in the street. When Thea went to visit her the next day she was perfectly compos mentis and in a furiously bad temper.

The ambulance – 'Can you imagine that noise, a siren right in one's ears? And so uncomfortable! Clinging to that narrow bed like a limpet – I was glad when that was over, I can tell you. But you've got to get me out of here.'

She was in one of the circles of hell. 'Everybody rushing around, and so many people, one takes a blood sample, another uses the electrocardiogram, then you have an X-ray but nobody takes any notice of you. They talk over your head. I kept saying I didn't consent and nobody listened. I can't stay here, Thea. If I could walk, I'd walk out this very minute.' Thea went to talk to the ward sister, whom she found in a tiny cubby hole, a heap of papers and her sensible black shoes on the desk. She was massaging her stockinged feet.

'My mother wants to go home.'

'Oh dear no. There are still tests we've got to do. And she's not strong enough, Must have been kept going by willpower. I'm afraid your mother isn't at all well.'

'Could you tell her so yourself?'

Ruth Wade listened glumly to the programme. There were standard procedures, and she'd got herself caught up in them. Thea couldn't take her home, or, being so law-abiding, wouldn't. The next time she visited her mother, she found her attached to a machine and to a drip-stand. She turned her face away from her daughter, and muttered something inaudible. On the third day, still angry and unforgiving, she told Thea to go away, there was no point in her hanging round, living uncomfortably in her parents' retirement cottage and filling in time. 'Go back to work for heavens' sake, we don't want you losing your job.'

'But don't you want me to—'

'No. Go.'

Things had never been easy between Thea and her mother. Ruth was jealous of Thea's career. Ruth had dreamed of being the curator of a great museum and, uniquely for a woman, was actually in charge of a department at the National Museum of Scotland in Edinburgh when Magnus Wade asked her to marry him. It was 1941. He was a naval officer about to leave for the frozen waters of the North Sea and Baltic. The Russian convoys were notoriously dangerous. Ruth loved him. She couldn't refuse. It had not occurred to her that her post was a civil service one, and that women civil servants had to resign on getting married. It would be many years before the marriage bar was lifted, too late for Ruth to start again.

Looking after a house and a husband was simply not enough for her irritable intelligence, nor was looking after house, husband and baby. She filled in the hours, reading, knitting, bottling fruit and vegetables, doing 'good works' as she called them, but she had been foiled, as a woman in an as yet unliberated society, of realizing her personal ambitions. She became increasingly embittered. Life had always been a disappointment, as long as she could remember. Nothing would change that now. And while she was naturally proud of her daughter's success, she also felt pangs – no, *waves* – coursing through her, waves of jealousy, envy, resentment, that the next generation had all the chances and opportunities that her own had been denied.

Ruth's daughter Thea had realized all her mother's ambitions. She had enjoyed undreamed-of opportunities, achieved professional success at an unexpected level. But there was nobody else to take charge of her mother once she needed to be looked after. Ruth left hospital and moved into the room that had been John's, as his grandmother had called him from birth saying that 'Clovis' stuck in her craw.

Thea was desperately trying to think of an unhurtful way to get Ruth to move out again when she collapsed in the kitchen and was taken back into hospital.

And when the results of the tests came back, it suddenly became clear that hospital was where she would be staying. Once recovered from major surgery she had chemotherapy which gave her sores in her mouth, a rash like a burn across her body, the itching was unbearable, and extreme fatigue. As soon as one problem was resolved, another occurred or recurred. More surgery. More medication. No privacy. No control over her own actions. She was told what to do as if she were a child: wake, eat, bath, dress; share your bedroom with a stranger. In effect, Thea sometimes thought, during the final year of her life, Ruth had been tortured to death.

Thea tried to think dispassionately about this realization, like a scholar, not an undutiful daughter. Ruth had been caught up in a process hardly known until the twentieth century: the long medical battle against an incurable condition. There is no victory possible against dementia, advanced cancer or organ failure, since death trumps all, but that inescapable truth doesn't stop the medical profession trying and their patients hoping.

Thea remembered those two years more vividly than she would have chosen. In her own 'living will' and in the official advance directive she had written that if found unconscious she was not to be taken to hospital; no surgery was to be permitted. 'I had rather die' she'd added, and meant it. After the number of graves, grave goods and skeletons Thea had excavated in her life, she truly believed that she was not afraid of death, only of the process of dying. Which brought her thoughts, in a neat circle, back to square one.

WHEN HELGE ARRIVED for work the first morning she had to run the gauntlet: curious stares from the receptionist, the residents, the nurses, in fact everyone who had heard of the tragic new inmate.

The problem of finding him accommodation had been solved by throwing money at it. Three times a day and twice every night a pair of agency nurses would turn Davy's dead weight of a body and replenish the drips. Once every other day a doctor would look in on him. And Helge would be with him eight hours a day, five days a week. Davy's mother had arranged for the room to be redecorated in as un-institutional a style as she could think up. The pictures from Davy's room at home, mostly marine prints, were brought over to replace the innocuous flower paintings, and hung within his line of sight. His own curtains were cut down to fit the windows. There was a comfortable sofa for visitors and a music centre loaded with the tunes he used to love.

The target of all this effort remained unresponsive. Inert. As one of the agency nurses offensively remarked, he seemed brain dead.

'Much they know about it – I don't think!' Helge hissed. She perched her bottom on the narrow windowsill while the last of the accumulated junk was carried in. 'I'll deal with it all, just leave it,' she said, and heaved a relieved sigh when the last stranger left the room. 'I thought they'd never go,' she said, plumping herself down on the bed beside her patient.

'You know what, Davy boy. Now I know you can hear and understand me, we'll be having proper conversations in no time.' She put her hand in front of the bulging eyes, and moved it away again. 'You've got a squint. I wonder if you did before. Some people do.'

She took his face in both her hands and moved his head so he was facing the window. 'Look, can you see outside? We'll get you out there soon. Somehow. I wonder which is the dominant eye. Davy, if you're hearing me, if you understand, move your eyes again, move them like you did before. Move them just anyhow, try. Come on, try it for Helge, you can move your eyes, Davy, they're moving now. Is that you showing me they can? Good. That's brilliant. Now show me you can stop them moving too. No? I don't believe you. Come on, show Helge. Keep them still for a moment. No, they are swivelling like – like a wind-up toy. Come on Davy, aim your eyes. You can see me, can't you? And we're all alone, there's nobody else watching. Just for us, Davy, you and me against the world. Prove that you can understand what I'm saying, look into my eyes Davy, look at Helge.'

They were bloodshot, naked-looking eyes, the pupils tiny now, the lids fastened open with sticky tape, blue, with a couple of yellow specks in the right eye. She watched it moving from side-to-side, an uneven, rhythmless dance. And then ...

'It's a miracle,' she breathed, clasping his inert hand in her warm grasp. The eye was momentarily still. Both eyes. They had developed a squint, and can't have been focused, but the response was undeniable. He'd heard her, he'd done what she said.

The staring blue eyes had swivelled right and then left and then right again. 'Yes!' She stood up, her clenched fists above her head, grinning madly at the empty room. 'A result, that's what it is, a result!'

She sat down on the bed again. 'Show me what you can do Davy boy. Can you look up? Down? At me? My God, you can, you really can! I knew there was someone at home, first time I saw you, I knew it!' She got up and danced rapidly round the room, too elated and excited to keep still. 'Ages and ages you've been lying there and nobody's realized you were conscious. Listening. Taking it all in. Right? All that talk of turning off the machines or keeping them on, your parents, the medics, you've heard it all. Now we've got to work out what you heard, how you can tell us. We've got to find a way to communicate Davy boy.' She did a few twirls in the empty space by the window, her red hair and her blue overall flying out behind her. 'I'll tell you what, Davy boy, we'll keep this quiet for a bit. Our secret, mmm? It'll only upset them that they never noticed it for themselves.'

The tape that held the eyelids open had to be removed every quarter hour to lubricate the skin and eyeballs. The hospital doctor had explained it to Helge. They wouldn't normally tape any patient's eyes open, paraplegic or not. They had decided to do so in Davy's case because his eyes were the only moving part of his body. But without the frequent soothing and smoothing of the eyelids on the eyes, they would become dry and painful – if the boy still felt pain, or felt anything, which the doctor seriously doubted. Eye drops could be used for extra lubrication, but every fifteen minutes the eyes were to be untaped and allowed to fall closed.

My God, Helge thought, if he'd not had a doctor who insisted on taping them open he'd have been lying there blind. Aware, conscious, and deprived of all his senses. A knock at the door, immediately followed by someone coming in.

'Oh hi, d'you need...?'

'Hi, you must be Helge. I'm Gloria, and it's me that'll be doing nights for your patient this week. So I thought I'd come and say hi.'

'Oh isn't that nice. Davy, look, this is Gloria ... what's wrong, Davy? Does something hurt?' Davy's eyes were swivelling as if in panic. 'It's all right, Davy, Helge's here, don't you worry....' She crooned comfort to the unresponsive carcass.

'You don't really think he understands, do you?'

'Actually, Gloria, I do think so, even if he can never express it. You will treat him like a person, won't you?'

'Rather than an animal? Or a hunk of dead meat?'

'You know what I mean.'

'Yes, I do. Don't worry, we'll be fine. Won't we, Davy boy?'

When Gloria had gone, Helge packed her rucksack to go home. I'm really excited, she thought. This is going to be mega. Maxi-mega. Sensational.

Helge's sensation. Helge's secret.

She saw the words in her mind's eye, emblazoned on a poster, a book jacket, a newspaper headline. She said, 'A sensation. A phenomenon. Just you wait.'

TEA WAS ALREADY laid when he arrived so all he had to do was make a ritual protest – 'You really shouldn't have bothered' – and push the trolley towards the high-seated wing chair, where she sat. Coffee cake, chocolate biscuits, and 'you like cucumber sand-wiches, don't you, Doctor?'

'You've got a good memory.'

'There's nothing wrong with my memory. It's about the only bit of me left that still works properly.'

She managed to lift the teapot using both hands and did not spill very much as she filled two cups. 'I like to see a man eat,' she said. 'My husband had such a hearty appetite it was a pleasure to cook for him.'

She had told him about her husband and his hearty appetite several times, but the doctor nodded sympathetically and looked attentive as she again described her life before he died, when her days were busy and meaningful. 'You should have seen me then, Doctor, running around like a mad thing to get everything done. I don't think I ever took a day off, but then I don't think I ever wanted to. Please help yourself to the cake, it's your favourite, coffee. Of course, in those days there was so much to do. We had all the staff in for their dinner almost every day. Sixteen, seven-teen, sometimes even twenty of them, and I did all the cooking.'

He nodded and smiled, he ate and then he ate more.

'You know Doctor, when you come here it's the highlight of my week. You are so kind to me, letting me rabbit on like this.'

Stuffed like a turkey for Christmas, he forced himself to swallow the last mouthful of chocolate biscuit and said, 'Well, let's be having a look at you.'

Knuckles and finger joints hugely swollen; increasingly incon-tinent; decreasingly able to walk and entirely dependent on the kindness of neighbours for shopping; she was a prime candidate for a place inside the care home which, at the age of seventy-four, she absolutely refused to consider. No children, apparently no relations; at least, she never mentioned any. What was the point of going on living?

'This looks painful,' he said.

'As a matter of fact, it hurts dreadfully.' Her face had crumpled and tears began to flow. 'I do try not to complain.'

'Well, let's see what we can do about that.'

It wasn't easy to find a vein but he did in the end, and she thanked him with passionate gratitude as the merciful morphine began to work.

He loaded the tea trolley, putting both their cups and saucers on the top tray, tidying up the raw edge of the cake. Then he went to the window and drew the curtains against the gathering dusk.

Someone was knocking at the front door. Not the brass knocker in the shape of a hand, but knuckles sounding out the familiar pattern. Rat a tat tat. He walked to the door and opened it.

'Oh!' A little woman, her face about level with his lapels. 'Oh Doctor, it's you! I was going to check on Rosemary.'

She was trying to see past his bulky figure. 'I'll just have a quick—'

'Better not,' he said firmly. 'We haven't finished.'

'Oh, well, in that case, of course, later perhaps, I could look round ...'

'Tomorrow,' he said firmly. 'She's very tired, when I've gone she'll be asleep. Come in the morning.'

'Yes. Yes of course, just as you say.' A sudden screech. 'Goodnight dear!' And more quietly, 'God bless you for coming, Doctor. I'll look in tomorrow morning.'

He put the door chain on and shot the inner bolt. Do not disturb, he thought as he went back into the sitting room. Rosemary Maitland was slumped in the wing chair, her eyes closed, her breathing irregular and very slow. Several times she stopped breathing, as if she had forgotten to do it, and several times after a long silence she did eventually take another breath.... He'd been so concentrated on her eyes and her mouth, it was as if he needed reminding that this was – this had been – a real woman rather than a forensic enterprise. Dr Macintosh's eyes were fixed on his patient, whose breathing became softer and less hoarse until, really relatively fast, she ceased to breathe at all.

It was a very peaceful end. No jerking, he thought. No involuntary movement. No pain. Equally, there had been no drama, no extravagance.

If he was Greek he'd be tearing his clothes.

Better just make sure, he thought, and went through the little house without touching, turning on lights or standing by a window. No, all perfectly safe, nobody was there. On his way out he glanced in through the open door of the sitting room. Then he moved to open the front door before calling. 'Goodbye Mrs Maitland, I'll be back tomorrow.' Then he paused, looked like a man listening, and called, 'What's that? What did you say?' Another pause. 'Oh – I'm not quite sure I'm afraid. I'll try to make it before lunch. See you then. Bye now.'

He pulled the front door shut and walked down the path, not at all surprised to find that the neighbour was hovering by his car.

'How is the poor dear now, Doctor?'

'I'm afraid she's been in a good deal of pain,' he replied.

'I know, it's such a shame, one can't help noticing. Perhaps I ought to just go and ...'

'Leave it for tonight, don't disturb her now, she said she was going to bed as soon as I left.'

'Oh, she can do with every moment of sleep, I'll keep clear for a while.'

'Probably best,' he said. 'I'm sure she'd appreciate it if you go round in the morning.'

The neighbour was called Pinkie Thornton. After breakfast the next day she picked some fragrant roses from her garden, went back into the house to tidy herself up because that was the sort of thing Rosemary noticed, walked down her own garden path and up her neighbour's and knocked loudly on the front door. After a moment she knocked again, before lifting a particular stone in the rockery, feeling around underneath it with her fingertips and drawing out a key. Then she rapped her knuckles on the door – long short, short long – and let herself in, calling out as she did so, 'Don't worry, it's only me.'

Rosemary Maitland had not gone to bed the previous night. She was still seated in the high, winged chair in the sitting room, still fully dressed in the previous day's clothes. But her head lolled forward, chin to chest, and she had lost control of bladder and bowel.

'Oh my dear,' Pinkie Thornton whispered. Being a thriller fan, she'd read about finding dead bodies. She'd always known that she might be the one to find Rosemary's and had tried to prepare herself for it. But she had never actually seen a human corpse before and it had a violent effect on her. She realized that she was breathing in little short gasps, her hands were shaking, her lips were trembling. 'Oh, my dear,' she repeated, and found to her own surprise that tears were trickling down her cheeks.

What am I supposed to do now? she asked herself. She knew the answer perfectly well but just at this moment was so discombobulated that she couldn't recall what it was. Should I dial 999, or ring the doctor's surgery, or try to get in touch with Rosemary's family? Pinkie realized that she was shaking so much that she must sit down, and collapsed gratefully into a brocade wing chair. It was very warm in the room, with the gas fire still on. Momentarily closing her eyes, Pinkie actually went into the sleep of the shocked, her head tilted back at an uncomfortable angle, to be woken by knocking at the front door and a loud voice calling 'Mrs Maitland, madame, I come in, all right?'

For a moment Pinkie couldn't think where she was. Then she struggled to pull herself onto her feet just as the new arrival came through the door. A thin little woman with bright, inquisitive black eyes: Rosemary's carer.

'I think there's something wrong.' But before she could say anything else, the other woman had seen for herself. She took Rosemary's wrist and tried to take the pulse. Then, very gently and without saying anything she used one hand and spread fingers to close the lids over Rosemary's staring eyes.

'Poor lady,' she said. 'You find her, madame?' The carer was from the Philippines and whoever had taught her English had done so as if his pupils were going to England to get jobs in a stately home circa 1911. 'You call police already? Doctor?'

'No, I haven't done any of that, I felt too upset.'

'OK, now I call.'

Pinkie tried to pull herself together, literally by standing up and buttoning her coat.

'I don't need to stay, you know where I am if anyone needs me.'

Two cars turned into the yard just as Pinkie was putting her front door key in the lock. Pinkie went into her kitchen and put the kettle on. Then she walked across to the telephone to cancel her lunch date, a regular monthly meal that she and an old school friend had been sharing for the last few years. 'I simply don't feel up to it,' she admitted.

'You've had a shock. And at our age it's not so easy to get over. Make yourself a cup of something hot, heat up the sitting room and have a decent rest.' Which was good advice and Pinkie was taking it, dozing on the sofa when she was brutally woken by banging on the front door.

'All right, all right, I'm coming.' She lurched and stumbled to the front door. Unsteady on my poor old pins, she thought.

Someone was watching her, kneeling down outside and peering through the letter box. When the door was open she saw that it was a young man in some sort of blue uniform.

'Stephen Collis, Police Liaison,' he announced, holding up a card that, without glasses, was just a blur to Pinkie. But behind him she saw two police cars, one with lights flashing, and official-seeming figures were talking on the pavement.

'Come in,' she said. 'Sit you down. This will be about Rosemary. Mrs Maitland.'

'We were informed that you found her.'

'It was such a shock. She seemed all right yesterday, really cheerful in fact. I was quite surprised. Anyway, I'd done her shopping, we had an arrangement, I'd go to the supermarket and get what she needed as well as my own things, and she would pay for a taxi to bring me home. Yesterday she wanted a cake, and biscuits, because the doctor was coming at teatime. Dr Macintosh. She always had an eye for a good-looking man, did Rosemary.' At this point Pinkie began to weep again. 'I shouldn't have said that, you didn't write it down? Please forget what I said, will you? Can you? I don't want to speak ill of the dead, specially not Rosemary, she was a good friend to me.'

'So when you went round to her house this morning ...'

'I always looked in on her when she was a bit poorly.'

'She'd been unwell? More so than usually?'

'I thought so. She never complained, stiff upper lip and all that – her father had been in the Indian army and brought her up to behave like a little soldier. But I could tell when she was in pain. And she'd asked the doctor to call. But I didn't realize how ill she was. If only I'd known I could have ... I don't know what I'd have done. But I wouldn't have left her to die alone.' Sobbing, she wiped her eyes with a sodden handkerchief. 'Nobody ought to die alone,' she sobbed. 'It's what I always dreaded, living here on my own. Who'll be there for me when I wasn't there for Rosemary? Who? Who?' Pinkie's tears turned into loud wails and her hands began to tear at her hair and her jersey, like the heroine of a Greek tragedy rending her clothes.

A PERSON WHO never cooked without a recipe and read *Vogue* as if it were an instruction book was unlikely to take her own life without acquiring instructions telling her how to do it. A surprising amount of advice was available, books on open sale not

173

only through the internet but in shops on the high street. Detailed information on how best to commit suicide, written in the same style and tone as a cookery book. Thea Crawford had bought herself several of them. Not all survived the first reading. One of them concentrated on increasingly peculiar methods. It was quite amusing to read about a man in Southern California who collected rattlesnakes as a hobby and allowed one of them to bite him several times, which did indeed kill him. It was depressing to read about a man who deliberately drove his car into an oncoming train at an unattended level crossing. It was truly horrifying to read about the corrosive poisons that some wretched suicides forced themselves to swallow.

Leafing through the next chapter she found numerous bad examples: people who jumped over cliffs or from high buildings, some of whom survived, injured and maimed. Others who drank household cleaning fluids and suffered agonies before dying; those who believed themselves to have found deadly poisonous plants, others who had saved up deadly poisonous pills. Poisoning oneself, it turned out, was not all that easy. Very few poisons assured death, and the chances of failure and of long-term harm were too high for anyone sensible to risk. In any case, if the pill or potion was guaranteed to kill you there would be a horrible mess to clear up. That was not something one wished to leave behind. In fact, what did one wish to leave behind?

Nothing disgusting. Nothing filthy. Was it a romantic fantasy, the idea that it was possible to fall painlessly into perpetual sleep?

A woman sleeping in a bed. A stack of envelopes on the table, addressed to family, friends, and officials. No blood, no bodily fluids, no mystery.

Thea addressed herself with professorial firmness. Get down to work, do your homework, make a decision.

She sat at her desk with a lined foolscap pad of paper and two pens. Beside her was a pile of books: *The Savage God, A Study of Suicide* by the poet Al Alvarez; The *Peaceful Pill Handbook*, by

Drs Philip Nitschke and Fiona Stewart, whose cover proclaimed 'banned in Australia'. The contents listed fatal drugs and drugs which did not guarantee death. The style was that of a cookery book. The next one was called *Final Exit* by Derek Humphry, and subtitled 'The practicalities of self-deliverance and assisted suicide for the dying'. Rather to her surprise Thea had found an enormous number of relevant books. Not all of them were instruction books. *When We Die* explained what happened to the body after death; *How We Die* was described on the cover as 'a series of portraits or analyses of dying as powerful and sensitive and unsparing and unsentimental as anything I have ever read.'

She began to make notes on the first book in the pile.

Passive or active euthanasia; suicide with someone's assistance, or suicide alone. An anecdote appeared every few pages, or a cartoon, or a little piece of verse. The author was trying to lighten the tone. The story of a Harvard professor aged seventy-nine, still working but in the last stage of cancer. One August day in 1961 he completed the index to a seven-volume collection of his scientific articles, posted it to the Harvard University Press and then shot himself. He left a note saying, 'It is not decent for Society to make a man do this to himself.'

No, Thea thought, nor to make a woman do it to herself. Surely doctors used to help their patients to the inevitable end? But that was in the days when a nurse or practice assistant would have kept her mouth shut. We are too democratic for that, nowadays, Thea thought. What medic would risk everything to help a patient escape early, when all it would take to ruin their own life was one disgruntled employee or fundamentalist nurse? No wonder the only people left to turn to were those much-publicized pedlars of death, the talk-show doctors who conceitedly call themselves deliverers as they publicize their favoured methods: canister of gas or plastic bags. She read a few more pages. Testing the method, experimenting. It all sounded like hard work. Perhaps it would be less trouble to let nature take its course. Idly turning the pages, she came upon a picture of a man wearing what looked like an enormous, transparent chef's hat. What on earth … Oh. A polythene bag to suffocate in. Fastened with bulldog clips. Charming!

She riffled through the pages, looking at chapter headings.

Helium.

Drugs.

Plastic bags.

Compression – what did that mean? Was it hanging yourself?

Starvation.

In their macabre way these books were fascinating. But they all left her with a problem: she simply couldn't see herself making the preparations described. There was something grotesque, even laughable, about the solemnity with which the mechanisms were explained; flipping through to find the illustrations, gas cylinders, to fill helium balloons, or a little ancient car described as 'test vehicle with BBQ charcoal burner', Thea found herself giggling. It seemed that the recommended method involved cylinders of an inert gas, argon, neon, nitrogen or helium, this last easily available because small tanks of the stuff were sold along with helium balloons for children's parties.

Take pliers to pull off the extra-wide rubber nozzle, connect a four-foot long piece of thin vinyl tubing to the canister and put the other end of the tubing in a plastic bag, taping it firmly to the inside.

At this point came a discussion of plastic bags and their rival merits. How big? How thick? Black, opaque or clear? 'Experience tells us that the plastic should be clear so that patient and family may see each other.'

Thea paused in her reading to muse on this sentence. Shouldn't it be 'agent', not patient? And if by some ghastly aberration the agent/patient had his/her family in the room, how could they go ahead with their plans at all?

She returned to the text, to examine the illustrations. 'Place the elasticated opening of the bag on forehead, also covering hair and ears ... lean back and turn the gas on ... when bag is fully inflated with helium [and here the illustrations showed an androgynous figure with a kind of mitre on its head and a seraphic smile] exhale, pull the bag down to neck, fasten strap snugly round the neck and inhale deeply.'

Turning the page Thea discovered that the person 'self-delivering', as the suicide was always called, must practise and rehearse repeatedly, which was a downer. Even more unenticing was the advice that when 'the person' was dead, a family member switches off the gas tank, removes the plastic bag and disposes of all this evidence.

It was impossible to see any of this as practical, sensible advice, to be followed step-by-step as one might (or indeed, had) a recipe by Elizabeth David or do-it-yourself instructions on say, gardening. Rephrase, Thea told herself. I can't read it seriously. It's too ... too undignified.

In any case, how could I possibly bring gas canisters through the college and up into these rooms? As for the idea of asking Clovis (no, sorry, she apologized to her absent son) asking John to join in was grotesque. Selfish. Out of the question.

She picked up another of her haul of textbooks. This one, which boasted on its dust jacket that it was banned in Australia, showed more pictures of gas cylinders, tall and thin like fire extinguishers, or short and fat.

Does it matter what you look like when they find you dead?

It was a question that many, perhaps most people would answer with a resounding 'No'. But Thea Crawford, who had excavated so many skeletons, her brush moving over the bone, her professional attention total – the world could have come to an end and she wouldn't have noticed, one of her assistants once said – had retained the belief that these remains must be treated with reverence, accorded due dignity until they could be re-interred. And she had always thought that even more strongly when the body had been buried adorned. The scattered beads, dulled and drained of colour by their centuries underground, a brooch, a belt buckle, such grave goods reminded the digger that this had been a person and that someone else had cared enough to send her decorated into her eternal sleep.

I don't want them to find my body looking grotesque or ridiculous, she thought. There must be a better way than that.

She shook herself physically – jerking her shoulders backwards and forwards, making her head circle and flapping her arms – and mentally, by walking to the window and breathing in the sea air.

Am I really sitting here learning how to kill myself? It's too ridiculous! Stop this, Thea, she admonished herself.

Thea had closed the outer doors – 'sported her oak' in the old-fashioned college terminology – which was supposed to be sufficient indication to anyone that she did not want to be disturbed. So why was someone knocking on the outer door? Surely nobody would open it. Was that actually someone now knocking on the inner door? Now, not knocking but actually turning the handle and trying to come in?

Really, this is intolerable!

'Who is this? What do you think the closed door means?'

The intruder was full of apologies, and, coming forward into the light, proved to be Tamara Hoyland.

'Good lord, Tamara, what are you doing here?'

'I was in Cornwall so I thought I would come and see you. Is this a bad moment?'

'It's just unexpected. Wait while I get my head round it, I was miles away.'

'I'm so sorry for interrupting your work.'

'Oh, nonsense, it's so nice to see you.'

'It seemed far too long since we met.'

'Yes indeed. So why don't you sit down? Here I think, it's just about OK, though the whole place was designed for something other than comfort. I'll just get ...' Without finishing her sentence Thea gathered up the books into a pile and took them with her into the bedroom. She was pleased to see Tamara and quite pleased to be interrupted in her macabre research, but she definitely didn't want Tamara to know what she was researching.

'IT'S GOING TO be exhausting,' Helge said. 'For me as well as you.' She had brought in a large case full of equipment. 'We'll try these out, see which suits you best. I'm excited and I bet you are even if you can't show it. But there's a lot of hard work ahead.' The first thing was to find out how much Davy could control his eyes. Eventually it became clear that he could make his right eye move to the left or right and the other one would usually follow. But the process was constantly interrupted by the need to untape the lids and let them fall over the eyeball. Then Helge had the idea of artificial lubrication. She got a bottle from an optician, saying her elderly grandfather had been advised to try it, and experimented on Davy with an eye dropper. That seemed to work OK, but it couldn't be done all the time. In fact, never when anyone else was watching. Helge was not expected to introduce innovations. It took ages to work out how actual communication could be achieved. Eventually, after many failures, and frequent total exhaustion, she reached a conclusion. The weaker eye, and she would have to do some trial and error tests to be sure which it was, should remain closed. With the other one, Davy could turn his eye away, if a suggestion was the wrong one, and stare at it, or the person in front of him, if it was correct.

Helge started making an alphabet out of cut-up paper, until she suddenly realized that she was creating unnecessary work for herself. She went to a toyshop and bought several sets of brightly-coloured letters, upper and lower case, all of them fitted to magnets. They were meant for fridge doors, but would work very well on any metal.

The next day she arrived at work with two heavy carrier bags, one from the toyshop, the other containing a large oven tray, from a kitchen supplier. Before doing anything else she opened the cupboard, which held only a dressing gown, slippers and pyjamas. Davy's mother had bought them and taken them to the hospital, in the very early days when she still believed in cures, and in hope. Ever since then David had worn only hospital gowns, or T-shirts. Helge made a space big enough to hold the stuff she'd bought and crossed her fingers in the hope that Mrs Canning wouldn't look in the cupboard. She was very much looking forward to surprising Davy's parents with his communications.

'Now then, Davy. Here goes.' She held up a plastic letter block. 'Keep your eye on it if it's the right letter, turn it away if it's not.' A: the usual swivel eye; B and C, swivel again; D: his eye fixed on the green plastic and stayed there.

'D for Davy!' Helge cried. 'Oh this is so exciting!' She put the D on the oven tray, held up a red A, and waited. Not A. 'I thought it was going to be your name, Davy.' It was not until she reached the letter I that he stared at the red plastic. The next letter was E. 'Die? Davy! What do you mean, you telling me to die? No? Well then, who? What's the next letter?'

Slowly she realized that the letters were M and E.

'Oh Davy, it's you. You wish you were dead!'

Later, when Helge herself was exhausted, Davy was asleep and the letters and tray were hidden away in the cupboard, she found the copy of *The Diving Bell and the Butterfly*. Jean-Dominique Bauby, his brain unaffected by the massive stroke that paralyzed his limbs, had managed to become the author of a masterpiece by blinking the only functioning muscle in his whole body, his left eyelid, As its blurb said, the book was about the ability to invent a life for oneself in the most appalling of circumstances. It had become a best seller in many languages. It's called a win-win situation, Helge thought. But there was no need to tell anyone else about it yet. This could be her and Davy's little secret. Just for the time being.

TAMARA HAD LISTENED with great and genuine interest to Thea's account of the work she was trying to finish. 'Some archaeologists I have known, I like that idea.'

'It's not exactly scholarship. But it's as close as I'm prepared to go as far as personal memoirs are concerned.'

'Did you think of writing an autobiography?'

'No – more than one publisher has suggested it, and I've always said no way.'

'Perhaps when you've done the others you could turn to that type series of clothes you once thought of, I've always thought I'd like to read it.'

It was usually taken as axiomatic that objects developed logically and incrementally. Take, for example, a cauldron for cooking. Gradually improvers would try out a lid, a spout, a lip, a flat bottom – until one day there was a saucepan indistinguishable from those in use today; or think of a pair of scissors, their shape unchanged since the first shears were made. It was assumed that the same process governed the development of nearly every object.

However Thea, being interested in clothes, used them as an analogy to contradict the dogma. Shoes, for example, did not progress from low to high heels in a neat and predictable pattern. A season of flatties would be brought to an end by their opposite, stilettos. Wearers of heavy winter boots were more likely to change into strappy sandals than a thinner pair of boots. You could rearrange the cooking pots in a completely different way, and suggest the pendulum of fashion swung backwards and forwards, not in a straight developmental line. And the fashion argument could apply to serious objects, whose type series were set out in museum cases.

They began to discuss the ways in which long-accepted series could be rearranged. Half an hour on, Thea sighed, 'It would certainly set the cat among the pigeons. Think how many accepted beliefs it would overturn.'

'Which you've been doing your whole career.'

'You make me sound very destructive.'

'I didn't intend to. Iconoclastic, perhaps.'

'Even that ... Am I so destructive, really?'

'No, Thea. Just clear-headed.'

'That's what I'm trying to be.'

'Is there ...' Tamara began, pausing because she didn't know how to express it. 'Thea, I really don't want to interfere or tread on your private affairs – but I have to ask – are you all right?'

She began to give her usual all-purpose reply, a quelling assurance that she was perfectly fine, delivered in a way that made sure the questioner would know better than ever to ask her that again. As she opened her mouth to utter the soothing lies, something stopped the words coming out. Something? It was a sweep of emotion rushing across her consciousness. She had been acting like a zombie, not allowing herself to feel anything for fear that she'd also feel self-pity. But why shouldn't I be sorry for myself? I'd be sorry for anyone else in my position. Why shouldn't I accept some sympathy? I've offered enough of it in my time. Her voice hoarse and hesitant, she uttered the words that she'd planned never to say.

'Tamara, I'm ill. I've got something wrong. It's incurable. I've got cancer.'

MAC'S COME UP with some news that worried him.

He had to begin it with a confession, but cheered up lots when

I said I'd already guessed and it couldn't matter less to me.

When you see someone hesitate before answering to his name it's not genius to guess he's using an alias. The only interesting question is *why*? And he's going to tell me later. When we've done the job. It's that Olga on the first floor. She's completely away with the fairies, wouldn't even recognize her own face in the mirror. But, bad news for us, she's not one of the demented oldies whose families dump them here and scarper. She's got sons who look in occasionally and daughters who keep on coming even though her brain has rotted away and she doesn't even recognize them. I wouldn't bother if I was them. What's the point?

Anyway, her family know Mac, as he says, 'In another context'. And he definitely doesn't want them to know him in this one.

'I've got to stop them coming here,' he says.

'Well, they won't come here once the old woman's snuffed it.'

'Maybe, but ...'

'What's the prob?' I asked.

'If anyone saw me going into her room ... they've got a webcam.'

'Infirm of purpose, give me the dagger,' I declaimed. I was good at theatre studies at school.

'What?'

'Lady Macbeth.'

'Oh Jesus, Gloria, you shouldn't quote the Scottish play! That's really unlucky.'

'Not this time, matie. You've had a stroke of luck – which is me saying I'll do it. You get hold of the doings – something she's taking anyway in case they do a post-mortem – and leave it to me.'

They had made the old woman's room much nicer than she needed, since she'd obviously never noticed and never would. When I went in she said something that might have been 'Hullo' and I burbled on – the weather, her flowers, what a beautiful dressing gown, and what a lot of photos. She must have lots of grandchildren. Might I look?

Almost every room in the place is plastered with pix of babies and children, all much the same, healthy middle-class kids with tramlines on their teeth. While I was facing the table, covered with so many framed photos that it was hell to dust, I looked round to find the webcam. It took a moment to find because it was disguised by one of those magnifying mirrors, hung by the washbasin on an expanding holder.

Got you!

The basin was in the corner of the room, with, on one side, a small bathroom-style cabinet holding, as I knew from other rooms, a few sticking plasters, a black eyeshade, a spare tube of toothpaste and cake of soap, and on the other side a trolley with a kettle, sachets of tea, milk and sugar and there would have been biscuits too, except that I'd noticed the crumbs and the torn wrapping on the armchair.

I said, well, this won't do, and started dusting and wiping. When I got round the room to the basin again, I ostentatiously wiped my forehead on my sleeve. 'God it's hot in here,' I muttered and then took off my jersey and hung it on the webcam.

I took out of my pocket a piece of toilet tissue wrapped round about forty gel-wrapped tablets. Screwing each one into two pieces, I poured the powder they contained into a toothmug, covered them with hot water from the tap and began to stir with the handle of the old woman's toothbrush. Once they were a nice smooth paste I poured in the contents of two sugar sachets and two of powdered chocolate.

I have to say that I'd expected trouble when it came to making her drink it and was really surprised when she gulped it down greedily. I cautiously tasted the dregs: very sweet, with a metallic aftertaste. 'More?' I asked. She smiled at me and in a momentarily normal voice said, 'Yes please, it's delicious.'

Actually it was beyond disgusting, like a puree of artificial sweetener. But I was happy to wash out the cup and make more, because it meant I could be pretty sure that they would find no trace of any foreign substance when they analyzed the contents of the cup.

TAMARA'S SYMPATHY WAS always practical. Hearing of something awful happening to a friend, she was sometimes perfunctory in expressing dismay or sorrow, but immensely energetic in trying to think of ways to help. So Thea had cancer – what a bummer – but there must be something that could be done about it.

'Does it hurt?'

'Occasionally. Not often. Most of the time I feel perfectly OK.'

'You're sure they are right? Did you get a second opinion?'

'No, but I saw the scan results. There didn't seem much point, after that.'

'Oh Thea, you're so unworldly. It might be benign, there might be ways to shrink it, you can't take it on trust, one man's – I suppose it was a man? – one person's opinion.'

'He said it was inoperable.'

'By him, maybe. But who knows if someone else ... I'm going to ring my brother.'

'Tamara—'

'Yes, I know I'm interfering. But someone's got to. Honestly, Thea, look at you, holed up in the middle – no, at the very end of nowhere, miles from your friends and family, brooding about a diagnosis that could easily be wrong. I want you to come back to London with me and go and get a proper second opinion. I'll ask Paul who you'd best see. He'll know. It might even be him.'

It was not until the following day, when they had been driving for a couple of hours, and Tamara was feeling homesick at the sight of the glossy thickness of Devon's trees and hedges, that

Thea eventually said, 'Actually, Tamara, you're quite right. I know I've been rather churlish.'

'Not at all,' Tamara said.

'I went sort of numb after seeing the last specialist. He just came out with it, no wrapping it up in nice words. And it seemed to be – I don't know how to put it – a kind of confirmation. You know, one gets older, and then you're at retirement age and everything is valedictory, as if it's all over, so what's after that except for death?'

'Oh, Thea please! If academics retire in their sixties they've got decades of working life ahead. Or can have.'

'Unless they get something incurable.'

'OK.'

'Or start losing their marbles.'

'At least nobody could say you're doing that,' Tamara said a little grumpily.

Thea closed her eyes when Tamara reached the motorway and was lulled into a brief sleep. Tamara sneaked glances at the shuttered face. Thea looked quite formidable. And as a matter of fact, Tamara thought, formidable is exactly what she is.

THE NIGHTS WERE so long. Maybe if he could just sleep he'd feel better, but whoever was on duty had to wake him up every two hours to turn him. Tonight it was the nasty girl again, the one who thought he should be left to die. Actually it was what Davy longed for himself, but he didn't like hearing someone else say so, either to him or about him. One of the oddities of Davy's state was that his hearing seemed, mysteriously, sharper than ... than before. A perfectly useless ability; there was nothing cheerful to be heard. And there he was, accumulating information he could never use or share. Such as, that the nasty girl was going out with the doctor. They were quite unembarrassed, taking no more notice of Davy than if he'd been a statue, or a fish. Tonight they'd actually done it in his line of sight, she stripping to a thong and shelf-bra, he taking off his suit, shirt and tie and then she moved, deliberately he thought, right into Davy's line of vision, bending over his bed, while he came up behind her, his hands either side of her body holding him up as he jerked up and down, faster and faster, until she groaned and then he groaned, and for a moment they were still, in a sweaty heap, on Davy's bed.

She lifted her face and stared at Davey. She said, 'He's jealous.'

'I daresay,' the doctor mumbled into the blanket.

'I wonder if he's still got any feeling ... you'd think it was the last thing to go.' She slid out from under the man, and moved close to Davy. The she pulled back the single cover, and looked with curiosity at Davy's crotch. 'Not that I can see anyway,' she concluded.

She put her hand forward, out of Davy's line of sight. He couldn't feel anything, but realized what she was doing when the doctor asked her to stop.

'OK. It's not working anyway. I just thought, a final moment, you know, go out on a high.'

The doctor had dressed himself again, and she pulled on her black trousers and white shirt. Then the doctor took something out of his briefcase. 'This should do the trick.' He was loading a syringe with liquid. He squirted it experimentally. He dabbed something onto something white and then smeared it on Davy's arm. At that moment loud voices were heard outside the room.

A loud male voice, posh accent. 'It's really very good of you to spare the time to show me round, you must have been off duty hours ago.'

'Not at all, it's my pleasure. Now, this room ...'

'I don't want to disturb anyone.'

'Don't worry about that. I'm afraid this patient is long past noticing.'

By the time Mrs Bussell had opened the door, the nasty nurse was fully clothed and the doctor was dressed and checking the dials on the life support system. 'Come you in,' she said, taking no notice of the nasty girl. 'Oh Doctor, you're here again!'

'Still, not again. But I'm on my way now.'

'And I'm due to go off duty,' the nasty girl said. 'I just wanted to make sure that this patient was all right. He's so vulnerable, the poor boy.' Then, looking at Davy, she said, as if it were a light farewell, 'We'll try again another day.'

TAMARA SUGGESTED THAT Thea should come and spend the night with her, rather than be left on her own, brooding. But Thea Crawford disliked staying with other people. She very much preferred her own bed, her own bathroom, the elegant comfort of her flat in Bayswater. 'You can come round tomorrow morning if you'd like to,' she told Tamara. But her mask was already back in place.

Tamara drove slowly home to Putney. It had rained continuously from Exeter onwards, and she felt the rhythm of the windscreen wipers had become part of her.

In I go, she thought, have a hot bath, change my clothes, pour myself a drink. A leisurely programme. She felt restored and awake again, once she was wrapped in her cashmere dressing gown with sheepskin slippers and with the electric blanket warming up her bed. She went downstairs, clicked the on-switch to boot up the computer, poured herself whisky with ginger wine and took the mail through to the kitchen table. So much had been delivered during her brief absence that it took a good half hour to open it. Bills, and more bills. Credit card statements. Bank statements. Appeals from all the local estate agents to put her flat or house in their hands.

She knew that these computer-generated messages should neither be answered, nor taken at all seriously but she did find herself looking at the website of one of them which advertised 'Pretty pottery made to order in a pretty house with studio'. It was a way of putting off the awful moment of checking the leak from the washing machine. The utility room might be full of water by now.

I'll just check the emails first, she thought. Oh, at last! A message from I. Harper. But it wasn't from Iona.

Dear Dr Hoyland, it's kind of you to want to speak to Iona, but she's too upset to get back to you. It would probably be best if you leave it for quite a while. Thank you for the kind thought. Yours, Ian Harper.

Well! As brushes off go, that was pretty thorough! Then another name leapt out at her from the long list of surplus-to-requirements junk.

M. Solomon! Max! He had answered her letter!

My dear Tamara,

Jonathan rang me from the train to tell me he had been with you earlier that evening. I was delighted that he had met you, and even more delighted to receive a letter from you today. I frequently recall our adventures in Egypt[4] all those years ago and am regularly overcome by sadness to think that I shall never see such a place or feel the hot sun again, for the infirmities of old age forbid such adventures; I shall be 85 next month.

Jonathan tells me that you look exactly as you did twenty years ago, unmarked by time – but that you are the mother of teenaged sons. I congratulate you.

And now to respond to your question or request. I became well acquainted with the man you knew as Mr Black, and even (but I write this for your eyes only) carried

---

4 *Death Beyond The Nile* by Jessica Mann

out a couple of small commissions for him. We still meet from time to time. As far as I know he holds no official post, though I believe he is frequently consulted by highly placed officials. I do not feel that I am free to pass on to you his address, but I am certainly free to pass yours on to him should you wish me to do so.

In the hope that we may meet again in the not too distant future, I remain yours most affectionately, Max Solomon.

'Gosh!' Tamara said aloud. 'Golly gosh!' A schoolgirl's response to this curiously pompous missive seemed appropriate. Surely he used not to be like that? Was this the effect of literary success?

That aside, it was a thrilling and very satisfactory message. Would Mr Black get in touch if he knew Tamara was interested again? She turned off the lights and went upstairs to her bedroom, where she undressed in front of the full-length mirror. Then, watching her own body with a hypercritical eye, she began to perform a series of the most challenging exercises she could remember.

'WHERE THE HELL were you? Where've you been?'

'Sandra?'

'We've been ringing and ringing. Your mobile, the landline—'

'Why? What's happened? What's the matter?'

'Oh, Tamara....' Alexandra sobbed into the handset.

'For God's sake, what—?'

'Tamara? It's me. Paul.'

'Paul? What—?'

'It's Mum. They found her this morning. She died.'

Tamara put her hand over her mouth, pressed hard against her lips thinking, *I won't cry, I won't.* She heard a moan and realized it was her own, the sound of shock and misery forcing its way out.

'Are you all right?' Paul asked.

'Yes. No. I don't know. What happened?'

'Nothing dramatic. She was put to bed last night and didn't wake up in the morning.'

'It's a good way to go, Tamara. And you know, she wasn't ...'

'I know, it's what people call a blessed release, and one couldn't wish it on her, to go on as she was, but oh, Paul ...'

'I know.'

They were silent for a moment, and then Paul said, 'Where are you?'

'At home. I was in Cornwall, and then I turned the phone off when I was driving back, and I forgot to switch it on again.'

'OK, listen, in the morning I'm going to go to the home and collect Mum's stuff.'

'I want to come with you. Will you pick me up?'

Paul turned up in his 'consultant surgeon style' car. He was a big huggy-bear of a man, and Tamara felt remarkably comforted by his embrace. He said, 'I'm glad you're coming, I haven't any idea what Mum had with her, what we're supposed to collect.'

They arrived at the Helleborean at about noon, and found the car park unusually full. Paul drove slowly round, overtaken at one point by a snazzy yellow, loudly roaring two-seater which paused at the space painted with the word 'Doctor'. The driver's face was invisible behind a beard, sunglasses and a baseball cap, but his head movements showed that he was looking round for a space. 'I bet that bloke will squat in the doctor's space,' Paul remarked, but was immediately proved wrong when the yellow car was propelled out of the car park and quickly disappeared from sight and very slowly from earshot.

'You're a doctor, why not go there?' Tamara said.

'Certainly not,' Paul said virtuously. 'I'm always really pissed off when someone parks in my space.'

He drove back to the access lane, which looked only just wide enough for the statutory fire engine, and parked in a field gate, from which it was a ten-minute walk to the care home's front door.

'You're so law abiding,' Tamara said.

'Aren't you?'

'Actually, no,' she replied, remembering some of her exploits for department E.

She had contrived the death of the two terrorists who had murdered her first boyfriend. She had smuggled a wanted suspect out of the country. She had impersonated, used a false identity, broken and entered – I'd be facing a lifetime in prison, she thought, and said, 'No need to worry, big brother, I don't have a criminal record or even any points on my driving licence.'

He took her arm, and they went together into the large and still quite elegant entrance hall, the part of the house that had been changed the least, still a country house's room, Wedgwood blue with white plaster mouldings, and always decorated with several vases of expertly arranged seasonal flowers. Today, Tamara noticed, there were roses and heavy-scented syringa.

It was lunchtime for the residents. Most of them were in the dining room, arranged in tables for four with the food laid out on a central counter, where white-coated staff would put the chosen item onto plates and carry them across the room. 'We want it to seem more like a homely hotel than a nursing home,' Tamara remembered being told, back when she and Alexandra were quartering southern England in their search for a place where they could bear to leave their mother.

The girl at the reception desk had recognized them as they went into the building, and buzzed for Mrs Bussell, who almost immediately came running down the stairs. Her condolences were well practised, striking a tactful note somewhere between 'a tragic loss' and 'a blessed release'. Olga's possessions would be packed up straight away, and could be sent if not taken away now. Olga's body was already at the funeral home, where they could go, if they wanted, to see it. The doctor's certificate was in this envelope. The death had been registered by Mrs Bussell in person and here were several copies of the death certificate. And this envelope ... she tactfully refrained from mentioning that it contained the final invoice.

Paul said he'd like a word with his mother's doctor.

'Of course Dr Macintosh was here yesterday, he had to ... well, you know, and he was in here early this morning to sign the certificate, but this next fortnight he's on leave. He asked me to send you his condolences. But Gloria is here, your mother's usual carer – would you like to speak to her?' She picked up the phone, pressed a couple of keys and said. 'Gloria, dear, Mrs Hoyland's family would like to see you.'

Gloria was in her dark blue nurse's uniform, her colourful hair scraped back in an elastic band. She said, 'Good morning, Mrs Hope. I'm very sorry for your loss.'

'Thank you, Gloria. This is my brother.'

'How do you do? My condolences.'

'Kind of you. Do you want to tell us...?'

'Well, your mother's friend, you know, Mrs Maitland—'

'You remember Rosemary Maitland, Paul,' Tamara said.

'Of course.'

'Well, Mrs Maitland hasn't been too well recently, and in fact she sadly passed away on Wednesday. Olga, I mean Mrs Hoyland, she became quite anxious, she was restless, uncomfortable, you know? And then she started sneezing, in fact her cold was bad enough for the doctor to come and see her – that was on Monday, and then he was with her on Thursday again and did a full examination, he said she had a lung infection and prescribed antibiotics and said we should keep her warm indoors. She didn't seem seriously ill, I promise you, I'd have got Mrs Bussell to warn you if I'd thought for a moment that she ...' Nurse Gloria's voice had been growing more strained as she spoke, like someone trying not to cry, and at this point she couldn't hold back her tears which spilled out and rolled down her cheeks. 'If only I'd realized ...'

'It's all right, Gloria,' Tamara said.

She sniffed, took a tissue from one of the boxes that were provided in every room, scrubbed at her eyes, and finished in a choked voice. 'I wasn't on nights this week but I thought I'd better check on her again before I went to bed. And when I went in to her room the lights were still on and she was lying on the bed, not in it, still dressed. And she was ...' (more sobs and sniffs) '... she'd passed away. I'm so very sorry.'

Upstairs, they found that packing boxes had been delivered and were stacked up outside the room.

'Terribly efficient here,' Paul said approvingly. Then, his hand on the door handle, he hesitated for a moment before going in. The room had already been tidied and cleaned, the bed covered with a blue cloth, flat and taut on the mattress. Surprisingly many possessions were piled on the tables, some powerfully and painfully familiar. In the attempt to remind Olga of herself and her own life, visitors had brought too many momentos: dozens of framed photos and several thick albums, favourite pictures, familiar clothes, Olga's usual armchair, a gaudy pottery bowl that had, at home, always been hospitably full of fruit, and a faded Persian rug. The flimsy institutional curtains had been removed and replaced by the blue and white glazed chintz from Olga's bedroom at home. Instead of the fake-wood laminated bedside cabinet there was a walnut sewing table. Only the bed, high, hard and infinitely adjustable, had been a reminder that this was not home, but a care home.

On the way back to London with Olga's personal belongings filling the boot and jam-packed on the back seat, Paul was silent for a while. Then he said, 'You know, once Mum started losing it I really prayed for her to die. I couldn't bear to think of what she was becoming, all the lights switching off one by one until there'd be nothing left of the person who'd been Olga Hoyland. I mean, this is a merciful release, I'm glad she's gone. But all the same, I can't bear it.' He took one hand off the wheel to wipe his brimming eyes. In harmony, Tamara wept with him.

THEA FOUND THAT the specialist recommended by Paul Hoyland had a very different desk-side manner from the elegant and unconcerned young man who had delivered the diagnosis before. This one was a gentle, stout man, wearing a sweater with food-stains, with bubbles of white curls on his head and shining pink cheeks. When the nurse came in to chaperone his examination, she spoke to him in the indulgent tone of an affectionate nanny.

He'd read the correspondence between consultant and general practitioner, which Thea had not seen, and handed the letters across the desk, excusing himself for a moment, obviously intending to give her a private moment for emotion. In fact the letter did not include any information Thea hadn't already known, having done her own on-line research. The most welcome line was at the bottom of the page. 'Dame Thea made it abundantly clear that she would choose a shorter life of good quality, rather than extra years as an invalid.'

When he came back into the room, he didn't start with her medical condition. Instead, standing by the window with his back to Thea, he began to talk about the changes he'd seen in his time as a medic. The progression from the doctor as omniscient deity, doing what he thought best without fear of any consequences; then came the era of democratization, when the nurses and clerical staff learnt to believe that the medics were no better than any of them, and if some injection or medication was given to ease pain, tales might be told, to health service bureaucrats and even the press, of excessive doses or dangerous drugs. 'Now we're getting into the third phase,' he continued. 'It's accepted that we relieve pain and discomfort. That's what we can do when surgery and medication have done all that can be done. Patients in my wards or inmates of the hospices I have anything to do with, choose for themselves. Relieve the pain and take the consequences; or persevere with treatment until it ceases to have an effect.'

'In other words, you'd help me to die.'

'No, Dame Thea, that's not what I was saying. In other words, I'd help you to live comfortably until the end.'

It's a narrow line between them, she thought. But this was no place for semantic argument. She said, 'Do you promise?'

'Yes,' he replied, 'I promise.'

She thought of the books piled in her bedroom in Buriton. The do-it-yourself suicide manuals, the discussion volumes about the morality of assisted self-deliverance, *Final Exit*, *Five Last Acts*, *The Peaceful Pill Handbook*, *How We Die*, *Why We Die*, *Deadly Doses*. 'That's a piece of research I'll be happy to abort,' she said, forgetting that the doctor had no idea she had been doing it. But he was a man of unusual perception, as Paul had said when recommending him. And now he showed it by asking if she meant the do-it-yourself end-it-all books.

'They aren't all quite accurate, you know,' he warned.

'I'm not surprised to hear it,' she replied.

The doctor came to the front door with Thea, and warmly shook her hand, repeating his promise to fit her in for surgery very soon.

It wasn't a reprieve, she was in the same condition as yesterday, no better, no worse, but she felt very much better. She'd been an individual. Previously she had felt and been treated like a faceless, characterless collection of signs and symptoms; while in the queue to see the previous specialist she'd heard him telling a nurse, 'Next, I've got the ovarian cancer, and then there's a vaginal prolapse and a couple of coils.' Thea felt so much the better for being treated like a real person, not a medical condition on legs, that she decided to potter down Marylebone High Street, and have a look at some clothes.

HAVING SET IN motion the tracking down of Tom Black, Tamara suddenly lost her nerve.

What have I been and gone and done? I must have been mad. What if he does get back to me, what possible use could I be? A suburban, middle-aged housewife. People like me come by the dozen. He's probably employed dozens of young action-women since my day. I've got to offer him something else. What can I show him?

Her mind was wandering erratically over recent and less recent experiences. Metal detectorists? No. A transgender man/woman? Hardly. The murder of Vera Fleming? Still under investigation, months on. And despite her special status, Tamara had been told no more than the fact that inquiries were proceeding. And Gordon's death? Nothing to report.

Tamara realized that her own subconscious had reached a conclusion, though her conscious intellect recognized it only now. She was certain that Euan had done something to hasten his father's death, if not exactly to kill him – manipulated the machine's dials, or put something into the drip. She was not certain, but thought it very likely, that Euan had killed Vera, either in revenge because she had been given money he expected to inherit, or because she knew too much about him. But she hoped that the police didn't share her view. And she certainly wasn't going to be telling her potential boss about a murderer in the family.

Mr Black just might be interested in the death café and the part-heard conversation that seemed to be about importing drugs. She rather thought that some of the people present might have been customers. Small, not to say puny, as operations go, but relevant. Better than nothing? Possibly. No, raise that to probably.

197

But not surely. Worth a try, anyway.

It was raining again, or still, as Tamara walked from the station to the middle of Oxford, but this time it was soft, pervasive dampness, from which umbrellas and macs were little protection. The first thing was to find the same café. Where was it?

I parked in a metered bay, she thought. Here, this was the one. And then turned north, through a giftie shop – yes, here it is. One couldn't forget those crocheted sausages, or that embroidered joint of beef. Then I'd walked through the Covered Market, wiggled my way to the High Street and was walking up it to do a big circle back to the car, along … yes, along here. I passed those two cafés and came upon – here we are. The pink one on the corner.

There weren't any notices in the window this time. Had the death café gone? She ordered Earl Grey tea and when the waitress brought it (was it the same woman? Yes, surely) Tamara said, 'Hullo again. I was here before, do you remember?'

'I'm not quite …'

'It was a meeting. The death café? About a month ago.'

'Oh yes, they're regulars now, some of them anyway. Look, there's a notice.'

The next death café session would be – oh. Tomorrow. It was mid afternoon by this time, and there was nobody at home to notice whether she was there or not. Tamara took out her phone and rang the hotel where she stayed when there was a work crisis on. They knew her well there, and said things like, 'As it's you,' and 'We wouldn't do this for anyone else.' Tamara looked in at M&S for overnight necessities and then walked to the Covered Market and through lanes and alleys to Broad Street and Blackwells, where she gave herself the treat of buying a book that had no relevance at all either to her work, or to any kind of literary improvement, a republication of the complete *Hornblower* in two volumes and a feminist re-imagining of Britain between the two world wars. Then she called to leave a message: she'd be coming to the office in the morning.

Tamara went down to the hotel's dining room for dinner. The food was excellent and Oxford residents who knew of it went there often. The professor count was never very high, for as Tamara knew, few of them had much spare money to flash around. But this time – what a coincidence! – one of Alastair's old friends was at a table on the far side of the room. Tamara was about to go and say hullo when she saw his companion in profile and realized that it would be impossibly tactless. Funny, she thought. All those years we've joked about Giles and Pauline and wondered how such a clever man could stay living with the squeaking nitwit he married, and now I see how he does it. Because that girl is obviously an undergraduate here. The polar opposite of 'a little bit of fluff'.

He's seen me. Damn. But he looks quite calm about it.

Giles smiled across the room, and raised his glass to Tamara, elegantly acknowledging a friend's presence without letting her muscle in on his evening. In any case, Tamara's evening was spoken for. The bed, with its excellent bedside light, and Hornblower's dazzling career from midshipman to Admiral of the Fleet, were waiting for her.

So were the office staff when she went in the next morning. It was a quiet place now, compared with the glory days, really not so long ago, when there was almost more rescue excavation going on than there were archaeologists to do it. Now, how the mighty had fallen. The best of them had jumped ship early and found other jobs, some with the rival outfit known as The Oxford Unit.

The worst of them had been 'let go' early on in the drawing-in-horns process. Those remaining were competent and perfectly able to do what they were asked to do. And pretty soon, they would be asked to go.

Tamara said nothing about that, or the future. Staff management was not her job. For that matter, she wouldn't have a job much longer either. Tamara worked in the office till late morning, clearing her desk up and her in-box out.

She arrived too early at the death café. In the window, facing out to the street, were posters advertising 'Dying Awareness Week' and somebody's 'Final Fling'.

Tamara went to the ladies' room, which was accessed through the bead curtain and down a dark passage, where she paused on the way out listening to the start of proceedings. A male voice, curiously high and with an old fashioned haw-haw accent.

'Listen up.' The chatter did not die down. Tamara heard, 'Hi, I'm Georgia.'

'Silence please, ladies, while I give out the notices.'

'Could be back at school.'

'Ladies. Please.'

'OK, Trevor, don't mind us, just go ahead.'

'Our Scottish brethren are holding a conference called Good Life, Good Death, Good Grief. I've arranged to go up and represent this Oxford branch of the society. Then there's another get together in Exeter, theme, You Only Die Once ...'

'Excuse me, Trevor.' A shaky female voice.

'Yes?'

'As far as I'm aware we aren't a branch of any society and if we were, we haven't elected a representative. This is a talking tea party, no more, no less.' A surge of comments and criticism. When it died down the same pale voice asked, 'Does anyone know where Lucy is?'

A general murmur of no, sorry or no idea. 'But she's coming, isn't she? We are expecting her?'

Trevor replied, sulkily, 'She told me she wouldn't make it today, that's why I was standing in.'

'But she's got to! She promised! I paid and she gave me her word, she said she could get them from Mexico no problem, where is she...?' The speaker sounded like someone who would burst into tears at any moment.

'Sit down, why don't you?'

'Barbiturates, was it?'

'Nembutal.'

'For you?' The woman nodded.

'I didn't get your name, you're...?'

'I don't think I should say. 'Cos if Lucy's been arrested or something ... I've heard it's a custodial sentence.'

'Crazy, considering you could buy them perfectly legally when I was younger.'

They were talking knowingly about potentially lethal drugs when the door opened to let in wind, rain, and a wind-blown figure dressed in black. 'Hi, hi, my lovelies, I'm so late! I'm here to stand in for Lucy.'

'Where is she?' someone called out.

'Well, it's not good. Lucy had a nasty accident on Sunday, actually she's in hospital, but she's getting on well and I'm here instead so let's get going. I'm Lezli, from New York City, but now of Oxford, come to help with all your dealings with death. Gather round, gather round!'

The staff of the café were in the main room pouring tea and handing round cake. The café had a back door opening onto an alley so Tamara slipped out. Next stop, the police station where she asked for Detective Constable Gilbert, who did eventually appear and even seemed quite pleased to see her.

'I just thought I'd ask whether you've made any progress,' she said, and added, 'and I've got another unconnected question.' He took her with him past the barrier, and into a small interviewing room.

'No two-way mirror or camera or recorder in here,' he said.

'Could you look up the surname of a young woman called Lucy who was taken to A&E and then admitted to a ward on Sunday?'

'If she was one of our customers I can. Were the police involved?'

'Yes,' Tamara said, crossing her fingers.

He fiddled with the computer, fingers moving almost too

fast to see. 'Lucy Donovan, born 18ᵗʰ May 1990, address in Woodstock. Unidentified assailant.'

'So she was attacked.'

'Beaten up. No permanent damage. That what you need?'

'Absolutely. Thanks so much.'

'So back to your own case. I'm glad of the chance to run some ideas by you.'

'Please. Go ahead.'

'We're now pretty sure, though it can't be proved, that someone turned the taps on your father-in-law's life support. Just for a moment, long enough to ...'

'Yes, I understand,' Tamara said.

'I'm sorry if this is upsetting for you, but he was almost certainly dying, so the fiddling with the machine could only have hastened the end, but—'

'But it's a criminal offence.'

'And in trying to find out "Who", we've got to find out "Why". And how, for that matter. There was a nurse in the room nearly all the time, a nurse or his housekeeper – someone. Anyone. Often enough it was one of the family. The point is, he was protected. So how could anyone—?'

'And what about poor Vera? Are you any closer to finding out what happened to her?'

'We've had Iona Harper on the phone so often I can say it in my sleep. There is no evidence to enable us to take the case further at present. I am very sorry.'

'So what happens now?'

'The keys to the flat are delivered to Miss Fleming's heirs – in fact, to Miss Harper – and the material goes into the unsolved crime file.'

'I wonder, do you think I could take a look at the flat?' Tamara asked, sure that the answer would be no. But this was another facility she could be afforded.

The building seemed in need of some love and attention, its

brass clouded, the wooden common staircase urgently in need of polish, and inside Vera's flat was, inevitably, a tip. Everything the police had taken away to examine had been returned in clear plastic bags. One, on the table, had photo albums inside. Tamara slit the plastic and opened the top one. Black and white snaps of unknown people in antique clothes, women wearing long skirts on the beach, men with hats wherever they went. As she opened successive albums the pictures changed, from black and white to colour, from fading to colourfast, the clothes from formal to normal. Here was Swallows. Gordon and Mary, side-by-side at the front gate. Alastair, reading on a garden bench. Euan, in the driver's seat of a long, low car, Euan laughing, Euan throwing a ball. Euan with his arm round a woman in early middle age. She was gazing at him with open adoration. Euan, in his shirtsleeves, a beautifully laid dinner table, champagne.

Vera had loved Euan once.

He was younger than she, of course, but not by so much. Ten years? Twelve? And a photo of Vera herself, smiling ecstatically, her hands on her tummy – her slightly bulging tummy.

AFTER THE BOARD meeting, which Mrs Bussell attended as an observer, she called a staff meeting. Those who were on rest-days or leave were invited to come back for the afternoon. Helge, and another independent helper who organized community singing and Scrabble contests, were also invited. Agency staff were taken on to hold the fort.

The employees congregated in the dining room, where Mrs Bussell climbed on a wooden chair to make herself taller than the crowd, and said, 'I'm sorry to have to tell you that the Helleborean is to be closed down.' She paused as the noise of gasps, groans and swear words filled the air. Then she went on in a louder voice, 'We've got till Christmas. Nearly six months.

During that time the board hopes that all residents will have found new homes. And that their carers will have found new jobs. Myself, I'm going to retire to South Devon and dig my garden.'

One of the male nurses pushed his way to the front and shouted, 'Comrades, listen to me. They can't just do this to you. There's rules and regulations to protect us.'

Helge was sitting beside one of the care workers whom she recognized. Gloria was one of the agency care workers. She and three other temps had been shown how to turn and clean Davy.

'Can't be much fun for you, spending every day shut up alone with a vegetable,' Gloria said. 'Bad enough just helping out the odd night.'

Helge bristled and replied, 'He's not a – not what you said. He's a clever person locked into a useless body.'

'Well, even if there is something going on in his head it doesn't do him much good. Or anyone else. I think you'd be doing every-one a favour if you switched off the machines.'

'Everyone?'

'Him, 'cos he's got nothing to live for. His family, 'cos they will never be free so long as he's alive. Or half alive.'

Helge had always feared personal confrontation, always walked away from a fight and chosen silence rather than argu-ments or ripostes.

This isn't my problem anyway, she thought; the Cannings were her employers not the Helleborean. Without saying anything else she swung her legs over the wooden bench and walked out of the room.

The protests and complaints went on for hours, which meant that the ambulant inmates, for whom a cold lunch had been pre-pared that morning, would have to picnic in the lounge.

The arguments were repetitive, so Gloria gave up on them. There'd be no problem finding another job which meant that none of this really mattered to her. She got up and left the room.

Standing outside the door, she took out the phone (property of the Helleborean and not to be used for private calls) and rang Mac's number. No answer, so she left a message.

'Hi, lover, it's your lover. Listen, I know you've already been in today but if you can skive off just now, we'd have the whole pool to ourselves. I'll tell you why when you come, if you come, oh please do come.' Gloria let herself into the giant conservatory that was the pool house, sniffed the steamy, greenhouse-scented air, took off some clothes, briefly admired herself in a geranium pink bra and thong, and lay down on the underfloor heated tiles beside the pool. This tiled walkway was well above the outside ground level so even lying flat one could see a good deal of what was going on outside, and quite a large area of the garden, which looked charming in the bright sun, the flower beds bursting with summer flowers, the lawns emerald green after the wet winter. Wooden benches and chairs were placed at tactful angles for the wrinklies to totter to.

Gloria was not interested in gardens. She was picking discontentedly at a corn on her little toe when she heard a familiar sound, the roar of Mac's sports car. I knew he'd come, she thought, as she saw the yellow metal flashing past and, its tyres squealing, skid round the corner into the car park. What she hadn't expected was to hear the engine revving and then to catch sight of the car racing away.

'What the hell ...' She pressed the speed dial on her phone. 'Mac? what happened? Where are you going, why ...?'

'I forgot something,' he said.

'Are you coming back?'

Mac told her he was too busy to come back again and he'd see her tomorrow.

Hurt, upset, angry – no, furious is what I am, she thought.

Fury was definitely preferable, an emotion that led to action rather than self-pity. Gloria had had her fill of being sorry for herself.

ALL THOSE YEARS, starting when she was eleven, years of fear and misery and – worst of all – shame; a shame that prevented her from telling anyone, or asking for help or even just running away. He was so strong. He knew everyone. He knew everything. There'd be nowhere to hide from him no matter how far she went. And at last the realization, far too late, that he was only human and fallible like everyone else. She needn't have put up with it, all those years, she could have run away long ago.

Her release came the day she found him ill in bed, so unusual an event that he thought he was dying, and the old childhood fears of retribution had come back.

'You won't tell?' he begged – actually begged! As if his vengeful god only knew what someone told him.

'I will too, I'll tell everyone,' Gloria said. 'I'm leaving today, I won't tell you where I'm going, and whether you live or die, believe me I don't give a damn which, I'm telling everyone who'll listen.'

He wasn't dying, actually, and if he'd kept his temper he'd have recovered from his illness, which was, according to the autopsy report, a kidney stone, excruciatingly painful, she was glad to remember, but not fatal. Men like that are greedy, they always overeat. None of their appetites are left unsatisfied.

But he didn't know he had a heart problem.

He started shouting at Gloria – who did she think she was, where did she think she was going, when he suddenly stopped in mid-sentence. Gloria looked at him, sweating copiously, panting, his hands clenched on his chest. She'd have dialed 999 for anyone else.

Instead, she took her suitcase downstairs and went to find her mother in the kitchen.

'I'm off,' she said.

'Off? Nonsense. Take this tray up to your father.'

Gloria wouldn't take the tray. Instead she made her mother listen, told her what her husband had been doing to their daughter all these years, told her that she knew her mother knew and that Gloria would never forgive her for not protecting her.

She started crying. She pretended to have known/heard/seen nothing, she claimed to be appalled. Gloria told her, 'I'm wiping both of you out of my life.' And she did.

THE PACKAGE, DELIVERED by a firm of carriers, was unwieldy and heavy. Tamara got the driver to carry it through the house to the kitchen table, where she slit it open with a vegetable knife. Young Mr Hardman, of Wootton Hardman, had rung to say that he proposed to return to Gordon's heirs the documents that had been stored at his solicitors.

Marriage licence, exams passed, insurance paid ... the written records of a conventional life. Here was an envelope containing letters of condolence on the death of Gordon's wife, Alastair's mother. Here were copies of birth certificates: Euan, Alastair, Gordon himself and – wait a minute, this one was for Iona Fletcher. This was the shortened form of certificate, in use from the seventies onwards, on which only one parent was named: in this case Vera Fletcher. Iona's adoptive parents had naturally changed her surname.

The document was stained, as if tears had fallen on it. Tamara turned it over and saw that something was written in faint pencil on the back. 'Father: Euan Macintosh Hope.'

WHEN HELGE WENT back into Davy's room, she found that his mother had arrived to see him. She'd already put the flowers in water, a huge bouquet of lilies and roses, their smell almost masking the other clinical and physical smells in the room. Polly Canning looked like a wraith in oversized clothes. She was sitting at the end of the bed, idly playing with Helge's magnetic alphabets.

'Hullo, Helge.'

'Hullo, Mrs Canning.'

'For heaven's sake, Helge, I wish you'd call me Polly.'

'All right. Thank you.'

'And what are these?' She had already spelt out Davy's name, and her own.

'I really wanted it to be a surprise for you and Mr Canning, we've been working on this for ages, haven't we Davy, but as you're here ...'

Helge had discovered that the best plan was to tape open only one eye, the apparently dominant one on the right. She had originally arranged the letters in alphabetical order and then changed them into what googling had told her was the order of their frequency of use in the English language.

'It's not perfect yet, but you'll get the idea. Look.'

She gestured towards the oven tray, where a row of gaudy letters of the alphabet was arranged in an unfamiliar order.

EARIOTNSLCUDPMHGBFYWKVXZJQ

'I don't understand. What's this for?'

'We'll show you.'

Helge carefully wiped Davy's face and administered the eye drops. Then she cut off a piece of sticky gauze and taped the right eyelid open. 'There you are, Davy, wide awake and raring to go. So what do you want to say to your mum?'

'What on earth—?' The blood had drained from Polly's cheeks.

Helge held letters in front of the single open eye, one after another, E and then A and then R ... the bloodshot iris, the tiny pupil, stared and looked away. I, O, T, N ...

'It's quite slow,' Helge said.

'Slow? What are you doing?' Polly's voice was hoarse.

On and on down the alphabet, C, U, D, P, M – and the eye fixed on the letter.

'M. Is that right, Davy? OK.' Helge clicked the letter onto the metal tray and said, 'Next.'

Polly was weeping silently, her cheeks bathed in tears, her shoulders heaving. Her words were hard to distinguish as she gulped them out. 'I knew it, I knew it, he's been there all the time, I told them, my Davy, my baby...'

She slid off the bed onto the floor, kneeling with her face pressed against the bedclothes. Helge had expected emotion, but this was over the top and she didn't know what to do about it. So she went on deducing letters. Davy's first word was 'Mum'.

'Do you think we need to tell them we're coming?' Alexandra asked.

'I wouldn't have thought so, there's always someone there.' Tamara said. 'As a matter of fact I'd be quite glad if they aren't there, the ones we know. Seeing them at the funeral made me ... uncomfortable.'

Olga's funeral had been in Devonshire, conventionally held in the village church, though she had never attended it, and, since they no longer had a house there, the reception was in a hotel about three miles away. They had laid on buses to ferry the congregation to and fro, and taxis to meet mourners at the station and take them back there later. In fact it had all been immensely efficient, but in many ways a truly ghastly day. For one thing, the ceremony marked the end of the Hoylands' association with the village they had grown up in, and with Devonshire. For another, so many of Rob and Olga's friends were infirm or housebound that the average age of the congregation was really noticeable: about a third of Olga's age when she died.

Sorting out hymns and readings, Tamara thought how much easier it had been to arrange her father-in-law's funeral, simply because she had not been emotionally involved. She remembered Vera's bustling figure as she trotted round Swallows getting it ready and felt simultaneously sad, and ashamed.

The funeral was the next day. The church was filled with roses, sweet peas and peonies. There was a general atmosphere of relief. Nobody could have wished for Olga's life to be prolonged, as Bessie Woods said, too loudly. Bessie was only three rows behind Tamara, who was sitting in the front pew. She heard the comment and couldn't help agreeing with it. I've changed my mind, she thought. Bessie was right, and all her gang. I was wrong to be shocked by them. Better to go at a time of your own choosing. Anything was better than Olga's fate. In fact Thea Crawford had been brave and sensible, rather than hysterical or silly, in determining to spare herself those last, wasted months or years. Tamara reflected guiltily that she might not have been doing Thea a favour, in arranging for her to see another consultant. I shouldn't have interfered, Tamara told herself.

They sorted Olga's estate, such as it was, very quickly. There wasn't much to do, as most of Olga's affairs had been handed over to her children years ago; and by the time she died, all her own money had long since been swallowed up by the cost of her care.

When at last Alexandra and Tamara found a day that suited both of them to drive down to the Helleborean, the pain of Olga's death was fading and both her daughters were able to think of her as she had been before dementia took hold. They had chosen a gift in her memory with the real Olga in mind, lively, clever, and passionate about her garden. In the back of Alexandra's four-wheel drive was a pair of wooden chairs for the care home's garden, engraved with Olga's name.

'Gosh, Sandra, your car!' Tamara said.

'I know, it's ludicrous. Like a tank. The whole family love it, except me. I think it's aggressive. It's even got a very warlike name, did you see?' The words 'Armoured Brigade' were attached to the radiator and the boot. 'I drive very slowly in it, and I'm always waving people to go ahead of me and stopping for pedestrians, 'cos I keep thinking how they must all hate me.'

They turned into the drive at about eleven, before the car park was quite full. 'There's a space, beside the yellow vintage sports car,' Alexandra said. 'Do you think I'm too big to fit?'

The yellow car was the one Tamara had seen before. It was parked in the space marked 'Doctor'.

The two women walked together to the front door. An unfamiliar face was at the reception desk. Tamara said, 'Is Mrs Bussell in?'

'I'm not sure, let me enquire.'

As they turned to the chairs set out for waiting relatives, they heard voices coming down the stairs.

'What do you think, Doctor, should he be in hospital?'

'I don't think it's necessary.'

I know that voice, Tamara thought. But I never met the doctor when Ma was here. She saw two people coming down the final flight of stairs, Mrs Bussell and – good God! It can't be. Tamara had time to tell herself it was nonsense, that she was imagining it, before they reached the bottom. But it wasn't nonsense.

She said, 'Euan.'

Mrs Bussell said, 'Oh, Mrs Hope, I didn't know you were here. Have you met Doctor Macintosh? What can I—?'

'Oh no you don't,' Tamara snapped at 'Doctor Macintosh' who had stepped to one side and was about to bolt for the door. An old skill returning, she grabbed his wrist and twisted his arm behind his back.

'Mrs Hope! What are you doing?'

'I want a word with him,' Tamara said through her teeth. 'Here, or somewhere more private.'

'You can go in my office, if you must. Doctor, shall I ring for—'

'No, it's all right, don't worry,' he muttered.

Alexandra followed them into the small room, and stood with her back to the door looking shocked. She began, 'What on earth—' but Tamara interrupted.

'You've seen him before, Sandra, across a crowded room. This is Euan. Alastair's brother. Euan Macintosh Hope, currently known as Dr Macintosh.'

'OK,' Alexandra said, still puzzled. 'Hi.'

'I'm perfectly entitled to use my second name if I choose,' he said.

'But you aren't perfectly entitled to practise medicine in this country, are you? How did you con anyone into giving you a job? Did you forge … oh.' Tamara paused, suddenly realizing what he must have done. Then she said, 'You used Alastair's certificates, didn't you? You impersonated him. And I even know where you found them.'

The attic at Swallows, Euan crouched over a suitcase that he claimed was full of old school essays, but in which she had glimpsed parchment and seals.

Alexandra had moved away from the door, and Euan seemed to have stopped fighting, so Tamara lowered her guard. He was a tall man and a strong one, and Tamara was out of practice and unprepared. Suddenly he swept his left arm forward. She flinched, which moved her aside so that his fist hit her shoulder rather than her face or neck, but the hard blow knocked her to one side, and he'd bolted past her and out of the building before she could catch him. She was still running towards the car park when the yellow sports car roared out onto the road and off, out of sight first and then its roar died away.

Alexandra had never been involved in the world of secrets that her sister and father had sometimes occupied. She hadn't even gone out to work since she was married quarter of a century earlier. But she was no fool and caught on fast. She waited until they were on the motorway to ask questions, but then made it very clear that she was going to have answers.

'Now then little sister, I've been doing what you say because you obviously know more than I do about what's going on. OK, you didn't think Mrs Bussell was the person to complain to. Fair enough. But we should be lodging a complaint all the same. Why aren't we at the police station at this very minute?'

'We probably should be. I'm sure it's a criminal offence to impersonate a doctor or prescribe drugs,' Tamara said. 'And we're committing an offence by not reporting a crime. You may feel you have to, later on.'

'You'll have to explain all this. Euan is qualified, isn't he?'

'He was. He could have been struck off, but I think they held back for Gordon's sake. So long as he didn't work in this country. That's why he went to the States.'

'So now he's back, how did he get a job? Don't doctors need some sort of documents?'

'He had documents. Alastair's. And he used Alastair's GMC number.' Alastair Gordon Macintosh Hope. Not so different from Euan Gordon Macintosh Hope, both names on the General Medical Council's register. 'It's the number that's the unique identifier. Anyway they look very alike, and nobody would have been surprised that he seemed older than the photo.'

'Don't they have to keep it up-to-date?'

'Every five years. And Alastair renewed it quite recently. Not that he wants to practise, if he can manage to find a research post, but it keeps his options open.'

'Is that what this is about? Not queering the pitch for Alastair?'

'Partly. But Sandra, think: there have been four deaths in that home in the last few weeks. Mum. Mum's friend Mrs Maitland—'

Alexandra interrupted. 'You don't think that Euan—'

'I wouldn't put it past him.' Tamara thought for a moment. Do I tell Sandra the other things about Euan? She'd insist on going to the authorities. Iona would find out that she was a murderer's

213

daughter. It would break Alastair's heart. Stalling, she said, 'And you know, there is an argument that he'd have been doing them a favour. A kindness. Putting them out of their misery.'

'I don't buy that one.'

'Nor did I, until recently. But I'm beginning to change my mind. Seeing Mum like that ...'

'You don't think he did anything to Mum?' Alexandra exclaimed.

'I don't know. He might have done. But would it have been so wrong if he did?'

Both women were silent, thinking of their mother, oblivious, unhappy and every day losing more of her faculties. There was no denying that her death was not unwelcome.

Eventually Alexandra said, 'So Euan came back from the States, and got himself a nice cushy place in a comfy care home ... not very arduous work.'

'And a new girlfriend. Did you see her?'

'That nurse? The one with red hair?'

'She's called Gloria.'

MAC SPOKE TO Gloria in the early afternoon. He was going to move on. France and points east. Would she come with him?

'You bet your sweet life I would,' she exclaimed.

'Meet you this evening. Bring everything you'll need, we won't be coming back.'

Gloria packed her stuff quickly, stowing anything illicit, mostly prescription drugs, in shoes. Then she went out to look around. Everyone's asleep, or out, she thought, as she walked along the corridor towards Davy's room. She had unfinished business with him. At this time of day, despite so much happening, the post-lunch nap silence still prevailed. It was an hour when nurses and carers were free, so she didn't meet any on her way. Slipping silently into his room, she saw him, as before, lying immobile on the bed with the machine that kept him alive bubbling and chuntering beside him.

'This is goodbye,' she told the unresponsive figure. 'I'm leaving. I know you can hear me, Davy, I know you're understanding me. I'm going to let you choose, 'cos I'm pretty sure nobody else will. Your choice is between going on like this for ever, or finishing it today. Your last chance of freedom. You want out? Then look straight at me, look me in the eyes, and if you do, I'll do it for you. Are you trying to thank me? Don't worry, I'm happy to help. Now, on the count of three. Look at me if it's a yes. One ... two ...'

The eye that looked back at her was bloodshot and unsteady, but it was aimed firmly at Gloria's own blue gaze.

I'm meeting your eyes, I'm looking at you as straight as I can, do it, do it, please do ...

Her hands went to the row of switches. If he swivelled his eye far enough he could just see the screen with its jagged record of his miserable life.

She switched off the machine at the mains plug, so that its emergency siren would not sound. In hospitals there was an additional attachment to a generator, so the machine went on working in a power cut. There was going to be a generator, it was to be installed as soon as possible, but it would come too late for Davy Canning. She counted the time. One minute, two. Switch on. Run to the door. There it was, flat line, and as the door swung closed behind her, the siren blared its warning. Out in the corridor, up the stairs, and just as she turned the corner, out of their line of vision, uniformed staff came running from both directions.

I hope he's safely gone, she thought, set free. She was surprised by her own benevolence. My good deed for the day.

❖

'YOU SHALL NOT kill; but need not strive officiously to keep alive,' the old man said, when Tamara had finished telling him about Euan and Gloria. Then he added, 'Arthur Hugh Clough.'

Tom Black must be in his eighties now, wrinkled, wizened, with trembling hands. But his eyes were clear and as perceptive as they had always been, and his voice as authoritative. Tamara felt a mixture of relief, pleasure, anxiety and awe. She said, 'So what should I have done? What should I do now? I believe that he's killed people – I know he did, perfectly legally, in Oregon – but his victims would have thanked him for it if they could. Even his father – though there's no evidence that his end was hastened – he might have begged his son to speed it up, if he knew what was happening. He wasn't going to recover and he'd have loathed being an invalid. It's just Vera. She wasn't ill, she wasn't old, and she was really looking forward to her new life. What had she done to Euan? Been given money he thought he should have inherited. I can't think of anything else.'

'Apart from his relationship with Vera Fleming, did he have a reason to fear her?'

'I can only suppose that she knew he'd pinched Alastair's certificates. I think she was going to tell me, so perhaps he went there to make sure she'd keep quiet.'

'Go on.'

'OK, as far as I know there's no proof of any of this. So suppose I tell the police about him anyway. No, to rephrase: I will tell the police, I can't not, no matter what it costs. And it will cost. Someone will find Euan, sooner or later, and the muck will spread. And poor Iona will realize not only that she's lost her birth-mother, but that she was murdered by her newly-found father.'

'And what about his girlfriend?'

'Gloria. Who knows? According to the local police she's left a trail of deaths behind her. There's no doubt that she killed the paraplegic rugby player. Or let him die. But he'd have thanked her for it. He'd have done it himself if he could. So if she's hunted down and tried and punished, will it be seen by posterity as equivalent to hanging homosexuals? Or burning heretics?' She sat still and silent for a moment, but couldn't keep her own selfish concerns out of the equation. She was almost crying, her voice thin and shaky, as she said, 'Worst of all, just think of the effect of this story on my husband's reputation. Alastair will have it hanging over him for keeps, it'll be the end of his career, because they'll be muddled up together, the two Dr Hopes, something seedy about one of them, details forgotten, safer to give someone else the grant, the job, the award. Just in case.'

'And the same applies to Dr Hoyland too?'

'Not necessarily, but it won't help – or wouldn't if there were any jobs going for field archaeologists.'

THE HEAVY SILENCE of the book-lined room descended on them. They were sitting in the library of what would once have been called a gentleman's club, the same one that Rob Hoyland had belonged to, and after he died, Olga, who, although her children all had comfortable spare bedrooms, had sometimes stayed there when she came to London, saying she wanted to be independent. The sun shone in through tall sash windows, illuminating the books' leather spines and the faded dragons on the carpet.

After a while Mr Black said, 'Turning to your drug smugglers.' She hadn't intended to tell him about the death café, having come to the conclusion that the people there were doing no harm, except perhaps to themselves. But she'd found herself blurting out about them too. It was what it must be like making your confession to a Catholic priest. Get it off your chest, relieve yourself of the weight of worry. He said, 'My department was never a law enforcement agency. You want to leave them to it?'

'Yes.'

'It's your decision.'

'It's something I've changed my mind about. After seeing my mother's faculties disappear ...' Tamara no longer felt shocked by the idea of cutting short one's own suffering. In fact she was beginning to believe in legalized euthanasia. But looking at Mr Black's wise, ancient face, it was instantly obvious that this wasn't the time or place to discuss it. He's a boss, not a father confessor, she told herself.

Outside there was a view of cream stucco buildings, most with gleaming brass name plates and shiny black painted railings. This was the London of nods and hints, of unofficial power and secret influence, the London in which Tamara could be advised by a senior figure in public administration that she needn't feel bound to report a crime.

'Leave it then,' Mr Black said. 'Let the police do what they can. Drop tactfully out. Keep your official profile low.'

'I'll do my best.'

'And wait a few days before talking to them about your brother-in-law.'

'You mean, give him time to get clean away?'

He didn't answer that question either with words or looks. He continued, as if she hadn't said anything, 'Find a research subject that you're genuinely interested in, because it's what you'll be working on most of the time. But make sure it's a subject that can plausibly involve site visits all over the country.'

'Do you mean – are you saying that I can come back? That you'll take me on again? I thought I was too old and out of practice.'

'My dear Tamara, your name was never removed from the list. It's been marked as inactive for a few years. But just think. If I want someone who goes unnoticed, a truly secret agent, who better than the mother of three, a doctor's wife, an archaeologist? An apparent herbivore in a cage of predators? I'm offering you a job.'

'Oh!' So unexpected a statement, so very much what she wanted to hear, made Tamara pause, unable for a moment to speak. Eventually she said, 'Thank you. I accept it.'

'You'll need refresher courses.'

'Yes.'

'And training sessions.'

'I know.'

'And you'll report directly to me. Welcome back.'

Alastair will be furious, Tamara thought, in fact, beyond furious. He'd be unforgiving. Well, that bridge must be crossed later.

'Lucky,' she said.

'What is?'

'Meeting you again. A stroke of luck that I was put on to Max Solomon. And also ...'

'Yes?'

'I'm better qualified than I was before. Because I can get into places your other operatives probably can't. And nobody's going to remember seeing me. I'll fly under the radar. You know what they say. Older women are invisible.'

IT WAS MIDSUMMER day when the long, low, vintage sports car in look-at-me yellow crossed from France into Germany. There were no border controls and the only sign of being in a different country was the language on shop and street signs, and the fact that in Germany, there was no speed limit on the autobahn. But an automatic sensor recorded all the car numbers that passed below it and the driver's photograph, and that of any passenger, were automatically snapped, and if a European arrest warrant existed for anyone in the car, a couple of lurking police cars were scrambled to intercept it.

Euan Hope saw them coming up behind him, but it never

occurred to him that it was his own car they were chasing. Next thing he knew, one was in front of him and one behind, and both were flashing all their lights. He slowed down, and further down.

'What are you doing?' Gloria shouted. 'Don't stop for them, drive on, drive! They'll arrest us, Euan, they'll separate us! Don't let them get us!'

Euan looked quickly around. Then he jammed the gearstick down and floored the accelerator pedal. The seats seemed to hit them on their spines as the big car leapt forwards.

'You pranged someone,' Gloria said.

'Too bad.'

It was early enough in the day for there to be little traffic. Most drivers got out of the way when they saw the blazing headlights and heard the almost continuous horn. 'Get out of my way, move it,' Euan muttered as he roared along in the fast lane, swerving to overtake on either side. There was a slight smile on his face. It was at such moments, when he was risking death, that he felt most alive. After a while there were no slower cars to cringe in the inside lane. 'They've closed the road,' he said. Then, over the brow of a slight hill, he saw a row of police cars parked door-to-door, blocking his exit.

'Don't stop, don't stop!'

Pulling on the handbrake while keeping his foot jammed down on the accelerator, the car skidded sideways, performing a complete turn-round and roared back the way he had come. Momentarily unpursued, he muttered, 'That surprised them!'

'Oh no!'

He heard Gloria moan, and glanced ahead to see why. Flashing blue lights, flashes from powerful spotlights, the shapes of many officers awaiting them. Euan glanced to left and right. 'Hold on,' he shouted and without losing any speed tugged at the wheel. The car skidded, was corrected and moved forward again, at right angles to the road, into the woody scrub. He steered between trees, wrenching the wheel to left and right, and by the time it could go no further was well away from the autobahn.

'Now we walk,' he said.

There was no reply. He turned to look to his right. Gloria was held to the passenger seat by the taut seatbelt but her head was hanging at an awkward angle. Automatically Dr Euan Hope checked Gloria's vital signs. He lifted her eyelids to look into her eyes, he put his ear to her chest and his hand on her pulse. He noted the inhuman angle of her lower leg and assessed the number of breakages as three or four. He thought the words, 'Death pronounced at 10.36 a.m.'

It was very quiet here. He could hear no birdsong, just the light wind rustling the tree tops.

Then he pushed the driver's door as far open as it would go, which was not very far, and managed to squeeze his bulk through the gap.

The trees were in full leaf, a small number beginning to change colour.

Once out of the car he hobbled round the long bonnet, intending to retrieve his iPad from the glove compartment and to find out exactly where he was. As he put his hand out to open the door, the silence exploded into noise and motion.

'Halt!' a German voice shouted.

'Don't move.'

'Hands up!'

Already dismayed by losing Gloria, himself black and blue with bruises and about to be violently sick, Euan just was not up to this new threat. I'm done for, he thought, and shouted aloud, 'Don't shoot. I give up.'

He was passive throughout the formalities of arrest and extradition, the flight (wearing handcuffs) to London, being taken from the plane to a police car that was waiting on the tarmac, the drive to Oxford police station and his first encounter with the very junior salaried solicitor provided by Wootton Hardman to defend him. It felt like those days had passed in a dream.

On the sixth day he asked for writing materials and began to write his confession.

LIKE EVERY PRACTISING medic, I have saved lives and I have taken them, some unintentionally, but most in response to the patient's plea to end his or her suffering. In doing so I may have broken domestic law, but I have followed the practice of good doctors from time immemorial. Guilty but justified.

I have carried out procedures that are hanging offences in some countries and routine procedures in others: that is to say, in one State of the Union where euthanasia by request is permitted, I have cut short the lives of those who begged for release. Guilty but justified.

Within the legislative restrictions I have performed abortions, sterilized women and prescribed contraceptives. Guilty but justified.

I admit that I hastened my father's end by altering the dosage in his drip. I did this with his knowledge and consent, to spare him more prolonged suffering before his inevitable death. Guilty but justified.

I am charged with causing the death of Vera Fleming.

It is true that I visited her and that I frightened her by turning up on her new doorstep. She didn't want me to come in, so she stepped out onto the landing to talk to me. I can't deny that there was animosity between us. We'd had a brief fling together. It meant far more to her than me, and she never changed her mind because of the result: her pregnancy. There was no way I was going to settle down with my parents' housekeeper, but I was quite unable to persuade her to have an abortion. I told her that I wasn't going to let my life be ruined by one evening's carelessness and she shouldn't either.

Eventually she told my parents and they supported her through the birth and kept her on afterwards. She never forgave me – and I, for that matter never forgave her. On the day she died, I had made a final appeal to Vera to let me off the annuity payment I'd been forced to enter into years previously. After cursing me, and shutting the door in my face, she slipped and fell, I failed to act. I left her lying there since I assumed that someone she trusted more than she trusted me would come to her rescue.

I admit to hastening the inevitable death of Rosemary Maitland by giving her sufficient morphine to deaden her pain. Her death was inevitable and would be soon. I spared her what would otherwise have been final agonies. Guilty but justified.

This confession is for the attention of men and women, most of whom are young enough to live and work and plan their own future. A merciful death, euthanasia, is not a relevant concept at that age or stage.

But imagine what it's like to be a boy totally paralyzed by an accident on the rugby field; or a woman who is disastrously pregnant; or a man or woman newly diagnosed with a fatal, painful disease; or simply being old and ill with nothing to look forward to except pain, suffering and death. Now choose your medical practitioner. Would you rather be cared for by a rule-bound stickler, or by me?

My conviction or acquittal depends on your answer to that question.